MONSTER, 1959

ALSO BY DAVID MAINE

The Preservationist
Fallen
The Book of Samson

MONSTER 1959

DAVID MAINE

ST. MARTIN'S PRESS ≋ NEW YORK

This is a work of fiction. All of the characters, organizations, and events portrayed in this novel are either products of the author's imagination or are used fictitiously.

www.stmartins.com

Book design by Jonathan Bennett

Words and music of "The Monkey" by Dave Bartholomew and Pearl King © 1957 (Renewed) EMI Unart Catalog, Inc. All rights controlled by EMI Unart Catalog, Inc. (Publishing) and Alfred Publishing Co., Inc. (Print). All rights reserved. Used by permission of Alfred Publishing Co., Inc.

Library of Congress Cataloging-in-Publication Data

Maine, David, 1963–
    Monster, 1959 / David Maine.—1st ed.
      p. cm.
    ISBN-13: 978-0-312-37301-6
    ISBN-10: 0-312-37301-5
    I. Title.

PS3613.A3495M66   2008
813'.6—dc22

                                             2007040721

First Edition: February 2008

10 9 8 7 6 5 4 3 2 1

for my teachers

HARRYHAUSEN PICTURES Presents

JIMMY STEELE

BILLY QUINN

BETTY DE LA MONTAIGNE

AND INTRODUCING: "K." IN...

MONSTER, 1959

Edited by JENNIFER ENDERLIN Produced by SCOTT P. HOFFMAN
Music by RICKY AND THE ROCKIN' CHAIRS
Written and Directed by DAVID MAINE Based Upon His Novel

MCMLIX CHARACTERS AND EVENTS IN THIS STORY ARE FICTITIOUS AND BEAR NO RESEMBLANCE TO ANY PERSON, LIVING OR DEAD. MOST OF THEM ANYWAY.

REEL ONE

MONSTER, 1955

I, that am curtailed of this fair proportion,
Cheated of feature by dissembling Nature,
Deformed, unfinished, sent before my time
Into this breathing world scarce half made up
—And that so lamely and unfashionable
That dogs bark at me as I halt by them—
Why, I, in this weak piping time of peace,
Have no delight to pass away the time . . .

— LAURENCE OLIVIER IN *Richard III* (1955)

Doc, didn't you say that among the lower animals
there were no natural enemies, as long as they were
well fed?

— CLINT EASTWOOD IN *Revenge of the Creature* (1955)

1. ESTABLISHING SHOT

In his dream, K. flies.

Below him is the island: verdant and vertiginous, lunatic with creation, lush like a scrap of Eden discarded and forgotten in the ocean's endless tundra. Trees flash by, rainforest-dense, tropical growth shrouding the hills in overstuffed quilted folds. Flocks of birds glitter like refracting jewels, like op art on the wing, *V*s and swarms and grand unruly mobs weaving from scarp to treetop to lakeside and up again into open sky. Toward K.

K. has no words for this. In fact K. has no words at all. The language center in his brain looks like a Jackson Pollack painting dropped from a great height. K. is preliterate, prelingual; in fact, pre–just about anything you can think of. His thoughts are the pictures he sees and the feelings they create. Sensation is his vocabulary: flavor, touch, sound, intuition, image. And smell most of all. In his dream, the heels-over-head feelings of floating, swooping, soaring are bereft of words to name them. The closest he can come is to grunt in his sleep, whimper and purr and coo and bleat. Slumbering high in his treetop nest, K. does just this. But in his dream, he flies.

Not all dreams are such. Sometimes he sees faces, figures of others like himself: huge, shambolic forms lurching across the primeval landscape. In ordinary life—though "ordinary" is a precarious

word to use around here—in ordinary life, K. wanders as solitary
as John the Baptist, so the feelings stirred up by these misty figures
elide into a whirlpool of difficult-to-understand emotions. In his
waking life, K. has never seen anything even remotely resembling
himself: an oversized, black-furred, butterfly-winged, fish-scaled,
hawk-taloned, insect-antennaed primate. Sometimes he wonders,
as best he can, why this is so. Such wondering is difficult without
words. Ideas like *species* or even *family* lie far outside his ken; he is
possessed of a rudimentary sense of *me* and a slightly clearer sense
of *them*, but abstractions of any greater complexity elude him. He
cannot know that he is a species of one, the first, last and only of
his race: a race that is over before it starts. The merciless demands
of natural selection have declared his impossibly overgrown,
jumbled-up self to be simply too huge, too ungainly and demanding—of nourishment, of physical space—to evolve further. The
other preposterous species of the island, the fish-finned insect-rats
and miniature, eight-eyed mole people, are similarly marked, but
possessing as they do even less self-awareness than K., they don't
know it either.

In his dream, K. circles high in the air, flirts with the clouds,
brushes the firmament, pirouettes like a deformed Nureyev before
flipping head-down and plummeting toward a lake. The water approaches with gut-clenching speed, and K.'s heart jolts into double
time. Waves glitter and smear across his vision. At the moment of
impact, K. jerks himself awake. The tree he is lounging in shudders as if struck, and a multitude of storks takes noisily to the air.

Around K. the island hunkers, observing him. Low morning
sun wrestles heavy clouds. Tropical forest, wet-earth smells, plenty
of bugs.

K. peers about groggily. His heart beats fast as if he is in danger, but he smells none, hears none. What dangers are there, anyway, for a creature such as himself? The insect-rats are too small
to mention, the dens of the mole people lie deep underground.

K. flicks his tongue and smells the peaceful air. Already his heart is slowing, the dream is fading, then faded, then gone: river mist that flees the sun. His blood pressure drops. He reaches for a nearby cluster of leaves and stuffs them in his mouth, chewing meditatively. An observer might be forgiven for thinking that K. is lost in thought. He is not. He is simply lost. Or more properly, he is waiting for a stimulus, internal or external, to prod him into motion. Perhaps hunger, or the approach of the flying lizard who occasionally torments him, or the need to relieve his bowels, or a thunderstorm.

K. sits patiently, chewing without thinking. Waiting, like one of Pavlov's now-famous slobbering dogs, for something to happen.

Later that day, something does.

2. A HELL OF A YEAR

Something always does. 1955 is a hell of a year, but K. doesn't know that.

It's the year that audiences shiver to *This Island Earth* and *The Quatermass Experiment,* while Clint Eastwood makes his screen debut in *Revenge of the Creature.* It's the year James Dean dies and Marilyn Monroe stars in *The Seven Year Itch,* the year scientists prove the existence of antimatter and use meteorites to place the age of the solar system at four and a half billion years. None of this matters much to a black American fourteen-year-old named Emmett Till, a Chicago native who is found drowned in the Tallahatchie River after being abducted and beaten for the crime of insulting a white woman. His alleged murderers, a pair of white men, admit to the kidnapping but are subsequently acquitted of the murder. Few people, if any, are surprised. Are you?

Lockheed produces the U-2 surveillance plane, one of which will soon crash-land in the Soviet Union. Scientists bombard uranium 238 with nitrogen ions and invent fermium, a synthetic radioactive element named for Enrico Fermi, the man who created history's first controlled nuclear fission reaction. If "controlled" is the right word.

Rocky Marciano defends his heavyweight title for the sixth and final time. Marilyn divorces Joltin' Joe. Fidel Castro gets out of jail.

Albert Einstein dies. France abandons its nine-year war in Indochina, but not its colonies in Algeria. (That won't come for a few years yet.) Ceylon, Nepal and Jordan join the United Nations; West Germany is admitted into NATO. President Juan Perón is exiled from Argentina by the military, with the help and support of the United States. A Korean general named Choi Hong Hi creates a hybrid of Japanese karate and Korean foot fighting, naming his new mutation tae kwon do.

K. knows nothing of all this. Would it help? Would a little tae kwon do come in useful, these next few years? Would knowledge of the UN's Universal Declaration of Human Rights (1948) be of any benefit? Or the Baghdad Pact (1955: Iraq, Turkey, Britain, Iran, Pakistan)? Hard to say, really. Or maybe not so hard: after all, look at the thousands of people who know all about these things, but who *aren't* being helped one jot. Not one iota, not one atom— of fermium, or anything else.

K. descends from the tree and stands upon the earth, upright but slouched onto his knuckles, browsing for breakfast among the succulent shoots that choke a small pond. When he notices the distant drums, his body pivots toward the sound, a murmurous droning like the beating of surf. But it is not surf. K. opens his mouth and his tongue detects faint wood smoke. K. does not panic. His primordial cortex recognizes forest fire smells and this is not that. This is the odor that comes just often enough for him to recall it, always from the same place at the far end of the island, the place filled with small swarming creatures. The place he never goes to, unless. Unless.

Unless summoned.

K. looks away from the sound, bends to the pond, cups water in his claw and drinks. Most of the water sloshes away before it reaches his lipless mouth. If he had a thumb he would lose less but he has no thumb. His tongue—forked, snakelike—flickers in-out as he raises his head and notices the drumming sound again, the sound he'd almost forgotten but not quite. The sound is a tick under his fur, or maybe a Volkswagen Beetle. Impossible to ignore for long. K. shifts his steps away from the river, away from the thicket where he has been enjoying his breakfast, insofar as a creature such as himself enjoys anything. Now his steps make their way toward the sound without his realizing it. (K. does nearly everything without *realizing* it.) His path is a rambling meandering indirect one to be sure, but inarguably in the right direction, toward the drums and the wood smoke and whatever else is to be found there. That thing which K. hazily remembers, from the last time, and the time before that.

Something has happened. Something always does.

Something happened a couple years ago, when the United States tested its first H-bomb not far from here. It was called Mike. No kidding: Mike. Somebody's idea of a joke. (But what do you expect? The test site for the very first atomic explosion, in 1945 in New Mexico, was code-named "Trinity." For Christ's sake, what sick bastard dreamed *that* one up?) Mike fell on an island somewhere in the South Pacific, vaporized the whole place. In fact it was spitting distance from K.'s island, geographically speaking, though K. knows nothing of it.

The detonation was considerably more ferocious than expected. Supposedly when they told Eisenhower what happened—the whole island gone—he turned pale and had to sit down.

At least Joe McCarthy is safely consigned to history's wastebasket, discredited and disgraced after accusing the army of treason last year. So he's off the scene, a positive development by any measure. But there will be plenty more where he came from. There's always somebody eager to clarify the border between *us* and *them,* to build walls (China 400 B.C., Berlin 1962, Palestine 2003), or drop bombs (not enough time to list, sorry).

McCarthy's gone all right but the Shah's been reinstated in Tehran. He'd been sidelined back in '51 by a nationalist prime minister named Mossadegh, who then had the nerve to nationalize Iran's oil—keeping it within the country for the country's own use. *That* hadn't gone down well with U.S. oilmen or the government they paid for, so the CIA promptly engineered Mossadegh's arrest and trial by military tribunal. Once the Shah got settled back in, he obligingly denationalized oil wells and went back to selling lots of cheap crude to white people.

Mossadegh got three years' solitary confinement. He came out looking shaky and gave up politics for good.

The Americans—and the Brits, don't forget the Brits—sighed in relief. For a while it looked tricky: gasoline might've cost more! But the niggers had fallen into line, predictably enough, and all they had to do was sacrifice any notion of representative government. And if anyone wondered how the States had gotten into the business of subsidizing Middle Eastern monarchs in exchange for cheap oil, well, he could keep those thoughts to himself. Democracy was all well and good, but some people just weren't ready for it. It's not like that crowd posed any kind of serious threat, anyway. What were they going to do—stage a revolution? Throw out the Yankees? Build H-bombs of their own?

3. ON THE ORIGIN OF SPECIES

To the human eye, K. is an evolutionary absurdity. A bad joke with a garbled punch line: something to cause Darwin to burn his notebooks and run shrieking to the nearest monastery. Nature couldn't make up her mind what to do with him—K., not Darwin—so she tried a little of everything, breaking her own boundaries, leaking from reptile to mammal, arthropod to vertebrate, insect to bird. The result is a Dali-esque construct of unexpected leaps and alarming juxtapositions.

It's a good thing Crick and Watson never set eyes on him, they'd have had to start all over again. *Double* helix? Not even close!

K. stands roughly upright, bipedal, forty feet tall from crown to toe. Claws instead of fingers, earholes like a lizard's, residual butterfly wings far too flimsy to support his mass, the suggestion of a dorsal fin halfway down his back. His bosom is dressed with an unlikely speckling of crimson feathers. Matted black fur covers the rest of him except for those wings—black-veined yellow, not unlike the delicate *Papilio machaon,* in K.'s case shoulder-width like a Renaissance cherub's—and the scaly forearms, patterned like an Amazon constrictor. Arms longer than the comfortable human proportion, nearly dragging on the ground even when K. stands erect.

Like enormous pistons, like nineteenth-century factory machines, K.'s legs carry his bulk over the earth. They are sheathed in fur right to the nails of the seven—why seven?—toes on each foot. His gait is slightly knock-kneed; two little bald patches have been worn away on the insides of his thighs. Sheathed between them, his penis remains unseen except for the very tip.

And how to describe the face? Imagine a block of granite, squarish and rough-hewn, with great round flat shark's eyes set forward. No nose, no apparent way to breathe except through the mouth, perpetually open. That mouth lipless but possessed of a family of teeth, an extended clan of teeth, spinster aunts and distant inbred cousins, old and young together, sharp and dull and chipped off, slashing incisors and rounded grinding molars jammed awkwardly together as if for a group portrait. The mouth defines the head and the teeth define the mouth.

There is something unfinished about K.'s face, as if nature gave up halfway through. Quitting an obviously hopeless job in favor of something more fruitful: flamingos, maybe, or eels. The fur peters out around his temples, leaving the crown exposed and bumpy, raw pinkish brown skin peeling and spotted. There is no neck: flesh and fur conspire to anchor the bottom of the head directly to the torso. Dangling before those serving tray eyes (unblinking, narcotic) flop a pair of antennae. Slender green tendrils, they bracket K.'s field of vision, swaying in front of him like the bangs of a fashionable London teenager.

The drums grow louder, insistent, as he fumbles his way toward them.

4. SEEN THIS MOVIE BEFORE

The setting now is as it ever was. Although K.'s sense of time is hazy, his understanding of *was* being primitive and *will be* nonexistent, still there is some rudimentary comprehension when he gazes upon this mise-en-scène: things are arranged according to plan, familiar in their contours, all the elements in place.

First there is the din of the drums, thrumming against his earholes, into his skull, lodging there till his jaw clenches unconsciously. It is the low murmuring rumble that has drawn him here in the first place, across the plains, through the narrow mountain pass and along the tortured contours of the river. Finally to this spot in front of a steep earthen embankment which, if K. were cognizant of such things, he might recognize as artificial. But he is not, so he does not.

Here, then. An earthen wall fully as tall as his shoulder; a jumble of rocks and boulders and steep cliffs that stretch away on both sides. Behind him, the familiar jungle, his home. And before him, on the far side of this rubble-strewn barrier? He doesn't know. He has never ventured there. A filmy odor hangs over the place, wood smoke and—somehow he knows this—burnt flesh. Mixed in with this, the scent of these swarming creatures that live in clusters. Not unlike the mole people but larger, with dark skin and only two eyes, and much more skittish. It is a place that simultaneously draws and repels him, a place he rarely thinks of except when the drums beckon.

The drums. They pound at him now, throbbing like the tide, only louder. They disorient him and blur his thinking, such as it is.

Today K. does not see the drummers. Sometimes they show themselves fleetingly, shiny-brown and furless as they clamber across the boulders, whooping and pounding their drums. Other days they remain hidden in the rocks, their noise lashing out like a punishment or a seduction, or some mutant hybrid of the two.

K. moves closer.

There is a small platform among the boulders and earthworks. Until K. sees it, he doesn't remember it. There is a figure bound there, one of the small creatures, tied in vines at wrist and ankle. This too is normal. Or if not normal precisely, it is what regularly occurs in this place and on these occasions.

K. approaches the platform. It has been erected at his chin height. Tall bamboo posts bracket the girl—for it is a female, maybe seventeen years old, though K. of course has no knowledge of years. The posts hold her wrists apart, so she forms a sort of Y shape. She is sharp-chinned and high-cheekboned, with braids to her shoulders and skin the color of last night. Her eyes are wide with anxiety that she struggles to control, for the most part successfully.

For a long moment they regard one another, the tiny female and the monstrous smorgasbord. K. faintly registers satisfaction that this figure does not make the insect-pitched keening that so many others do; nor does she flail and jitter like a moth in a spiderweb as he comes near. Neither is she limp and passive (red-eyed with the tranquilizing leaves that the village elders offer all the sacrifices), nor has she simply fainted dead away. No: this one stands upright, helpless but still, somehow, dignified for all that. She waits. K. feels a flicker of excitement in his core. Why, he does not know. Why the drums periodically call him to this place, why the rocks offer him these bound sacrifices, he lacks even the ability to imagine.

What has happened to the others, all the previous females he has taken away from here, it does not occur to him to wonder.

(There are many answers to that. Some, fearing gruesome mastication in his jaws, hurl themselves from the boulders the instant he snaps the vines. Others tumble from his claws, willingly or otherwise, or from the treetop he brings them to. Some manage to escape only to be eaten by the beasts in the forest. There have been heart attacks, strokes, snake bites, lacerations that turned septic. Many girls merely starve to death, unable to subsist on the handfuls of forest greens that they manage to snatch. None has lasted more than a week, except one.

Oshango understood quickly that K. was no god who needed appeasement, as she had been taught from birth, and understood also that to stay in his company meant only her own death sooner or later. She contrived a way to escape his treetop lair, and spent nine nerve-wracking days retracing the path back home, subsisting on roots, river water and unripe berries. Little more than bones, she made it back to the earthwall and wept hysterically when the perimeter guards appeared. Wordlessly they impaled her with their spears before she could do more than jabber hysterically, anxious lest the angry god manifest himself once more, seeking vengeance on the whole village.

In due reverence they left Oshango's body for the vultures, and disaster was thus averted.)

The drumming cuts off as if by a signal. In the silence that reverberates, K. feels almost compelled to act. He reaches forward and snaps the vines with a cleaver-like claw. In the same motion he scoops the female, her legs dangling in the air, her shoulders wedged beneath the curl of his talons. A stray breeze carries a gust of wood smoke from the other side of the barrier, and he pauses to sniff. There is another odor too, an unpleasant one. His stomach shudders a bit as he identifies the smell of roasting flesh. *Whose flesh?* It is a question that he can almost, but not quite, bring himself to formulate. This degree of abstraction is something K. has not evolved as yet.

In his hand the tiny female shifts a little, perhaps trying to get comfortable, or making herself more secure. She peers back at the earthen wall, the village hidden beyond it, and raises her arm in a feeble wave.

His business here is done. K. turns to go. Beneath his heel, Oshango's weathering skull shatters and is ground into the soft forest floor.

5. CONVENTIONAL WISDOM

This girl's name is Alensha. As K. carries her off, her mind flits across the landscape of her past, of the moments that have led up to this one. She tries not to vomit, or scream. She will not be another Oshango, of that much she is sure: she won't disrespect K. by abandoning him.

She is too young to have personally known Oshango, whose death was many years ago, but she's heard the stories.

Alensha has always been a bit of an oddball, by the standards of the island tribe. Her long serious face always possessed an inward-looking quality, and as a youngster she never mixed easily with other children. Her first word, at the age of eighteen months, was "Mama." All well and good; but her second word was "Kama ka"—the high priest's ritual name for K., and considered a poor omen when spoken aloud. Alensha's stepmother, fulfilling the role of stepmothers everywhere, declared the girl unclean and probably a witch, or at the very least possessed by spirits inimical to the interests of the clan. Plague and famine would inevitably follow, she predicted. Many agreed, but the high priest himself generously dismissed this as unkind gossip, assuring Alensha's father that all would be well though it might be best to go about begetting a few more children, just in case. Sons especially would be welcome. . . . Alensha's father did so, and none of the newborns died, so there the matter rested for some years. The stepmother's subsequent death (an unfortunate early-morning encounter with strangler vines, which did not go unremarked by some) encouraged this.

For a time Alensha's quirks, her fits of giggling and unwarranted sobs, her quick temper and solitary nature, were noticed and commented upon—as everything in the village was noticed and commented upon—but, in general, accepted. She was of the tribe, after all, her father well respected and her mother of a good family; and anyway she herself was a fine huntress, gifted at predicting both the coming of the rains and the movements of herd animals. But when she announced at the age of fifteen that Kama ka was her betrothed and she would marry him and bear his offspring, her declaration was greeted with universal revulsion and anger. There was little even the high priest could say in the face of such obviously demonic ideas. That the girl spoke with perfect calm and apparent sincerity didn't help matters. The tribe shuddered and Alensha's mother wept at night, but everyone knew that when the time came for another sacrifice to the god whose very name brought ill luck, there would be little discussion about who to choose.

And there wasn't. On her sixteenth birthday, Alensha was given what she had hungered after for years: private time with Kama ka.

The story recited by the high priest to explain K. is told only twice a year, after sunset: on the longest night of winter and the shortest of the summer. The whole village collects around the watchfire to listen, and shiver.

Since before humans existed there has been a struggle between Kama ka, the god of things living, and Komo ko, the god of things dead. (These names are taboo, the high priest reminds them in his urgent hiss, and are to be spoken only by the holiest of men; and even by them only during this twice-yearly recitation.)

So then. The battles between these two gods took place on the upper slopes of that mountain where the immortals live, whose peak is shrouded in perpetual cloud. For years beyond number the god of things dead won the battles, day after day, and the earth remained a place of stone and water and salt and stars. But one day Kama ka—the god of things living—tricked Komo ko by saying, I give up! You win! To which Komo ko said, Take then my hand as a gesture of your good intentions. But instead of doing so, the god of things living smote him a mighty blow on the head, using a turtle whose hard shell knocked Komo ko lifeless. Or so Kama ka believed.

Then the god of things living arrived on earth and found only a barren place and said, I will fill it with my children. From his feathered chest he pulled the birds and sent them into the sky in a great flock. From his butterfly wings he drew clouds of insects that filled the air, and from his antennae came armies of insects that crawled along the ground. From his glassy eyes he cried fish. From his scaly arms crawled serpents and reptiles of all sorts. From his furry anus dropped the warm-blooded, furred creatures. And from the tip of his loins spurted men and women, who coupled furiously and bore their offspring to faraway places.

For a time all was well.

Then Kama ka, the god of things living, returned to the high mountain whose upper reaches abide in perpetual cloud. And who should be waiting for him there but Komo ko, the god of things dead. An angry god was he. Oh yes. Komo ko held a heavy stone in his hand, and used it to smite his unsuspecting rival a mighty blow on the head. A stone however is heavier than a turtle shell. It sent Kama ka nearly unto death, and he fell clear off the mountaintop, all the way to this island.

Komo ko followed.

Thereupon followed a mighty battle. It was a battle beyond words. The sky was sundered; the ground trembled. Lightning bolts flashed and thunder howled and this was as nothing, these were the gentlest caresses of a devoted lover as compared to the awesome energies these two deities hurled at each other.

Fire filled the sky. Fire *was* the sky. Then cinders and smoke and furious winds that carried not sweet smells of flowers bloom-ing but the acrid stench of things dying and already dead.

In the end, Komo ko, the god of things dead, prevailed. Per-haps this was because stone and salt and water are stronger than bone and blood and flesh; because animals can drown in the sea or be crushed in a landslide or poisoned by a tainted stream. Or per-haps there was another reason. In any case Komo ko at last smote Kama ka—the god of things living—a mighty blow and left him for dead. Komo ko returned to the mountain in perpetual clouds and was never seen again.

But Kama ka, being a god, remained unkilled. Yet not whole either. Crippled now, he can no longer return to the mountain where he belongs; his injury ties him to this island where he can only wander and bellow and shake the very night with his rage. In his anger he has created companions to reflect his bitterness, com-rades too horrible to contemplate: an underground tribe of semi-humans, clouds of poisonous butterflies, carnivorous finger-fish. And much else, all awful. The human beings of this tribe built a mighty wall to keep these deformities at bay, but it is little use against the god himself.

Which is why we of this tribe (the priest intones grandly, meet-ing the eyes of each villager) must also perform our paramount duty. We must remind Kama ka that we know who he is and where he comes from. That we have not forgotten him. We must appease his hunger, slake his appetite, offer him sacrifices of that which we value the most. To do otherwise is to fail the entire vil-lage. The young women we place before him do more than just give up their lives. They deliver our entire community another twelve months of peace. They are our martyrs, and more than that, they are our heroes, as surely as the men who hunt our food or the women who bear our children.

And the rest of the tribe reflects on this, some with sadness, others with an undeniable spurt of excitement. And then, one by one, they agree that this duty must be fulfilled, that it is for the best. That a lesser evil must be accepted, to keep a greater one at bay.

Alensha heard this story twice a year, every year of her life. Felt her nerves quicken at the awe of it, the epic scale. Did Jean d'Arc feel the same when, as a teenager, the world spun and crashed around her? Did she feel the same impulse to hurl herself into the center of things? Did the kamikaze pilots, scrambling for their Zeros, feel equally caught up in an epic battle between life and death, good and evil? Alensha couldn't say. She had never heard of Jean d'Arc, or kamikazes, or France or Japan—or for that matter, white people or yellow ones.

Alensha knew only this for sure: that she yearned to be in K.'s presence. To be in the company of something undeniably greater than herself, greater than any member of the tribe. Not greater in a stinging-fire-lizard kind of way, sneaking up at twilight to burn your ankle and put you in a fever for seven days, after which you will either dry up and die or else live on, hobbling on your weak leg, crippled for life—no, not that. Greater in a different way altogether, a towering, lumbering, blot-out-the-sky-with-its-shoulders kind of way, a way to inspire awe or even worship, not disgust. Alensha was pefectly aware that many in the tribe felt revolted by her or even afraid. She'd never wanted that. She wanted only to be the companion of the god, the woman who—not who tamed him, exactly (for no man can tame a god, nor woman either), but who was companion to him. Who was—who accompanied him through his days. Understood him better than any other. Yes. Who made his way a little less lonely.

And hers?

Well, sure. Her journey through this world would, undeniably, be a bit less barren too, in the presence of a companion. Or companions. Alensha had a pretty good idea of what those companions would look like.

Alensha told none of this to the high priest. She simply presented herself one morning, when the mist was still heavy on the ground and the monkeys and birds were just beginning their daily squabbles. She arrived at the door of the priest's hut wearing only a cloth wrapped round her privates, and when the man appeared at the doorway she said.—When the time comes, choose me for I am ready.

Now the time has come.

She has seen K. before, at previous sacrifices. Alensha never understood why the other girls wailed and screamed and kicked and cried. It is obvious that he does not take them away to eat them: if he wanted to eat anyone, he would come every day at dusk to hunt like the island's other predators, and the tribe would have long since been eliminated. So obviously there is no danger. The stories of the living hell outside the village embankments are just that: stories, told not to enlighten the village children but to keep them from running away. There are no underground tribes of worm-skinned semi-humans, of this Alensha is certain; no flying monsters with snake's heads and eagle's wings; no befanged butterflies or killer fish in the rivers. All mere invention, she is sure, originally created to keep little children behaved and by now, generations later, believed by even the wisest of the village elders.

So when K. arrives like a drug-induced nightmare, Alensha feels no fear. None that she acknowledges anyway. Sure, her bowels tighten, acid dumps into her stomach, her breathing grows shallow and fast. This is not fear, she tells herself, but excitement; the urgency felt by a netted bird as it fights its way to freedom and the open, windswept sky. Kama ka is taking her away to heaven, or if not heaven then at least someplace very nice, much nicer than her dreary mud-walled village. In that place, she and all the other sacrificial girls—except the ungrateful idiot Oshango—will lounge all day slurping wild fruits and fanning themselves in the shade, feasting on suckling pig served on golden platters by well-muscled young men who look nothing like her dumpy father or the desiccated high priest or the bandy-legged warriors of her tribe.

But to be honest she's not ready for the smell.

She closes her eyes as K. reaches for her, snaps her restraints, lifts her clear. The stench slaps her and stings, it burns her eyes. Her stomach convulses, she can't help it, but nothing comes out: she hasn't eaten for days, so excited has she been.

The smell is something like moldering fish, mixed into a paste of dung and dead bodies and jammed by force into her mouth. It is more than a smell really, more than she's ever known a smell to be. It is the first odor that she has ever actually *tasted* in her throat; its toxic residue is left behind, paste on her tongue like the kiss of a corpse. Only worse, much much worse.

She fights back a scream. She forces herself not to kick: there is no chance, she grits to herself, that she is going to behave as those previous girls did.

From behind the topmost boulders of earthwall, Alensha sees the wide-eyed faces of her tribe, staring at her. Her, and Kama ka. The god of things living. They are watching, she knows, to see how she behaves. To see if she will kick and scream and panic and act pathetic. She will not. She isn't going to give them satisfaction.

She lifts her hand to them, as casual as Queen Elizabeth, and *waves.*

Nobody waves back.

At that moment Kama ka, the god of things living, lets out a belch that slaps Alensha's face like a waterfall. She feels it warm and wet against her cheek and the stench leaves her heaving. Alensha begins to wonder, then. Her stomach wobbles as the creature swings about, swinging her as casually as a piece of fruit. His claws are gritty and smooth, difficult to cling to; she props her feet against the enormous hand's leathery palm and secures herself as best she can.

K. turns to go and crunches something underfoot, rambling his way back into the forest. Earthwall drops behind and with it everyone Alensha has ever known. Still nobody waves. It seems unlikely, Alensha can't help thinking, that heaven would smell quite like this. For the first time, a little wriggling trickle of uncertainty worms into her consciousness, and she wonders if she's got her facts straight. If she had taken everything into account in quite the right way. Or if maybe the elders knew what they were talking about, all along.

6. TRACKING SHOT

The second day after the drums, K. has returned to familiar ground. The female he carries is still alive, though listless. Terrified? Resigned? Philosophical? K. would not know—these are unknown feelings to him.

Fatigue, however, is an old friend who walks alongside him now. Matches his lurching stride step for step. Compulsion has pressed him to leave behind the earthen wall and the drums as quickly as possible, so he has trundled on through the night, not pausing to rest or eat, following the river through the mountains and across the plains. Now, at the base of his tree at last, he is overwhelmed with the desire to sleep. It does not occur to him to wonder what the female might need, any more than he might wonder why he has taken her. Instead, he climbs.

The ascent is hampered by the burden he clutches. Single-handed, he pulls himself up in great lunging thrusts, like a salmon fighting the current. Around him branches rattle and crack, geckos scuttle for cover, parakeets spill away in squawking hordes. At the top of the forest canopy, a chance intertwining of branches forms an uneven cradle. K. deposits the human female there, perhaps motivated by some instinct that suggests she will be unlikely to tumble out of this perch. She reclines uneasily—it can't be comfortable—and grips the branches like the gunwales of a lifeboat, even as this extremity of the tree sways in the afternoon breeze as if on ocean swells. K. retreats a bit lower, finds a comfortable crotch to nestle into, and plunges into dreamless slumber.

He is awakened by screaming.

When he scrambles upward it is to see the female in the talons of his great winged rival. K. bellows but the beast tumbles skyward, the girl firmly enclawed. Watching the pair recede, K. feels any number of things he is unable to articulate. Rage is one of them; hopelessness also. Righteous indignation figures in there as well. And even, in some obscure way, shame at having fouled up again.

K.'s rival is more distinctly reptilian than K. There is the suggestion of the dragon in her, as well as the pterodactyl, though she is precisely neither. Her body is lithe and sinewy, but quadruped; her wings unfold like a glider, translucent and redly veined like great triangular sheets of flexible rose quartz. Her head is horse-like and beaked, the ur-mother of all eagles.

They have tussled before, K. and this other apparition. She is Stalin to his Eisenhower. Or maybe vice versa. They have met enough times, and she has bested him enough times, that K. now views his rival with something approaching hate. This feeling intensifies as he watches her glide off, loping and ungraceful, the very opposite of the swooping poetry of a raptor. The human female writhes, entrapped in her grip.

K. knows he is beaten. He pounds on his tree trunk and howls like Quasimodo cursing Paris; like Menelaus, cursing Paris.

Once, K. got the best of her. But only once. She made the mistake of harrying him in a narrow canyon, a rocky barren place. Without thinking he hefted a boulder the size of a Japanese car and hurled it at her. The rock only grazed her but it was enough to send her spinning like a leaf to earth. K. had nearly taken her then and there, but her huge beak held him off. It did not occur to him to batter her with more stones, Saint Stephen–style, once she was trapped on the ground. After a long face-off, he turned away, leaving her metallic shrieks to bounce crazily off the enclosing granite. Quite soon he forgot all about her. Until the next time. And then the time after that. And now, again, this time.

As K. watches, his rival gives a twist of its talons and Alensha's head pops off like the cork of a champagne bottle.

REEL TWO

MONSTER, 1956

We cannot subscribe to one law for the weak,
another law for the strong; one law for those
opposing us, another for those allied with us. There
can be only one law—or there shall be no peace.
—U.S. PRESIDENT DWIGHT D. EISENHOWER,
OPPOSING THE INVASION OF THE SUEZ CANAL
BY BRITAIN, FRANCE AND ISRAEL, 1956

But the Krell forgot one thing . . . Monsters, John!
Monsters from the id!
—WARREN STEVENS IN *Forbidden Planet* (1956)

7. STAR QUALITY

This female is different.

K. does not notice right away. So much else is the same: throbbing drums, earthwall, wood smoke. The female bound up in the usual place, in the usual way. Yellow sun in a blue sky throwing a thick pall of forest-shadow across the scene. (Not that K. can see or understand colors: his worldview is black and white, as grainy and poorly focused as a moldy movie print.) This female gets his attention though: she screams as if she is being eviscerated, her intestines extracted an inch at a time. She shrieks and wails and twists against the constraining vines while tears streak her face like a monsoon. No philosophical resignation for this one. No going gentle into that good anything.

—Help! Oh God someone help me!

Her words rattle off him like hailstones. K. doesn't recognize the sounds as being any different from the usual moans and whines and wailing. He does notice, however, that this female in some way looks different. That she is—how to say it? If he had the vocabulary to ascribe color to the world, he would have perhaps described her as light-skinned, or pale-cheeked or blond. Or even, to use a sloppy, shorthand and patently inaccurate term: white.

—Johnny, where are you? *Johnny!* Get this thing away from me!

K. swipes with a claw and snaps the vines, scoops the female—
older than a girl, more precisely a woman, though the distinction is
a bit fine for K.—and intuitively clutches her tight. Intuition serves
him well: she flails her legs and pounds his claws like a battery-
powered toy, like something cheap from Taiwan. No doubt she
would flail and pound herself right into open air, into the long void
and the big sleep at the end of it, if he let her. As it is, her legs kick
nothing but empty space and her pounding is as effective as a spar-
row pecking a Panzer turret. K. turns his back on the earthen embankment and regains the forest, a wake of trampled shrubbery and
snapped branches marking his path. It does not occur to him that
he is leaving behind an obvious trail. It does not enter his mind (his
mind?) that he might be followed.

It does not occur to him that this one white female might
prove especially . . . difficult.

It takes some time for the forest to recover after he departs. For
birds to chirp and lizards to scuttle and strangler vines to regroup.
Eventually, though, equilibrium reasserts itself and things get back
to normal. Almost normal anyway. K. doesn't know this, doesn't
even know that when he's around, normalcy has a way of fleeing
for the hills. Put simply, things can get downright strange.

For example: the men who watch him leave. Jaws hanging open
like Dust Bowl cottage windows, voices snatched away by shock
and dread and plain unbelief. White men for the most part, which
is strange enough, decked out in khaki jungle-duds and carting
enough firepower to level a small town. Nope, K. doesn't even notice them. And wouldn't know what to make of them if he did.

8. EXTRAS

There is so much K. does not know. What cinnamon tastes like, for example, or what a camera does, or where gravity comes from. What a chain reaction is. He has never heard of George Patton or Marlene Dietrich or Jackie Robinson or Benito Mussolini. The woman he carries knows about all of these people and many more.

Dates he is ignorant of, as well: 1066 and 1492 mean nothing to him, likewise August 1914 and December 7, 1941. Plus of course July 4, December 25, the fourth Thursday in November. The woman he carries clenched in his hand, Betty by name, finds all these dates significant, as well as many others. (Her birthday: June 10. Her wedding anniversary: July 15. Her father's death: June 6, 1944. Today: December 19, 1956.)

Most crucially, perhaps, K. lacks knowledge of current events. The Cold War is as foreign to him as the Montgomery bus boycott. He knows nothing of Soviet tanks parked on the streets of Budapest, or the impromptu riot at the water-polo match between Russia and Hungary at Melbourne's summer Olympics, "the first-ever games in the Southern Hemisphere!" The Suez Canal, Morocco's independence, the sinking of the *Andrea Doria* and "Heartbreak Hotel"—the year's number-one hit—are equidistant from his understanding, all of them as alien as Robby the Robot in Hollywood's latest blockbuster, *Forbidden Planet*. (You know:

the movie where the deadly monster is actually the manifestation of the evil scientist's unconscious desires. Sigmund Freud meets *The Thing from Another World.* That's the one.)

Around K. the jungle scampers with life. Most of it is engaged in a single activity: running away from him. Tailless herbivorous rodents, viperine lepidoptera, large variegated predators reminiscent of triceratops or saber-toothed armadillos—these are all as expected, they fall within the parameters of what passes for *normal* on this island. Likewise the eight-eyed mole people, the flying razorback lizard squirrels, the foaming hordes of slashing finger-fish swarming the river that K. unthinkingly steps through in a couple of strides. He gives little notice to these fellow jungle residents, and they (except for the finger-fish, who will mob anything and try to exsanguinate it whether they hunger or not) do their wary best to escape his notice. K. has never eaten a fellow creature in his life, his diet being purely vegetarian, but taking such things for granted is a poor way to pursue longevity on this island.

Had K. been possessed of a slightly more observant nature—ignoring the fact that this would have transformed K. into a different creature altogether, a non-K., an un-K., an anti-K.—he might have noticed the tiny creatures dogging his trail. Amid great fuss and hullabaloo, this band of diminutive bipeds had bubbled into sight like lava atop the earthen embankment even as K. disappeared into the woods.

Carrying the female.

Behind him, frenzied excitement: tart popping sounds of no account, and yapping, insecty whines:

—That thing's got Betty!

—Damn these savages! It's some kind of sacrifice!

—We should massacre the lot of them.

The lone black man among them says nothing but looks grave.

—I'm all for that! says another.—Let's start with that no-good chief of theirs! Giving us that drugged wine, so we all fall asleep for hours . . .

—So they could kidnap Betty without our noticing!

—Quiet, all of you. There's no time for that now. We've got to get her back.

—We're with you, Johnny.

—Come on then.

Like a cloud of wasps, the men storm ahead, laden with rifles and shotguns and a few concussion grenades. They scramble down the earthwall, slipping amid pebble showers and slick mud smears, clustering again at the bottom. Breathless, watchful. Guns in their hands like erections.

—Did you *see* that son of a gun?

—What was that thing anyway?

Had K. paused for a final look back, he would have seen fourteen men disperse in a rough line across his broken-ferned wake. Would he understand that their faces are set into grim lines, that the angle of their shoulders and heft of their guns indicate a deadly intent against himself, the kidnapper of the blond, milk-limbed woman he clutches? Probably not.

Why would he? He's never been tracked before, followed, chased, hunted.

K. splashes through the river that first afternoon. It barely reaches his knees, and the finger-fish gnaw uselessly at his heavy fur for only a few seconds. His pursuers reach the river some time later. K. does indeed pause, at that moment, to remark the wailing screams rising behind him like a curtain of bats. Ascertaining no threat, he strides on. The woman lies limp in his palm, clothes and hair matted with her own vomit.

Had K. doubled back to the river and taken the trouble to check, he might have seen the fourteen men enter the silty water, rifles held aloft soldier-style. The finger-fish cut down the point man so fast he doesn't even holler.—What's this? he says. And then is gone, just blood and froth spinning down the current.

The others have plenty of time to scream.

Men drop as though shot through the knees, contorted limbs slapping the water, red slicks on the surface like oil. Witnessing this carnage, many of their comrades throw themselves flat into the river as if seeking cover: precisely the wrong response to a cloud of rampaging carnivorous fish. Men writhe in the water like shock-therapy patients, dying too fast to drown. Somebody thinks quick and tosses a grenade; this rips open a couple of the thrashing hunters but clears a path to the far shore as well, and those who can still wade or dog-paddle surge ahead and claw their way to the river-bank as if pursued by nightmares made manifest. There they collapse, gasping, staring around them as if for the next horror.

—The hell was that?

—God knows.

More gasping, catching of breath. Heartbeats thrumming in their ears like subway tracks.

—How many did we lose?

No one wants to count, or even meet the eyes of the rest. Johnny grows impatient. —Well, how many of us are left?

The survivors squint at each other surreptitiously.

It is Cooke, the black man, who finally speaks.—Eight. Plus Willis there.

Willis has no legs and is spilling into the mud like a piñata.—Save me Jesus, he whispers.

—Wharton gone first, Cooke continues.—He was at point. I saw van der Lundt and Rostov go down too.

Johnny nods.—And Martinez. Did anybody see Lebeau?

Nobody saw Lebeau. He must have died, unnoticed, amid them all. Somebody says, Maybe the grenade took him out.

Clients, all of them. Johnny clenches his jaw so hard the muscle juts from his cheek like a ping-pong ball. He has sandy blond hair and a chin like a leading man's.—Dirty niggers.

Cooke coughs softly, his round face looking sad.

—Nobody's blaming you, Coco. You're different, you're—civilized. Not like these—these—*savages*. Back in America, we'd have 'em on a chain gang good and proper.

—'Sall right, Cap'n. I got a few words to say to that chief, mysef.

Johnny takes a moment to collect his nerves.—How are we for weapons? Everybody still have what they brought?

—Uh—I lost my gun.

—Me too. Dropped it in the river when those things started rippling me.

Silence a minute. The men take a quick inventory, trying to ignore the scuttling sounds in the jungle around them.

—Looks like four rifles, Johnny. And my shotgun, might be wet. Billy and Cooke've got a few grenades still.

—So do I. Well, nothing for it I guess. We'll be more careful from now on. Consider yourselves warned, gentlemen.

You mean we keep going? blurts Lashman, incredulous.

Johnny blinks. He had never contemplated any alternative: this is his expedition and it's gone to pieces. If anybody's going to haul it back from the edge of disaster, it'll have to be him.

Besides, there are other reasons.—That's my wife out there, Lashman.

The others watch uneasily. Professional hunters, most of them. Johnny's employees, rough men. And a couple of well-heeled clients, rough in their own way, high rollers who paid big money for an adventure safari. They're getting one all right.

—We just lost half our men almost, says Lashman.—Been out here, what, an hour?

—Not good odds, grunts another, one of the surviving customers. Johnny searches for a name: Munir. Lebanese high roller.

Another man might rethink his situation on this island—six

men dead, a woman abducted, nightmare monsters on the hoof—
and consider what he's doing wrong. But Johnny is the kind of guy
who alters his course of action only slowly and with great effort.
Setbacks make him stubborn.—That thing's got my wife, Lashman.

—Sure, but—

—You want to go back?

Johnny's finger stretches toward the river they have just escaped, calm on the surface but with ripples and eddies revealing
unknowns beneath.

Lashman says nothing. He thinks Johnny is stubborn enough
to get them all killed and too pretty by half, but the idea of re-
turning to the water makes his bowels loosen and he soils his
pants right there. Lashman goes hot with shame but fortunately,
everyone is too keyed up to notice.

—It's like this, says Johnny.—We don't have much chance out
here, that's obvious. But we've got no chance at all if we split up.

The high rollers are watching him. His employees—trackers,
snipers, killers—are frowning into the woods as if calculating the
odds should they ditch him. Willis stares at the angels overhead
and whispers, Save me Jesus, fainter and fainter.

—I'm coming out of this jungle with my wife, Johnny says, or
I'm not coming out at all. It's your decision whether you want to
chance it on your own.

Notwithstanding the tough words, Johnny speaks plainly,
without bravado. The men are silent as if embarrassed by his sincerity. Johnny looks to Billy, who is neither customer nor employee, merely a friend who came along on this trip for a lark.
Entertaining the boys with dirty stories and snapping photos of
everything in sight. —Maybe sell 'em to *National Geographic,* he
had said.—Make some money from going on vacation.

Some lark. Some vacation.

The men continue to sit in silence. If anyone is planning a rebellion, he keeps it to himself. Johnny wonders what he can say to reassure them. He feels like an actor who's forgotten his lines.

Billy breaks the silence.—I propose we push on a little. Follow the trail and get away from this water. Who knows what comes down here for a drink at sunset.

The men murmur agreement. They all stand except for Willis, legless.

—How is he, Billy?

Billy checks.

—He's dead.

They stalk up the trail, eight of them, quieter now.

9. A LAND WITHOUT A PEOPLE

A night and a day and another night and a morning. Betty opens her eyes, hoping the nightmare is over, and is disappointed yet again. K. stands at the bottom of a tree, gazing upward. In his claw, Betty moans and writhes. She can't help herself.

—Johnny Johnny Johnny . . .

It rained the night before. Betty finds herself lowered to the ground and by chance her face flops against a fallen leaf the size of a car door. Wet. The water revives her somewhat. She stops moaning and lifts her head, spies a hollow in the roots that has filled with rainwater. She heaves herself toward it, ducks her head, slurps like some animal. Her head clears. What kind of parasites lurk in there, she wonders, what worms and amoebae and multi-legged microorganisms? But is past caring. She drinks more, guzzling greedily, vomits with no warning, yellow and watery right into the water she is drinking. *Bye-bye, nematodes,* she thinks. Still clearheaded, she finds another puddle and sips carefully this time, barely allowing the drops to trickle down her throat. Rustling noises flutter in from behind her: K., whom Betty refers to mentally as *the monstrosity,* fossicking about in a thicket nearby. She hopes he will just go away and leave her alone: she is also, more than anything, terrified that he will do this.

Worms and microorganisms are not, Betty suspects, the worst that this jungle has to throw at her.

K. plucks a fistful of blood-red berries and drops them into his maw. Stems, leaves and all. He stoops for more, stripping as he does so a long streamer of leaf from a second plant and munching that too, like an aperitif. He rumbles from tree to shrub to pencil-trunked sapling, a gourmet in his kitchen, helping himself to a seven-course meal on the vine. Betty watches while hunger swells in her belly like a fetus, kicking, demanding, dilating. Betty is no fool: she understands that K. is not going to feed her. Such understanding of her needs is beyond him.

She does not know, yet, whether he plans to kill her. Lord knows he's had plenty of chances already.

Shakily she gets to her feet.

The berries are sweet and a little cloying, not unlike cherries. Unable to moderate herself, she stuffs in a mouthful, then another, like an addict. She hopes they do not kill her. She wonders fleetingly if in fact she hopes they do.

—Oh cut the drama, Cleopatra, she tells herself.

K. stops eating and peers at her quizzically.

—What are you staring at? she demands, and K. looks away as if baffled.

Betty possesses strengths unexpected to those who judge her by externals (prim mouth, unlined complexion, slight frame, heavy bosoms, blond cascade). These strengths include self-reliance, mental toughness and an unflagging optimism. She's not had an easy life, though it must be admitted that compared to a Bedouin nomad's or Colombian street waif's, it hasn't been hellish either. Nonetheless, Betty is resourceful and smart, doesn't get rattled easily, and possesses both a strong stomach and a master's degree in botany. Her cardinal weakness, if such can be so neatly identified, is a tendency to place her trust a little too easily and too fully in men who are kind to her. For that matter, what qualifies as "being kind" is a touch murky too. Her botanical knowledge serves her well now, as she scans the surrounding foliage. Settling beside a leafy bush, she tears off a fistful of greens and considers them dubiously. Salad has never been her favorite but this seems a poor time to be particular. She nibbles, grimacing at the wet-leaf taste, and absently wonders what that rushing sound is behind her.

The snake rises from the very earth, the color and consistency of a cement wall. With his back turned, K. doesn't notice this monster writhe out of the soil, great sheaths of dirt sloughing off like old skin. Betty barely has time for a sharp intake of breath before its enormous coils wind about her with suffocating force. She has no way of knowing this is a full-grown, hundred-foot burrowing corkscrew serpent, nemesis of the mole people; a creature who generally keeps a healthy distance from K. but who, upon spying Betty, has responded with typically reptilian vigor. Betty knows only that she is being crushed in a vise of cold-blooded muscle, dull-green-and-graphite scales twisting the life alarmingly from her, while over her hovers the distended jaws of altogether more snake than she has ever wanted to see. She cranes her neck at the face floating overhead, leering down like a mural by Diego Rivera.

Betty screams.

The constrictor's body tightens around her: it's like being group-hugged by the Green Bay Packers. Betty tries to inhale and fails. A beaded curtain of black spots swims across her vision. Urine gushes from her like lemon juice. The thought runs through her mind, *This isn't what I bargained for when I signed up to volunteer at the orphanage!* Later she will feel guilty for not having nobler thoughts, *I will love you always Johnny,* or better still *Lord, into your hands I commend my spirit.*

A roar batters the air like a truncheon. Through the curtain of spots Betty sees K.'s looming shadow towering overhead, arm upraised, a vengeful Statue of Liberty. He moves with astonishing speed, or perhaps it only appears this way to Betty, who is experiencing life in a kind of slow-motion bubble. K. sweeps his claws across the constrictor's coils, laying its guts open to the world. With a flashing *snick,* the serpent is left disemboweled and bloody, great wet chunks of its innards soaking into the earth. Instantly its grip on Betty loosens. Her vision clears and she staggers clear of the snake's thrashing death throes.

It seems to take forever to die. K. helps it along like a nine-year-old sadist tormenting some vermin in the basement. Even as it convulses, flies are collecting, hopping from exposed organ meats to congealing puddles. They buzz away, spreading word to their comrades, and return in hordes like teenagers at a drive in. The noise of their wings soon drowns out Betty's gagging.

Finally the serpent is still. Betty crouches against the bole of K.'s tree, breathing deep, willing her heart to slow. It cooperates eventually, and with this her hunger returns full bore, as if fighting for one's life is the kind of activity that works up a hearty appetite. K. seems to agree: he squats among the underbrush and returns to his grazing. Betty follows suit. Ordinarily her imagination might be tickled by the stained-glass flicker of insects' wings, but today her concerns are more immediate.

One of the leafy greens is chewy and redolent of spinach; she gets a few mouthfuls down before her stomach, still unsettled from the attack, refuses more. She pauses for a few moments before continuing. The next shrub is fuzzy-leafed and bitter and she spits it out. Hard-shelled nuts hang in clusters off a low-growing bush, and she greedily cracks them open between stones. The meats are small and frustrating but she needs all the protein she can get, so she keeps at it.

—Not much eggs and bacon out this way, she reminds herself.

She hums softly, unself-conscious, as she works. Nearly an hour it takes her to sate her hunger one demi-mouthful at a time, then to stuff her pants pockets with nutmeats. Her blouse burgeons with berries and wadded-up jungle spinach. No telling when she'll get another chance, she figures.

—One day soon and it won't be long, uh-huh, oh yeah, mm-hm, that's right, she sings under her breath, you'll come looking for me but I'll be gone, mh-huh, oh yeah, mm-hm, that's right . . .

She has a hunch she'll be eating when *the monstrosity* does, and who knows when that will be? She wishes she had some way to transport water, but the natives who sacrificed her to this thing neglected to provide a canteen.

—Probably just as well, she says aloud, thinking about the dysentery, and returns to half humming, half singing:—You'll ask yourself, what'd I do wrong? Uh-huh, oh yeah, mm-hm, that's right . . .

The song has been running through her mind for half a day now, an endless loop of rockabilly doggerel she had heard somewhere. Now, as she picks through the shrubbery, augmenting her supplies, she gives fuller voice to the words, the lilting tune. Her voice is like a soft breeze against the ferns.—And you'll sit and you'll cry and you'll sing this song—uh-huh, oh yeah, mm-hm, that's right!

She becomes aware, suddenly, of stillness, and looks up from her gathering. The creature sits on the ground, legs crossed like Buddha, watching her. Enormous eyes gaze with an indefinable gentleness. It seems absurd, but it is undeniable too: her lilting voice, unpolished though it is, simple though the melody might be, has had a calming effect on the monstrosity. Betty can hardly credit this. It seems some fairy tale conceit, something from a bad Roger Corman movie. Nonetheless, she tells herself to remember this piece of information, to store it away someplace. It might just be useful, should the thing grow agitated.

—What's this about? Music soothing the savage beast?

The monstrosity does not answer. Neither does it look away.

Betty's eyes play over the enormous, misshapen body, trying to make sense of it and failing. She's had enough biology to know the impossibility of what she's looking at, the surrealistic slides between phyla and family, genus and class. *Class war,* she thinks wryly to herself. *Family feud.* She's reminded of a movie she saw a couple years ago with Johnny, a silly thing called *Them!* about monstrous irradiated ants that migrate to Los Angeles from New Mexico's nuclear test site. The ants themselves had been laughable—just big puppets, you could see the wires—but still, something about the movie gave her the creeps. Then there was that other giant-monster movie, what was it called? *The Beast from 20,000 Fathoms.* That was the one that ended up in Coney Island, smashing the roller coaster. Or wait—was that *The Thing from Another World?* No, that creature was different. And so was —she felt pretty sure—the monster in *It Came from Outer Space . . .* or was that *It Came from Beneath the Sea?*

Betty sighs. Johnny loves all this silliness, all these dress-up-and-act-scared monster movies. Well, here she is living through one of them. And where is he? Wherever it is, she hopes he's enjoying himself. Down in the front row, popcorn in his lap and his arm around a—

Stop it. She takes a steadying breath and the annoyance passes. There is nothing Johnny could've done, she reminds herself. Nothing any of them could have done. They all came ashore and encountered the natives—the last thing any of them had expected. Met the chief, ate at the feast apparently held in their honor. To refuse seemed a bad idea, an affront to their hosts who, after all, far outnumbered the visitors. And then after the feast, or maybe during it, they had all gone to sleep. And she, Betty, had awakened to . . . This.

It just goes to show, Betty figures, that her mother had been right all along. You couldn't trust foreigners. You left the boundaries of the USA *at your own risk.* Germans had killed Betty's daddy and Japs had drowned two uncles at Pearl; her friend Janie's fiancé was done for by the Chinese somewhere in Korea. Now here she is herself, in a pickle the likes of which would be unimaginable to anyone back home.

As if on cue, K. snorts softly and Betty looks up. The monstrosity's gaze remains fixed on her, as if he's some smitten teenager unable to divert his acne-pocked face. Betty finds the flatness of this stare unnerving, just as she would've found the stare of a pimple-scarred hot-rodder, and turns back to her berry gathering. But the tune has left her, and as she gets back to work she does not resume singing.

10. DON'T TREAD ON ME

K. has long since finished eating and feels faintly anxious, wanting to climb the tree and gain the lofty perch from which he prefers to view the world, but some impulse prevents him from interrupting the female. She needs to eat: he intuits this. Moreover, the sounds she makes weave a sort of spell on him, one he is hardly aware of and unable to question. So he waits. But the moment she pauses in her song he lunges for her, scoops her in a claw, hauls himself a few steps up the tree.

—Darn it! squeals the female.—I thought we were getting somewhere. Can't you just relax a little?

K. says nothing, pausing to sniff the air with a snap of his tongue. Something faint, something unfamiliar has snagged his attention.

—Though I suppose I can't complain. If that snake's any indication of what else lives on this island, I'd be jumpy too.

Yes, definitely a scent he can't identify. Scents. Meat and sweat and smoke, and other things.

—Betty!

It is a male voice. Something registers. K. pauses, squints through the underbrush. Snake-tongue lashes the air. If K. could frown, he would.

The female stirs but doesn't speak. Perhaps her ears haven't quite captured the sound.

—Betty, hold on! We're here!

—Johnny?

K. takes another half-step upward, still looking over his shoulder, back and down. Fighting through the surrounding foliage, perhaps a hundred yards away, comes a quartet of figures not unlike the female he carries. Not exactly the same either.

—Johnny!

—Betty!

K. hears a popping sound, feels a stinging against his thigh.

—Stop that, Lashman! He'll drop her!

—Hey, whazzat? Lying on the ground up there?

—I don't know, but it's moving.

K. bends to inspect his leg, still gripping the tree with one claw. The other cantilevers into empty air for balance, and the female with it. She shrieks.

—Johnny don't startle it!

—Hold on darling!

Other voices:—Hey you guys, lookit this! Zat a *snake* moving around up there?

—Biggest snake I ever seen. And it ain't moving, it's covered with flies.

—What a stink!

The pain is fading like the sting of a wasp, only K. has never felt any such, not with his mat of fur and scaly hide. But although the pain has already diminished, hovering now on the threshold of memory, like the sun about to be extinguished by the curve of the sea, still there is some slight perturbation of mind. These four creatures, these—males—with their nagging insect voices and popping stings, crash closer to him. They are insignificant, they pose no threat. Nothing has ever posed any threat. And yet.

In the far recesses of K.'s brain, that clammy region where little-used mechanisms like alarm and fear and flight are stored, a synapse closes, an electrical impulse skitters across the gap. Intuition and instinct urge him back to the tree. He climbs.

Scrambles in fact: pitches upward as fast as he can. Beneath him the tree judders and jounces, its length vibrating like a tuning fork. Sinewy boughs bend under his weight, snapping back like catapults. K. and Betty, together, are the projectiles so launched: in something under a minute he has scampered nearly a hundred yards straight up. They are very nearly at the summit. The tree is hardly thicker than K.'s ankle at this height, dissolving into a fireworks display of canopy another twenty yards above. The whole thing sways precipitously beneath their unaccustomed weight. Betty has long since stopped screaming and has settled into a steady, purposeful sob. Perhaps she had thought her ordeal was over, down there with Johnny at the base of the tree. K. sets her in a little cradle of branches up amid the canopy and she clings, hysteria lending her energy: to sleep would mean to slouch would mean to fall.

Betty and K. are surrounded by a vista of incomparable beauty and power, which makes no impression on the woman other than to ratchet up her fear. Low mountains to the west, where they have come from; rumpled quilt of forest canopy in all directions; sea hazily glimmering to the east. In the distance, jagged cliffs rise from the forest, slam knife-edge into the ocean: waterfalls fling themselves like suicides from the summit. Nearby a forest of naked granite pillars rear skyward, like the ruins of some ancient race of Roman Titans. It is a sight to take away one's breath. Betty pays no attention.

K., having arrived, is as uncertain what to do next as a tourist who has lost his guidebook. His attention flickers here and there like a butterfly, east, west, seaward, skyward; settling finally on *down,* where he continues to hear those voices.

—Hold on Betty, we're coming up!

—Somehow . . .

The female does not answer. Perhaps she hasn't heard, or doesn't believe, or has long since stopped hoping for anything good to happen. Perhaps her ears are not as sensitive as K.'s rimless holes. (In fact they are not.) Perhaps she has sought refuge in unconsciousness or prayer.

K., however, is a wide-awake agnostic. He descends a few steps, peering through the tangle of branches to see if the others are indeed climbing up. Not that he understood their words; but he is a creature of intuition, and his gut tells him that these males, who showed up out of nowhere and—somehow—stung him from far away, are not finished yet. They might yet sting him again.

Or sting the female.

This idea fills him, suddenly, with unaccustomed anger. A kind of cloudiness seems to fill his mind then, different from the cloudiness that is usually there. His breathing comes fast, as though he has been fighting or fleeing. The reaction is new to him and strange. He does not question it. He does not, as a rule, question anything.

He climbs lower.

K. has many flaws, the most important being that he doesn't learn very fast. Certain things happen to him with mindless repetitiveness, as sadly predictable as the beat of a pop song or the plot of a B movie.

As an example, take K.'s rival, the flying reptile-dragon-dinosaur-eagle. One might have expected, after the many previous incidents when K. put the females in the crotch of the tree only to have them snatched up, snapped like birthday crackers and swept away to the creature's cliffside aerie—one might expect that K. would have, finally, *figured it out.*

K., however, has not done so. Figuring things out is not his strong suit.

K. is halfway down the tree when he hears squeaking overhead. With a sudden jab to his stomach, a loosening of his bowels, he clambers up again.

—Help! Oh God, not this! Somebody help me!

There she is, the female, snug in the talons of his flying rival. The lizard-thing hurls a taunting screech his way, cartwheels in the air, beats off laboriously to the distant, sea-facing cliffs.

—There, heading out to sea! Do you see it Billy?

—I see it all right.

—It's the thing that killed Munir.

—I couldn't forget that, Johnny. It tore his whole head off.

K. ignores the voices. The flying thing has taken the female, as it has done—now he remembers—many times before.

—Everybody down. We've got to get out of this tree.

—Johnny, you look like you have a plan.

—That's all we need. Another plan.

—Mistah Lashman, I've had an *earful* of your bellyaching.

—Is that so? Just what're you gonna do about it?

—Believe me, I'm a-thinkin!

—Easy, you two! Lashman has a point, Coco. I've had a job to do and so far I've only made a hash of things.

K. watches as his rival dwindles against the lowering cumulus. Part of him knows, somehow—instinct? observation? memory?—that she is flying to the cliffs, to the rocky ledges that dot them. There she will find a nest of some sort, a den or rookery or simply an empty patch of ground. Where youngsters of her own perch hungrily, waiting. How this knowledge has come to him, K. could not have said, but being who he is, he doesn't stop to wonder.

K.'s descent of the tree accelerates.

—Down, everybody! Big boy's coming through!

K. trembles: something he has never done before. For some reason, this female evokes a reaction in him. Is it simply her strangeness, her bizarre albinism, that makes her stand out? Or maybe the presence of these males, pursuers of himself while he had her and now, presumably, of her new abductor. Does this competition set him on edge? Who can say. Reasons are not important to K., but this female, for whatever reason, is.

He stands on the ground now. The remains of the corkscrew serpent lie scattered like pieces of a broken train. It glimmers with insects and soaks darkly into the soil. Among the wreckage stand the human males; K. ignores them and will continue doing so as long as they don't hurt him. As if sensing this, their guns remain mute.

—Wouldja lookit the mug on this fella! He even uglier than *Lash*man here.

—Quiet, Coco. Billy, what's your thinking?

—Well, Johnny, it's like this. That bird-thing, or whatever it is, has Betty. If we want to find her, we have to find it. That won't be easy on our own.

—I got a hunch you're right.

—To my way of thinking, our best bet is to follow big boy here. That's assuming he goes after her.

—And when he finds her with that other monster . . .

—Then we let the two of them duke it out, and sneak off with Betty.

—That's as good a plan as any. The *Ocean Princess* is out there somewhere, if we can get her attention to pick us up.

—That's hoping we don't get eaten alive by them rat-things, like Ritter and Butch. Or choked on those killer vines, or attacked by them poison butterflies like Hawkins was.

—Shoot, Lashman, you carp worse than a *woman*.

—Why, I oughta—

—Knock it off you two. Billy, give me a hand with these rifles. Lashman, you got a better plan, I'm all ears.

Silence then.

—*Thought* so.

Cooke smiles and Lashman stares back with fury. Cooke, aka Cookie, aka Coco, doesn't care. Coco/Cookie/Cooke is privy to Lashman's dirty little secret, which is that the boy has been walking around stone petrified for the entire duration of the safari. Not just this last day or two—who *wouldn't* be afraid of that?—but ever since shipping out of San Diego. The boy was wetting hisself while the boat stopped for refueling in *Hawaii*, for Pete's sake. Cooke knows all about Lashman's tender stomach, his night sweats and tremors, because it was Cooke's job to keep the head clean on board the boat. A man doesn't keep many secrets from the hired help and that's for sure. So Cooke knows all about Lashman's weaknesses, his diarrhea and vomiting. Lashman knows he knows, and hates him for it.

And another thing: Lashman is petrified of germs, of getting sick. Funny thing for a big tough safari hunter but there you go. Maybe that's why he taught himself to be such an expert with all those weapons? But it was no help *here*, for sure. Slopping through this muddy undergrowth, these rivers, sleeping with these parasites whispering in your ear when they weren't busy crawling up your ass—shoot, it musta been a lot like Lashman's idea of eternal damnation.

Cooke chuckles. More like *internal* damnation.

—What's so funny?

—Oh nothin, Mistah Lashman.

Cooke had been keeping a close eye on him ever since Hawaii. Why? Because Lashman is a nigger-baiting cracker who'd be happy to put a bullet in his head, or—around here—push him into some of those strangler vines. Cooke grew up knowing plenty of guys like him. Texas this was. Big-mouthed tough guys who'd walk around with a rifle on their shoulder, right next to the chip they always carried there. Not a combination that made for peaceful times, and Cooke had expected problems with Lashman before now. So far, though, all his observations had only led him to realize how weak Lashman really was.

Not harmless: just weak. Cemeteries were full of guys who couldn't tell the difference.

Cooke was too smart to make that particular mistake, though not too smart to get stuck on this lousy island. Ain't none of them too smart for *that*, and that's the truth.

So he smiles now at the squinty-eyed little man with all the weapons and equipment. And Lashman says nothing, only glares back furiously.

K. ignores the men as he might ignore insects. He has reached a decision unlike any he has ever made before. It is a decision to do with things he cannot see or hear, unlike food, rain, the land, the drums. It is a decision made in the abstract, about the female he no longer holds, the rival he no longer hears and her nesting ground to which he has never gone.

A line has been crossed in K.'s understanding of the world.

K. possesses a perfect sense of direction. He knows where his rival's nests lie, and how far they are. It will take roughly half a day to reach them. He does not know whether the female will be alive when he finds her. If he had the ability to imagine an answer, the ability to make a prediction based on past experience, he would be forced to admit: probably not.

—Looks like he's made up his mind. Any idea which direction, Billy?

—Nope. Our best bet is to follow *him*.

Knocking aside trees like drapery, K. fixes his memory on the female, and gropes his way toward her.

11. LIBERTY OR DEATH

How K. gets there is irrelevant. The men follow.

They find a sheer cliff, hundreds of feet tall, facing the sea. The men stand at the top and gawk over the edge. Below the lip of the cliff, halfway down, a thin ledge extends out, barely deep enough for Betty to lie on, but long enough for her to stretch. She huddles there, still alive: pressed against unyielding stone, naked legs curled under her skirt. A thick-boled evergreen juts from the cliff face, and Betty hunches unmoving in its shade. Dotting the cliff below and beside her are other such shelves. A few dozen, all smaller than her current perch. Most are occupied by gulls, cormorants, auks, guillemots. Two are home to the offspring of the dragon-raptor herself. Each as big as the captive, they eye her hungrily, shrieking to each other: their scratchy voices lacerate the air like photograph needles skidding across vinyl.

Far out to sea, something white floats.

K. stands at cliff's edge, looking down. Gusts buffet him, sending him back on his heels. His head is ringed by a halo of gulls floating motionless on the currents, feathered intimations of martyrdom and sainthood.

—Johnny, Billy! Out there!

—Well I'll be damned, it's the *Princess.* Billy, there's our ticket home.

The men gather at the cliff, not too close to K.'s ankles, and stare out at the boat while K. gazes down at Betty, pondering.

—Let's start a fire or somethin. Make a signal to tell 'em we're here.

—Hold your horses, Coco. We've got some rescuing to do first.

—And then there's the little matter of how we get down from this cliff, ourselves.

—Aw hell, says Lashman.—I got rope.

The men stare at him and Lashman lets them. This moment has been a long time coming and he basks in it. Lashman is a short, bandy-legged fellow, broad across the shoulders but ugly as sin and he knows it. He's never had any luck with the broads except those he's had to pay for, and not always them, even. (That hooker in Tijuana still gets his blood boiling just to remember her, but he made her sorry all right.) As if to make up for this shortcoming, his life has been dedicated to the manly arts, shooting and tracking and hunting, and he's turned himself into the best in the business. Johnny knows it too, which is why he hired him even though they hate each other. And then what happened?

Then Betty smiled at him early on in the voyage, across the mess table, and Lashman fell for her, hard. Sure she was married to Johnny but accidents could happen couldn't they? A smile like that gives a guy ideas, more than ideas. Gives him pictures and scenarios and stuff to think about late at night. Like something out of the movies. Makes a guy forget his inadequacies, his weak guts and diarrhea and nightmares of being chased and held down.

Then all this brouhaha on the island, the native tribe discovering them, throwing that big banquet and drugging the wine; the men waking up to find the monster making off with Betty. If he, Lashman, turned out to be the fella to rescue her—well, a gal might forget Johnny's handsome jaw for a few minutes, even a whole night. And show a little gratitude, no?

K. shuffles a few steps to one side, peering downward. The men follow suit. The cliff face is sheer, with few handholds except for those little ledges starting about halfway down. Along the cliff's edge grow a smattering of scrubby bushes and gnarled, man-sized trees.

Finally Johnny's curiosity gets the best of him.—Rope, Lash-man? How much?

Fumbling with a rucksack.—See?

—Not enough to reach bottom.

—It doesn't need to, says Lashman. He grins, making his hideous face even uglier.—We just need to get to that ledge where Betty is. You go first, Johnny. Tie this end around your waist, loop the rest over this tree here and drop the other end for Betty to hold.

—She's too weak to secure it, Johnny protests quietly.

—Don't matter. It's just something else to grab in case you slip. We anchor you up here, play it out as you go down. Once you're down, me and Cookie will anchor Billy, and then you two down there will play out the rope when Cookie climbs. I'll go last and we can pull it after us once we're all on the ledge.

—Why not just tie it onto the tree here? asks Cooke.—Safer that way.

—We do that, we can't take it with us. We're gonna need to do this trick a couple times to get all the way down.

The men are hesitant but Lashman figures they have no choice.—Trust me, he says, knowing they don't.

The males buzz about like dragonflies. K. ignores them. Impo-tent, he pokes at the cliff edge with a seven-toed foot. (Why seven?) There is a small avalanche of stones and dust.

—Hurry!

K. peers down again. The female is standing now, staring up at him. He assumes it is at him. He feels an impulse to do something, to—greet her somehow, but he does not understand this impulse or how to act on it. There is so much he does not understand: how to warble hello like a bird, or bump heads like a cat, or wave his hand like a human being.

—Don't let me drop, boys.

—Not to worry, Johnny.

K. gazes round-eyed at the four males. As he watches, one of them disappears and they become three males. K. registers this as strange, then forgets it.

A shadow passes overhead, broad-winged, lithe.

On the ledge below, Betty awaits Johnny. For a time he dangles on the rope like a half-finished spider. Winds buffet him. Pebbles and sand, kicked loose by his toes, plummet to oblivion. His arms clutch the ropes and quiver visibly.

Atop the cliff, the others lean back on the rope, hauling against his weight.—Careful Johnny! cries Billy.

Cooke mutters, Don't startle him.

Suddenly he's there on the ledge. Johnny and Betty embrace, they kiss. As if magnetized, his hands fall to her backside, cup it, squeeze.

—That's enough down there! We gotta train to catch.

—Sorry!

Up on the cliff, Lashman murmurs, Can't blame the guy, though.

—Ain't it the truth, grunts Cooke.

The rope is hauled up. Billy ties it around himself and goes down next. K. watches, puzzled but curious. The shadow passes over him again, larger.

Billy makes it down. Cooke follows, stocky but agile. Lashman pins the rope with his feet at the top while Johnny and Billy anchor it down below. The ledge is getting crowded when Cooke drops onto it too. He hugs Betty briefly, tightly, and furtively squeezes her rump. He pretends it's an accident. Betty pretends to laugh. The white men pretend not to notice.

—Okay Lashman, your turn.

Lashman is knocking something into the ground with a stone: a pulley wheel, set on a peg that can be hammered into the earth. Why he has carried this in his rucksack the past three days, only he could say. He finishes in moments and then he lays the rope across the groove of the wheel, testing that it can move freely.

—Okay, I got the rope so we can just pull it clear. Otherwise it'll get snagged on the tree.

—I take away all the bad things I ever done said about you. And believe me there was *plenty*.

Lashman laughs.—Thanks, Cookie.

He steps to the cliff edge, takes a rope in each hand. Down on the ledge the others lean into both the rope tails, anchoring them. Lashman hasn't tied off around his waist, preferring to scamper down unhindered. It's more dangerous but that's the kind of guy he is. Later, they know, he'll brag about it.

—Take it slow, Lashman. Mind your footing.

—Don't fret about me, Johnny, says Lashman.

—Don't fret about me, Johnny, says Lashman.

In a few moments he will be dead but he doesn't know that. Ironically, Lashman has never felt more vital, more alive, than at this moment. The wind knifes across him like an icicle, sets every nerve to tingling; the ropes thrum with tension, resisting his touch like a woman's thighs. He feels immensely powerful. He imagines Betty looking up at him, biting her lip, praying for his safety; imagines that by now the men have told her: Yeah, this is Lashman's doing, Lashman's rope, Lashman's courage. Lashman's rescue. You can thank him when he gets down here; thank him (this with a significant look between Johnny and Betty) when he gets us all onto that boat.

And Betty looking up at him, teeth against flesh, his silhouette powerful against the sky. The mug so tough he didn't even tie off. Who let the others go first. The guy unafraid of standing up here, alone with the monster, while the others bolted for safety.

Betty biting so hard with her perfectly square incisors that she tastes blood.

Lashman grins and imagines her wet beneath him.

When he leans back into the abyss, the ropes sturdy in his hands, cutting red-raw against his palms, the flying reptile-dragon veers in from out of nowhere and snaps her horse-headed eagle beak across his shoulders. Lashman's head jolts back like a Pez dispenser before tearing off raggedly, his already-dead hands clinging by reflex to the ropes. Blood bubbles onto the rocks, then his fingers loosen and the body falls.

K. watches it drop past the ledge with the cringing female and males, bouncing into the sea. He sees the flying lizard as it skims over the waves like an immense saurian pelican, turning back to the island and beating its heavy wings to gain altitude, to return to the cliff to where he stands waiting.

Far below, a squealing voice:—He's dead! That thing killed him!

—They're all dead, Betty, we're the only ones left. Now get a grip on yourself.

—The way that thing—it just—oh my *God*—

—Forget him, Betty, he was bad news. Anyway, crying won't bring him back. Now help me with this rope, boys, I think the ship's spotted us!

K. is ready for the flying lizard's first pass. He sets his haunches and leans forward: as she swoops overhead he leaps toward her, but she pulls up abruptly and he nearly overbalances, nearly pitches over the cliff. The fall would cripple him at least. Snarling, he jumps back. The lizard rasps victoriously and pinwheels against the sky, then folds her wings and drops howling like a Stuka over Poland. K. pitches into the dirt as an eagle beak snaps at where his head had been.

Prostrate on the ground, K. can squint over the cliff. The female is no longer on the ledge—she huddles on another one, farther down. The males are with her, trying to disengage the rope from the gnarled tree they have wrapped it around. Their movements are jerky, uneven.

K. sees why. The dragon-lizard has broken off from harassing him and now flutters along the cliff face, an ungainly hummingbird trying to hold its position long enough to snap off the heads of the three males. And the female.

The female—

Frantically, K. lurches to his feet, stomps the ground, bellows. It is a sound fit to unsettle demons, but there are no demons around, and he is ignored. A kind of rage rushes through his blood like heroin, interfering momentarily with his vision. He scrabbles at the earth, peeling up strips of sod, loose pebbles that sift through his curled claws, mocking his helplessness. He howls.

Down below: pop-popping, tat-tatting sounds. The sound of brittle things shattering underfoot, but for some reason it drives off the flying lizard. She banks hard into the sky, clutching one of the males in her talons. Frantic wiggling, cries of dismay. She rises hundreds of yards into the sky, drops the figure, then folds her wings and dives to snatch it again. The wiggling and shrieking are suddenly cut off. She deposits the limp figure on the ledge harboring one of her infants, who lunges into it amid rasps and grunts, while the other offspring, unfavored and unable to fly and so eat, looks on and keens in banshee wails of humiliated rage.

The remaining humans, two males and the female, are barely visible now. Having descended with the help of the rope and a few fortuitously protruding stones, they have nearly reached the sea.

Only belatedly does K. realize—dimly, hazily—what is happening. That white floating object out on the water—stone? whale? tree?—has moved closer. The female waves frantically. The males clutch her as she kicks and screams. K. hasn't worked out the details yet, but it is clear that floating thing is approaching to take the female away, possibly to harm her. This he cannot allow.

A resolution of sorts forms in K.'s breast, gelling, firming like mortar. This resolution makes him brave, in a way. Bravery is new. Bravery has not been much called for in the daily life of a forty-foot-tall, claw-fingered, mammalian-reptilian-insectoid gargantua with feathers.

K. resolves to *make his move* then and there. And although he doesn't know why, he prepares himself for this by taking a deep breath.

A sharp report, like a slap: out at sea, the floating bobbing thing has drawn closer to shore. Figures visible on its surface tumble back and forth like disturbed ants. A line of them holds those queer smoking twigs that K. is, belatedly, beginning to associate with noise and stinging pain. He fixes his eyes on this boat, these figures, those sticks, and further puffs of smoke dot the air, followed moments later by a series of clear crackling *snap!*s like dry leaves being trod upon.

It does not occur to K. that they might be shooting at him.

How fortuitous then that they are not. With a frenzied spasm K.'s airborne rival, the flying lizard-thing, the creature of nightmares (not K.'s but assuredly now the woman Betty's, the men Johnny and Billy's) twists like a crumpled ball of crepe paper and drops into the sea. In moments it disappears, thrashing, below the waves, enormous wings spread for a time like newsprint trying to blot a spill. They twitch before disappearing. K. watches them go. Then, bellowing, he hurls himself feet-first over the edge of the cliff.

It is an impulsive act. He would be the first to admit it, if he could. The nearest ledge is halfway down, perhaps a hundred feet; the drop is the equivalent of a jump from a second-story window for an average-sized man. Except that the target is not smooth flat earth but a tiny ledge of stone barely wide enough to accommodate his feet, and beyond that, another hundred-foot drop to the stony seaside and foaming surf.

He scrabbles at the cliff as he slides down, gouging out furrows of dust and stone and loose grainy earth. Great clods are hacked away by his clawed heels. Thinly rooted pines slow his progress momentarily before snapping violently or tearing loose. K. slams into the stone ledge like a juggernaut, like a localized monsoon, like every bad idea at once. The stone holds for a precious twothreefour seconds, then cracks somewhere unseen under the earth and tilts, spilling him in a crazy somersault of windmilling arms and fluttering (first lacerated now shredded) butterfly wings and grime-streaked fur. The whole process repeats itself, a slow-motion cavalcade of monstrosity and dirt.

Somewhere below him people scream. Gulls whirl like snowflakes. The ocean is a roiling cauldron as boulders crash into it; the waves toss the boat with seasickening shudders and drops. As for the rowboat that has been sent by the larger vessel to pick up the castaways clinging to the cliff, it is little more than a cork, a scrap of timber in a torrent, its crewmen reduced to clinging for life to the gunwales.

K. dimly registers this on his way down. It's surprising the details he is able to take in, like the faces of the two men and the woman, torn open in ricti of terror as he sails past. For he is falling now. The last sixty feet or so, everything gives way beneath him and he falls, artlessly, gracelessly from the last-ledge-but-one (the humans huddle on the last) into the shallow water that awaits, rock-lined, low-tided, tide-pooled.

Imagine a grown man dropping from a second-story window into a wading pool holding two feet of water. It wouldn't kill him, maybe.

For a time after his impact, K. clings to consciousness. He can't move much; he can barely lift his head. But his eyes work, so he watches. First all the water around him goes away. Then it comes sloshing back, a sloppy caress that ruffles his fur and cools him and makes him feel, partly, better.

He hurts. Especially his legs, especially his ankles. Also his lower back, come to think of it. (Think?) For the most part, shock numbs his body, keeps pain at arm's length. This will not last forever.

Movement catches his eye. The humans are descending. From the lowest ledge, barely twenty feet above the water, there is a narrow path down to the edge of the sea. The way is slick and it's necessary to cling to the cliff face in order to avoid a nasty slip into the rocky shallows, but compared to what Betty and Johnny and Billy have been through, this is putt-putt golf. They make their way slowly at first, tentative, like flowers uncertain whether to bloom this day or wait a bit longer. As K. watches, unmoving, their movements grow more confident.

—That fall's stunned him, folks.

—You just watch yourself, Johnny. We've come too far to let anything happen now.

The words bounce unheeded off K. His eyelids grow thick and his body starts to hurt in earnest: aching, shrieking in places. He is barely aware when the rowboat bobs past his head—within easy striking distance, if he cared to strike—and collects the three traumatized human beings. He totters at the edge of awareness when the rowboat passes him on its return journey, to deposit these same three on the deck of the steamship. And he has well and truly passed into oblivion's sweet embrace when, after a lengthy and heated discussion aboard that same steamship, some of its crew return to where he lies, breathing but motionless, and begin the delicate task of lacing his legs and arms and torso with an extensive shroud of ropes and nets.

It had never occurred to him to expect this.

Everything fades then, slowly, to black.

REEL THREE

MONSTER, 1957

Three monkeys sat in a coconut tree,
Discussing things as they are said to be.
Said one to the others, "Now listen you two,
There's a certain rumor that ain't be true:
That man descended from our noble race.
The very idea is a big disgrace!
No monkey ever deserted his wife,
Starved her baby, or ruined her life . . .
And another thing: you will never see
A monkey build a fence around a coconut tree
And let all the coconuts go to waste,
Forbidding all other monkeys to come and taste . . .
Yes, man descended —the worthless bum;
But, brothers, from us he did not *come."*

    —DAVE BARTHOLOMEW, "The Monkey" (1957)

Can you imagine an army of these things
descending upon one of our cities?

    —HANS CONRIED IN
    The Monster That Challenged the World (1957)

12. LOCATION SHOT

—Oh Johnny, he's awake.

K. lies on his back under an ad hoc tangle of cables and chains, helpless as Gulliver and twice as confused. The restraints that bind him have been scrounged from the lower holds of the *Ocean Princess*, as have the pontoons, oil drums, planking, metal beams and—unlikely bit of cargo, this—the collapsible helicopter landing pad upon which K.'s upper body now rests. The captain had told his men, If it floats, I want it on deck on the double! and they responded with the alacrity of sailors promised bonus wages. The oddball collection of flotsam was welded and bolted and bound, and now K. lies strapped to it like an ambulance case on a gurney. Not that he is familiar with ambulances, or gurneys either. Nor again hospitals, pre-ops, invasive surgery, sutures, flatline, postmortem, malpractice, brain death, vegetative states. His education is just beginning, and he has so much to learn.

—Stay right here, darling, nothing can happen now. You're safe.

—I wish I could be sure . . .

—Trust me, Betty. The nightmare's over.

His cobbled-together raft—his gurney—is attached by a long umbilical cable to the stern of the *Ocean Princess,* a steamship twice as long as he is but barely half as wide. From the sky, the ship looks like a blunt cigar towing a roughly rectangular float carrying . . . something that looks like K. (Metaphors fall short at times. Nothing but K. looks like K.) Sapphire ocean all around. The float drags awkwardly, slowing the steamship's progress. Her engines grunt as she labors, and thick runnels of white water blow into the air past K.'s shoulders. K. however seems to register none of it: neither floats nor boats nor seawater. He just lies watching the sky. Clouds litter it like corpses.

—I know I'm safe now, Johnny. It's just—seeing it again brings back such memories. Not that they ever go away anyhow.

—Put it out of your mind. Think of other things.

—How can I? It plays over and over in my head like some terrible movie!

His current situation is incomprehensible to K., but the things he does understand are more basic. The required texts for Existence 101. Hunger, for starters. And fatigue, heavy on him now, crushing his ribs as if the sky has turned solid and bears down on his sternum with its full weight. And oh yes, pain.

—That's why I'm not so sure it's a good idea for you to be out here in the first place. After what happened, him taking you away like that. Carrying you in his hand like—I don't know what. But I do know you should be resting.

—You're probably right. It's almost as if . . . I feel drawn to him somehow. I know it sounds silly, but—it's almost a compulsion.

There is a pause.

—Compulsion, huh?

The *Ocean Princess* has been on the water for weeks. K. barely notes the passage of time, slipping in and out of awareness like a kayak shooting the rapids. The captain of the vessel has had a hard time of it from the U.S. Navy, from the Coast Guard, from customs; since entering territorial waters he's faced a steady stream of tight-lipped, gray-faced officials. The captain claims that he plucked K. from the ocean, an assertion backed up by his crew and passengers. Strictly speaking, this is true, so technically K. is salvage. He's the captain's property to do with as he wants, and what he wants is to sell him to Billy for an exorbitant amount of money. He has reportedly done so, though the crew knows that really K. was Billy's property all along and what he's paying for is towing. The gray-faced officers on the mainland don't like it one bit but there's little they can do short of torpedoing the vessel and drowning everyone on board. This they are reluctant to do, although they discuss the possibility with grim earnestness—and before it's all over, more than one shaking, shaken admiral will wish he'd had the nerve to give the order.

—This sun's killing me, Betty. Let's get back to our cabin and lie down.

—How can I lie down? Every time I shut my eyes I have nightmares.

—Who said anything about shutting our eyes?

—Oh God, Johnny, not *now*.

There is a pause.

—Anyway I might as well stay out here and have him right here in front of me. It's all I see anyway, no matter where I go. At least this way it's more realistic, like one of those new 3-D movies playing out right before my eyes.

—Take it easy . . .

Meanwhile the engines drink gas like a Russian slurps vodka. A couple weeks back the captain arranged for a midocean fuel delivery, which took time—and money. For some days the boat floated more or less adrift, hundreds of miles south of Honolulu. Once the fuel arrived, the engines roared to life again.

The captain's been doing a lot of calculating, figures he'll be doing a lot more.

Still K. waits. His conscious mind, such as it is, is taken up with the more pressing demands of Existence 101. ("Broken bones take longer to heal when the patient is starving to death. Discuss.") The tribulations of the captain and the other humans on the boat are as opaque to him as the six o'clock news. ("Nasser and Nehru's Non-Aligned Movement threatens both American and Soviet hegemony by rejecting the notion of a zero-sum approach to Cold War international relations. Therefore, the NAM will never be allowed to survive. Discuss.")

—I heard a rumor that Billy's paying the captain an awful lot of money for this, Johnny. Is it true?

—Well, I guess he wouldn't do it for free. All those Coast Guard stiffs are giving him what for. You ask me, somebody somewhere's taking a payoff.

—I wonder what Billy has in mind.

—Well . . .

—You know something, don't you? Tell me.

—I'd rather have him explain it.

There is a pause.

—From the look on your face, Johnny, I have a feeling I won't much like it. What*ever* it is.

K. shifts his head, slowly. The pain takes his breath away. ("Injuries located in the lower half of the body lead to surprising amounts of discomfort in the upper half. Discuss.") Two humans sit in a small boat, bobbing some distance from his floating platform. From this angle they seem to dance amid the sparkling waves, their small skiff jostling in and out of sight. The waves pain him with their refracting-jewel glare. Sapphire, blue topaz, aquamarine. Jewels of course mean nothing to K., nor do colors; but the unrelenting brightness hurts his eyes.

The humans are watching him. Tiny things that they are, they have somehow gained the advantage. K. recognizes this. He understands in some primal part of his brain that he is here because of them: aching and immobilized beneath the heaving sun. He doesn't understand, though, how these things have come to pass.

He never will.

The humans have broken off their conversation to stare at him.—Boy, he's an ugly sucker.

—Don't talk like that Johnny. Can't you see he's hurt?

—Feel sorry for him do you?

—Of course not, but . . .

K., who is not a predator though he might look like one, is unable to appreciate the predatory instincts of others. A wolf would understand its role in this scene, even a python would, perhaps a shark. For that matter a prey animal would have a pretty good idea of how to play it, too. Not K. Having lived his life as neither killer nor victim, his instinctive understanding of such things— what would be his race memory, if he had a race, or a memory— is vestigial, dormant, rusty.

—But what?

—When he took me away that day, you know, he never actually tried to hurt me. He even saved my life. There was a snake, and then that flying thing—oh God, Johnny, that flying monster! What it did to poor Coco—it could've just as easily done the same to me!

—Easy darling, I'm here.

K. had forgotten the female. This is not surprising, as K. forgets everything with enviable swiftness. He is in fact halfway to forgetting the island on which he has lived his whole life. But now, seeing the white female with the shiny hair, the spark of recognition reignites: vague associations from the past well up again, feelings of longing and protectiveness. K. sees the other human move close to the female, wrapping his arms threateningly around her. The female responds by making soft whimpering sounds of dismay. Clearly she is trapped, frightened—

K. snarls at the male, who jumps back, releasing her.

—Sounds like he's waking up all right! So much for your gentle giant, Betty.

—Will those chains hold him?

—The captain told me they're pure titanium. Beats me where he got them, but they'll hold anything. Still, it's best not to get too close.

The outboard emits a low insect whine, and white froth bubbles out the rear as the little boat buzzes a few yards farther off. K. looks away. Now that the male has released the female, K. forgets why he snarled.

He stares at the sky. Far overhead, an albatross is a speck against the sky's blue concavity, a Sputnik with feathers. It hasn't yet occurred to K. to wonder how he has been immobilized, nor does it occur to him that the albatross understands his situation better than he himself does: a body ensnared beneath a web of chains and cables on a makeshift raft, helpless. The raft trails a hundred yards behind the *Ocean Princess* like a dirty secret: a child born of incest, say, or an uncle with syphilis.

At this point K. experiences an abrupt new sensation, as his consciousness flickers across the receding memory of his island home, fading but as yet not completely gone. Perhaps the female has triggered it. He remembers the lush forests, the shimmering orange clouds of viperine lepidoptera, the strangler vines, the moon-eyed toad bats, and it all coalesces into a single idea in his abdomen: *home.* K. would rather be there than here, wherever *here* is. Wherever *there* is too, come to think of it. And for the first time in his life, K. experiences nostalgia.

This is big, this is important. K. is desiring something he can't see, smell or touch. He is thinking in abstractions. If K. were the type to keep a diary, this is the kind of thing he might mention in it.

Another voice impinges on K.'s awareness, but he ignores it. The words are meaningless, and it has dawned on K. that, apart from snarling, there is little he can do to influence his situation.

Anyway, it's just another boat come to join the first. A lone passenger in this one.

—Hey, I've been looking everywhere for you two!

—Hello, Billy. We were just talking about you.

—Nothing good I hope.

—No worry on *that* score.

—So what's got you two out here, anyway? Can't be the scenery.

—Betty wanted to visit an old flame.

—Oh darling, stop.

—So how's our Romeo doing?

—Waking up finally. He barked at us once but now he's playing hard to get.

—Romeo, I like that.

—Well Johnny, it's what the crewmen are calling him. The captain figures it's a good idea. Helps the men get over their nervousness if they can laugh a little.

—Smart fella.

—Yeah, he is that. So, Johnny.

There is a pause.

—So Johnny, you think about what I said last night?

—I'm still thinking, Billy. Don't rush me. I don't like to rush things.

—Don't I know it!

—I wish you boys would come clean and tell me what it is you're planning. I know you haven't gone to all this trouble for no reason.

More silence. The ship's engines chug against the wind and currents, while the outboards idle against the swell.

—Well Johnny?

—Yes, Billy?

—Looks like your girl here's smarter than the both of us.

—I knew that already.

—Shall I tell her or do you want to?

—You go ahead.

—Shoulda known you'd say that.

—You're the slick talker, Billy. I'm just the hired gun.

—Will you two *please* tell me what's going on?

—It's like this, Betty. Romeo here is our ticket to the good life.

—What on earth are you talking about?

—Think about it. There's not a man, woman or child in the USA who wouldn't pay top dollar to see an attraction like this.

—You can't be serious! You're going to put him in some zoo somewhere?

—Billy's got a point, darling. When he first told me his idea, I had the same reaction as you. But imagine it. Not a zoo, but a show traveling from city to city. Under the big top, like Barnum and Bailey, but bigger—lots bigger. What do you figure to call it, Billy?

—The Romeo of the Forgotten Jungle. It was the sailors gave me the idea. The biggest big top in history, thousands of people in every city and town in America. Two bucks to stand in the presence of the mightiest monster the world has ever seen. Picture it, Betty.

—Oh, I don't know, boys.

—Think of it as a revival meeting—if people don't come away from it believing in God, well, at least they'll have seen the Devil!

—Billy, the way you talk! How can a girl believe a single word you say?

—You can believe them *all,* doll. And Johnny, I had another brain wave when I was talking to the captain. I was thinking . . . If we have a Romeo, what else does the story need?

—Hey, wait a minute—

—All I'm saying is, run it up your flagpole and see who salutes. Think of the crowds we'll pull, with the Romeo of the Forgotten Jungle *and* the Juliet He Risked Captivity For!

—That's an awful idea. Darling, make him stop.

—That's more than I bargained for, Billy.

—Of course we split the take three ways, even-Steven. Does the thought of becoming rich really repulse the both of you so much?

—It's not the money, it's just, it doesn't seem very *kind.*

—Would you listen to that, Johnny!

—I guess I have to listen. We're married after all.

—Ha ha! That's a good one.

—But listen. Billy, from what I hear we've got a bigger problem than this.

—Bigger than Betty's scruples? Not sure I'm ready for that.

—I'm serious. I overheard the captain say that the creature's not eating anything. No use building dreams in the sky if your ticket to the good life starves himself to death.

—Hmm . . . You got a point there. Maybe I should have a little chat with the boss. With what I'm paying for this towing job, I want to be sure I end up with something to show for it.

The insect-engine roars louder, then fades.—See you kids later. Don't do anything I wouldn't do!

—That doesn't rule out much, Billy.

When the sound is gone, K. relaxes minutely. He doesn't know why: in fact, he doesn't even know it happens. Then a voice rattles in his ear like a pebble, the voice he has begun to associate with the female.—Darling, are you really going to go along with that?

—I don't know. Billy's a smart fella. . . . When I said it's more than I bargained for, I meant it. But he's got a knack for business, and after what happened on that island, I need a job.

—But you have a job.

—You can't be serious. After this trip, my business is bankrupt for good. Who wants a safari guide who feeds his customers to the animals?

—Don't even say such things.

—But it's true. They're dead, all of them, and so are my men. No one will ever hire me again.

—Oh darling! I'll support you!

—How you figure that? Volunteering at the orphanage won't put food on the table, good cause or no.

The voices drop away as the humans sidle off in their little boat. K. has long since stopped paying attention. He is not exactly capable of hoping for things, but in some dim recess of his mind lies the knowledge that he hasn't always felt this much pain, and to the extent that such memories can serve as a template for the future, K. vaguely desires that when he wakes up next, he will be returned to that happy state.

It is probably for the best that K. has no more than a passing acquaintance with hope. It saves him so much grief, such disappointment. It prevents disillusionment from flowering into cynicism and bitterness. Having few expectations—the absence of pain for instance, or a life free of coercion and unfairness—means that he has few expectations that can be dashed into countless fragments the size of subatomic particles.

He dozes fitfully.

13. WITH MALICE TOWARD NONE

In his dream, K. flies. It is only after some time that he realizes the impossibility of this: the sun burns hot against his retinas, while his flickering tongue registers more aromas than a dream should bring. Unfamiliar pungent petrol smells, dirty smoke, acrid mammalian reek that he is slowly identifying as *human*. Salt sea tang underpins it all.

Still, the sensation is one of soaring, floating the currents. But the sky is overhead; K. can see it, which is confusing. If he is flying, he should be up there in the sky, with the earth beneath him.

It's a puzzle he is unprepared to solve. K. possesses only the shakiest understanding of the three states of matter: solid, liquid and gas. Earth, sea and air. He is familiar enough with land, virtually unacquainted with water beyond the narrow boundaries of the odd stream and the buffeting surf of the island's coast. Gas is clean off the map, the idea that air is a *thing* pretty well beyond him. So too is the ability to picture himself floating on a makeshift barge as he is tugged across the ocean. The up-and-down sensation brought on by the ocean swells as he rides over them is inexplicable and thus unexplained.

He does know about pain. Right now he's learning more about it than he'd have ever believed possible: he is a student of pain, a doctoral candidate attending a seminar in agony using himself as its primary text. His head feels as though an enormous puffin is pecking at it. His wrists ache. Two of his claws have splintered. His shoulders and neck are motley with bruises, one ankle twisted, both knees lamed. The stubs of his demolished butterfly wings throb. Lacerations crisscross his back and legs: he looks twice trampled by Ben-Hur's chariot. Besides all this, K. cannot move beyond shifting his head slightly, and his muscles have cramped as a result. He does not know that this is a result of his being restrained. K. knows he can't move but doesn't know why not; he is ignorant of things like knots, chains, cages and confinement.

He will learn. O how he will learn.

K. is also innocent, at this point in his life, of fear. Anxiety he has felt a time or two, in the face of an especially powerful storm; ditto surprise, startlement, even free-floating edginess. Flat terror is something new, the kind of heart-racing fight-or-flight response that rears up when one's very existence is at risk. Not surprisingly, K. has not faced this threat for . . . as long as he can remember. In fact—because he can't remember much—for a great deal longer than that. So perhaps, then, it isn't surprising that even as he lies on this oddly heaving platform, immobilized and aching, K. feels none of the rage of the trapped beast, the rage that is bred of vulnerability and nourished by terror. For these are things that K. has lived utterly without.

So far.

When he wakes, the sun is closer to the horizon and his body still hurts. But not as much. This is a significant improvement, though his knees still torture him and hunger bores through his abdomen like a dentist's drill. He hasn't eaten for weeks, but his enforced idleness has allowed his body to heal itself somewhat, living off its own stored fat, melting down muscle to repair bone and blood. Consuming flesh to repair flesh. There is only so long this can last, but to some degree at least, K's wounds have lessened. He dimly registers the improvement, and dimly wonders if it will continue. And so his education progresses, with him now pondering the future in terms of things that might, or might not, occur.

Voices nearby. Also disgusting smells, old blood, carrion. K.'s stomach curdles like bad yogurt.—What do you think, Captain?

—I think he's been tied up for weeks, he should be plenty hungry. But he's showing no interest at all.

—One of the men was saying he's got a pet snake at home that only eats once every two months. A boa constrictor.

—This thing isn't a snake, Ash.

—Yes sir. I was only saying, sir.

K. turns his head. Beside him, within reach of his mouth if he cranes his neck, sits a tower of carrion. Beyond this, a pair of outboard motorboats ride idle on the water. K. hisses weakly and turns away.

—Picky cuss ain't he?

—Some predators will only eat fresh kill, Ash. They'd rather starve than eat something already dead.

—We don't have a lot of wildlife on board, Captain.

—Thanks for the reminder.

K. stares the other way, at the ocean. The wind is gustier now, the swell rougher, and when it rolls his raft sideways he has a view of blue water and whitecaps stretching on to infinity. Infinity being of course another concept that K. is incapable of understanding, but in this way he is no different, really, from anyone else on the boat.

—Load up that meat again. No sense letting it go to waste.

—Aye sir.

—Then find that Johnny fellow for me, and the woman if you can.

One of the small boats buzzes off, taking the dead flesh with it.

The smell is carried away on the sea breeze. K. adjusts himself beneath his bindings, minutely more comfortable now. He dozes again, waking hungrier than ever, but is distracted by the presence of the female.—The whole time I was with him, Captain, he never ate anything but leaves and fruit.

—You're saying this thing is a vegetarian?

—From everything I saw, yes.

—Another Gandhi, who would've guessed. Ash?

—Sir?

—Raid the mess. Tell the cook I'm commandeering all the fruit and vegetables. I want every can of peaches and head of cabbage set aside for the duration. The men will have to live on meat and bread.

—Aye sir. Potatoes?

—I want those too. And while you're at it, bring some greens and fruit back here on the double. Get the men to help if you have to.

—Aye sir.

Thereafter things get better. The food that is presented to K. is unfamiliar and for the most part not to his liking, and it is nowhere near enough to satisfy him; but it keeps him alive. Small piles, mouthfuls really, are left near his head, and he is able to scoop them with his prehensile tongue. Flick flick, it is gone, and he is left to savor the aftertaste of banana skins and pineapple rings, canned beets and raw onions and carrots by the bunch.

—Bastard sure can put it away!

—You'd think that's a appetizer steada three days' rations.

Observing K. becomes a favorite pastime for the off-duty crew, especially at mealtimes. They circle his floating platform in the two little outboard lifeboats, heckling him from the water. K. ignores them. His rapidly healing body cramps horribly under its restraints, but K. has accepted the idea that he is helpless. Until external circumstances change his situation, his situation will remain unchanged. So he lies and sleeps and eats and stares at the clouds, slowly regaining strength all the while. And he waits for something to happen.

Something always does.

14. CLOSE-UP

Were K. able to loose himself from his constraints, snap his shroud of chains and cables like the spiderweb it resembles, then make his way unmolested to the steamship towing his little raft, perhaps balancing on the hundred-yard towline or hauling himself hand over hand while his seven-toed feet kicked at the ocean fighting to swallow him—maybe he could then lower one flat round shark's eye to the little rear cabin porthole and squint into the dimness.

This of course could never take place. For a whole slew of reasons, not the least of which concern the alarum that would greet his resurrection, not to mention the unlikelihood of his balancing on the tether or clutching such a lifeline with clumsy claws. But just suppose it all happens. What does he see in that cramped cabin with the too-small porthole and too-hard bunk?

The female, Betty, fine-boned though to K. all humans are such; yellow-haired with a frank Grace Kelly kind of face and a ready smile which sadly, on this voyage, has been altogether too uncommon. Betty with her master's degree in botany and strong philanthropic impulse. She likes to think of herself as a person who throws herself into things utterly, emotionally speaking. She is prone to thinking in terms such as *It's worth doing right if it's worth doing at all* and *Some things require one hundred and ten percent effort.* She threw herself utterly into her boyfriend Johnny who later became her fiancé Johnny and now has become her husband of ten months, Johnny. This has not always been easy but, as Betty is quick to remind herself, marriage requires one hundred and ten percent effort or it should not be attempted in the first place.

Now Johnny sits beside her on the bed, smoking. Betty doesn't like cigarette smoke but she likes complaining even less, so says nothing. She tells herself that this is part of throwing herself utterly into her marriage, emotionally speaking. She can tell that her husband has been wounded on this journey, traumatized even. Not to say broken, shattered, left like roadkill sprawled in K.'s careering wake. Which is ironic, given that it was *she* who was abducted, but there you go. Men are such fragile things after all. Little boys really; no matter how strong or blustering or pompous they become, they all remain, at heart, children who want to be looked after by Mommy. Betty knows that it is up to her to take on Johnny's hurt as her own, to massage and caress it and chase it away. It's a duty she relishes, most days.

K. would be privy to none of this, even if he managed to somehow maneuver himself, unseen, to peer into the porthole. He would only see Betty and next to her, tousle-headed and unshaven, Johnny. A currently unemployed big-game safari guide; a man who sank his life's savings as well as his wife's inheritance into one ill-advised gamble in expectation of satisfied customers, massive profits and a rep that would set him up for the next ten years. Sold the car, hocked the wedding ring, the whole nine yards. Johnny is a man slow to develop enthusiasm for anything but who will, once that rare enthusiasm has developed, act far past the point at which many people would say: *enough is enough.* He is prone to binges, and not just with booze and poker and girls. It wasn't absolutely necessary to take out that second mortgage on the house just to finance this trip, was it? Not really. But with the extra cash Johnny was able to charter this ship, the *Ocean Princess,* far bigger than the one he could've otherwise hired. Private cabins for each passenger instead of shared berths. Huge stocks of champagne and twenty-year-old whiskey for his high-class clientele. A three-star chef. His plan was to treat these high rollers to a degree of luxury they had never experienced on a rough-and-tumble safari expedition like this one. And so he did. Unfortunately, however, the high rollers all managed to get themselves killed, so Johnny will never collect his fees (those monied clients were canny enough to insist on this arrangement), and he has lost everything. His customers have too, of course; but first they made sure to drain the bar.

Johnny of the jutting chin and thick-veined forearms, whose waist is trim and pectorals broad, currently faces destitution of a sort he has never imagined. Not to mention the interviews that await him, with the families. Twelve of them in total, six clients' and six staff's. I'm sorry, Mrs. Phelps (or Munir or Willis or Cooke), there's no easy way to say this . . .

—Christ, he mutters for the fiftieth time.

—What is it, darling?

He just shakes his head. He wants to say, I sure have made a hash of things, but instead murmurs, At least they can't sue.

—What do you mean?

He drags on the cigarette as if it's pure oxygen. It took him a long time to take up smoking, years and years. Always hated the taste, the wracking fingers in his lungs, but he loved the way he looked while doing it. Like a man's man, a Bogart or Brando. Now he devours fifty a day, unfiltered of course. He tried rolling his own but didn't have the patience.—They all signed waivers, clients and staff both. So there's no danger we'll wind up in debtor's prison. Do they even have debtor's prison anymore? Sounds like something from the nineteenth century.

—Oh Johnny.

He drops his cigarette and his head collapses into his hands. Shoulders shudder like an epileptic's.

—Johnny darling.

Long minutes slither past. Johnny stops sobbing. Betty knows what he wants, so she collects him in her arms and leans back. He mounts her and is quickly done, bellowing as if some demon is being exorcised. She gets pleasure from the pleasure she gives him. Not much else, but she reminds herself that she is the kind of person who throws herself utterly into her commitments. It is this same impulse that causes her to say, after Johnny has finished and curled up beside her like an infant, I've been thinking about what Billy said.

Without moving:—Oh?

—And I'm, I'm ready to try it.

—What are you saying, Betty?

—I'll be his Juliet. The monstrosity is Romeo, so all right, I'll dress up in some fancy ballroom gown and stand next to him and everyone can have a good laugh and take our picture.

—Knowing Billy, it's no fancy gown you'll be wearing. And you'll have to do more than just stand there.

—Whatever it takes, I'm willing.

Johnny sits up.—I'm not sure I like the sound of that.

—I'm sure I don't, she replies.—But he's right, it'll sell, and that's what we need. Now lie down and kiss me, darling.

His mouth tastes of ashes but his chest is broad and his shoulders hover over her, poised like a protective shield. She curls herself into his shadow, trying to feel safe, willing herself to believe that he will take care of her. He hasn't said that he can, but she expects him to. She waits for the words: *Everything will be just like it was before.* Or *I'll never let anything bad happen to you.* The words will come any moment now. It's the sort of thing he'd have said already, in times past.

She waits. And keeps waiting. And he keeps saying nothing, though after a while he does rouse himself enough to roll on top of her again, and she responds by doing what everyone—herself included—believes starlets are best at.

15. MONSTERS

The captain sits in the outboard, half aware of its gentle roll beneath him like a lover. That's what the sea is to him, he has allowed himself to think in the past, during starlit idle moments (starlet idol moments?) of the third watch. Now is not an idle moment, however, and the captain has no time for metaphoric musings or word games. He is busy watching K. where he lies strapped beneath his restraints. There will be time for metaphor later. Right now, reality demands his attention.

The captain prides himself on many things, foremost among them his calm external demeanor and restless interior determination, the kind of determination that turned a bullied child named Ernie into the commander of an oceangoing vessel with a crew of fourteen. Right now, however, fear has taken up residence in the captain's midriff, has cleared a nest in his belly, laid slippery eggs and now sits atop them like a doting parent-to-be, eager to incubate terror.

The genesis of that terror is easy enough to fathom.—Atomic power, says the captain.

Behind him, Ash shifts his backside against the sea's roll.—Sir?

The captain ignores his lieutenant for the moment. There are things Ash understands (few) and things Ash doesn't understand (many). The captain prides himself on knowing which is which, and knowing when something needs to be shifted from the second category to the first. Such things are rare indeed but, perhaps, the case at hand is one.

But not yet. The captain peruses K.'s prostrate form, from lumpen head, shark-eyed and snake-tongued, bald on top like Nanga Parbat, carpeted thickly where the neck should be, all the way to the emu-clawed, seven-toed feet. Why seven? he wonders. He takes in the red-feathered breast, the overlong snakeskinned forearms, all the rest of it. In his stomach he feels the infant terrors pecking their stiletto beaks at the eggshells in the nest, eager to hatch, to spread downy wings, to grow and strengthen and take flight. The captain, who takes pride in his ability to keep a cool head, clamps down on his gut and inadvertently farts.

—Atomic power, he repeats, hoping to distract his lieutenant from his indiscretion.—Ash, I want you to look upon the legacy of mankind's flirtation with the provenance of the Almighty.

Ash's eyes flicker to K. and back to the captain. His face, like a faithful spaniel's, reflects a great desire to please, but little comprehension. The last time he'd heard someone invoke the Almighty had been a couple years ago, when he'd been sitting in a movie theater in Toledo, watching *The War of the Worlds*. The Martians had just succumbed to bacterial infection, as he remembered, and humanity was saved. Or something like that. The Almighty was involved, if he remembered right.—Sir?

—This, this monster, the captain declares gravely.—Mankind's folly.

Ash frowns. He has droopy eyes and lips shiny from his habit of licking them, which he does now.—Not sure I'm clear on the folly part, sir.

The captain extracts a folded paper from his breast pocket.—I've just received word from U.S. Naval High Command. We are forbidden from going to that island.

—You mean, the island where we found this?

—That is correct, Ash. It's off-limits. That island and everything on it belongs to the government. We should have been intercepted, but we weren't. More federal efficiency for you.

Ash licks his lips.—Sir, there were people on that island. Natives I mean.

—That is correct.

—So they're citizens then. Americans.

—Hardly.

The captain inflicts his gaze on his lieutenant. Depending on the light, the captain's eyes can appear sea green or icy blue or battleship gray. Today they are the dusty blue of frozen flesh, of gangrene, of things long dead and only recently unearthed. Ash is reminded of the hulking monster in *The Thing from Another World*. That creature too had been buried in the Arctic, frozen, later dug up—with dire results.

The captain allows his eyes to rest a moment on his first mate's uncomprehending face.—Government property, Ash.

Ash looks away.—I see, he says. Clearly he does not.

The captain lays it out for him like a buffet.—That island is a testing site for our H-bomb development program. Not the detonations themselves, of course—that would vaporize the island entirely. But the aftereffects.

—You mean radiation, Captain?

—Correct. The results of long-term fallout exposure on plants and animals have never been comprehensively studied, so it was thought best to conduct these experiments outside the country, so no Americans would get sick.

Ash nods.—Well, that makes sense.

—The island's been swimming in radiation for years. Heavy ions, deuterium, you name it. And plenty you can't name too, count on it. This thing is the result. Some kind of, of bizarre mutation. Nature gone awry, with mankind's eager help.

Ash appears to be shaking a fly from his ear.—But—but tests

are done in deserted areas, Bikini Atoll, White Sands, places like that. Those people on that island, they'd be exposed.

—So what?

—So the Congress would never allow it.

The captain's eyes are pitiless.—Ash, you think the government gives a hoot about some jigs on a foreign island?

—Well sir—with respect, yes.

The captain nods: his assessment of his lieutenant had been correct, and he files this away for future reference.—They don't even let the ones in our country vote.

Ash was born and raised in Delaware and is unsure whether this is true. He's never actually had a conversation with a Negro.—Even so. That's different from killing them outright, sir.

The captain frowns, as if choosing his words carefully.—The government's been letting black men die of syphilis for twenty years, and lying about it. There's a special program. The men are told they're being treated. They're not. The government watches them die so they can chart the course of the disease. The men, and the women they've slept with, are dead now, and so are their children.

—Sir?

—I know some people involved with the project. Hundreds of citizens, Ash, dying so the government can collect information. That's classified by the way, and you never heard it. Bound to come out someday though.

—Uh, yes sir.

—Now tell me again: Do you really think those generals in the Pentagon give a damn about a bunch of niggers in the Pacific?

Ash looks like a puppy trying to decide whether to crap on the parquet or the carpet: Who the heck moved the newspaper? Trying to lighten the atmosphere he says, Next thing you'll be telling me to believe in flying saucers.

The captain squints at him closely.—You mean you don't?

Ash looks over the waves as if for relief.

—Repeat one word of this conversation, the captain says slowly, and you'll never work again. Got it?

—Yes sir.

—I'll have you blackballed so fast you'll wake up with your head thinking it's tomorrow and your ass stuck in last week. But I trust I've made my point.

—I understand sir. Don't worry about me, sir.

He's not. The captain prides himself on seeing things the way they really are and cutting through the crap when necessary, but he also prides himself on knowing when to keep his mouth shut. Ash doesn't worry him: if he did, the captain would have remained silent. What worries him at this particular moment is K. What worries him in the longer term is the direction the world seems to be heading in. Last year the Soviets rolled their tanks through the streets of Budapest, and still had enough pep left over to launch Sputniks 1 and 2. They're up there even now, spinning their threads around the earth like malevolent spiders, while the genius of America's industry introduced, for the lasting benefit of mankind: the Frisbee.

Sure, Stalin's dead. So what—Khrushchev's no better, might be worse if he decides he needs to prove himself. Meanwhile, armed paratroopers guard black kids going to school in Little Rock. . . . Sooner or later, that situation will blow up in the country's face, no question. Just like the business over in Tehran. The captain's got no love for camel jockeys—crazy bastards all of them, from what he can tell; they'd be dangerous if they weren't so backward—and he's cognizant of the need for cheap oil. But still, if a country has an insupportable government forced onto it from outside, it's just a matter of time before resentment boils over and people chuck that government out. It happened before, in 1776, and when it happens again, that oil won't be had for love nor money.

Speaking of boiling over: the radio carries news of more military advisors being sent to Vietnam. The captain can't make much sense of this. He is a libertarian at heart, as he believes most Americans to be. Let people do what they want, is his motto. Just don't interfere with *my* business.

What worries him is that since Pearl Harbor, the powers making the decisions seem less and less inclined to let people do what they want. Eisenhower's all right but he's in over his head. His country is dropping H-bombs on desert islands without knowing what's going to come of it. MacArthur wanted to nuke China over Korea, and rumor has it that Ike was under pressure to drop them on the Russians before they got strong enough to hit back. Or failing that, detonate one on the moon. That would've made a lasting impression: the moon with a little nip taken out of it. Right up there for everyone to see.

The captain grins without humor. Maybe they'll find a way to rig up a big neon sign up there instead. He can picture it, cursive letters flashing red-white-and-blue across the face of the damn thing. DON'T TREAD ON ME. I LIKE IKE. LIVE FREE OR DIE. I LOVE LUCY.

So the captain stands on deck and worries. When he's not worrying, he's doing figures: fuel consumed, fuel remaining. Crew's overtime, Billy's payments. Bribes for the Coast Guard, supplies for the crew, food for the cargo. In amid these calculations, these numbers floating over his consciousness like mist, he frets about other things. The world. The future. The past. The atomic-radiation monster hooked to the back of his vessel like a U-Haul.

Most of all, he worries because he's let himself be talked into taking this thing to San Francisco.

16. CALCULATIONS

While the captain stands on deck, adding and dividing, K. lies and heals and grows restless. What does he know of numbers? Nothing.

20,000: the number of years that Homo sapiens has lived on Earth. 4,500,000,000: the years that the planet had previously existed without them. Approximately.

70,000: the dead at Hiroshima. 40,000: the dead at Nagasaki. (Both these numbers are disputed.) 3: the number of days between the two detonations. (This number is not disputed.) 45,000,000: the dollars paid to Iran after the CIA reinstated the Shah. 10: the years he had ruled the country before Mossadegh replaced him. 25: the years he will rule after coming back.

6,000,000: the Jews dead in the Holocaust—although Holocaust deniers will, amazingly, dispute this. 9: the years since Israeli independence. 950,000: the Palestinians who fled the country as a result—though some Zionists will, amazingly, dispute this. Zero: The number of Palestinians whose existence will be acknowledged by Golda Meir, Israel's prime minister, when she says, straight-faced, to the London *Times* in 1969: "There is no such thing as a Palestinian people." And later, in the same interview: "It is not as if we came and threw them out and took their country. They didn't exist."

They didn't exist. In just two sentences, a whole nation is erased as if it's never been. Talk about efficiency. There should be a word for that—for making an entire people disappear. Don't you think?

20: the years since Winston Churchill compared Native Americans, Australian aborigines and Palestinian Muslims to "the dog lying in the manger." 7: the years since he was awarded the Nobel prize.

9 again: the number of black students attending desegregated high school classes in Little Rock, Arkansas. 1,000: the federal paratroopers required to protect them. 24: how many years a U.S. government project has been withholding syphilis treatment from Negro citizens—volunteers all—while telling them they are being treated for it. 412: the number of subjects in this study. 16: the years the experiment will continue. 40: how many years will pass before the government acknowledges it.

8: years before Congress will pass the Voting Rights Act that guarantees black citizens the right to vote.

4,000: the number of Soviet tanks sent to "pacify" Hungary. 13: the numbers of days that Hungary's abortive uprising lasts.

40,800,000,000: The U.S. defense budget, in dollars, for 1956.

40,800,000,000: The same, for 1955.

40,800,000,000: The same again, for 1957.

Ignorant of these numbers and any others, K. grows increasingly annoyed at his confinement. Gulliver's net has evolved from a mystery to an annoyance to a torment. It is time, K. thinks (thinks?), to make something happen.

17. DECLARATION OF INDEPENDENCE

K. has had enough. The strange diet he has been consuming for months, inadequate though it is, has restored much of his strength, and now his legs yearn to stretch. They are one long horrible cramp, a double-knot of discomfort from thigh to ankle. Pressure bruises dot his elbows, buttocks, back. His neck pains him no matter how he holds his head. The antennae sprouting from his temples abrade against metal cables and torment him ceaselessly.

He does not realize that for 120 days, the *Ocean Princess* has been parked off the California coast, while Billy negotiates contracts to house, feed and transport him. K. has endured vicious storms and searing heat, nights cold enough to set him shivering, seas rocky enough to bring up vomit. He knows nothing of animal-control laws or quarantine regulations, even less of the labyrinth of public health officials that Billy must cajole, bribe or tiptoe around. Just as well.

Johnny and Betty are nearly as ignorant, and the captain knows only that he has been instructed to maintain position per orders of the Coast Guard while Billy wriggles through the regulatory minefield. It's all the same to K., as long as the rations are placed near his head each day. Until he finally decides it's time to sit up.

K. inhales mightily and shrugs, snapping the cables that bind his chest. Flexes one knee, then the other, freeing his legs. Joints screech in protest even as an unspeakable relief floods him. He brushes off the cables as if dusting away scraps of straw. Titanium-steel chains tumble slow-motion into the sea and disappear in a blink.

Tentative, stiff, K. stretches: ankles knees backbone shoulders neck. If he could express his sensations as words, K. might think, or even say, something like: *Ah . . . much better.* But of course he can't.

He looks around him, waiting for something to happen.

Something already is. Reclined as he was, he didn't realize that the ship was within sight of land. Sitting up now, he can see it: a low green stripe along the horizon. K. stares, some dim consciousness deep in his lizard cortex trying to remember why this is important. (The island upon which he has lived his whole life, minus the past six months, is as distant to his recollection as the dinosaurs, the Precambrian explosion, the newly hypothesized Big Bang.) He straddles his float, legs dangling in the water, his attitude that of a bemused surfer trying to navigate the oxygen-thin heights of advanced calculus.

Between K. and the coastline swarms a hive of aircraft, small boats, Coast Guard cruisers, police helicopters, journalists, curiosity seekers, beach bums. K. is confused by the choppers, hovering above the waves like glassy-eyed dragonflies, kicking up plumes of spray. He recognizes the other boats as fellows of the craft he rides on. Everywhere scuttle the tiny human figures that he is growing to loathe, and if he cannot make out precisely where they have hidden their noisy, stinging paintthrowers, he is no less certain that they exist somewhere.

Now what? K. wonders wordlessly, not recognizing this as a breakthrough: he has learned to expect things to happen.

The feeling flutters in his belly like a moth. It's not an entirely pleasant sensation. All things considered, a person could be forgiven for thinking that K. was better off—more at peace—back before he'd learned to think of *the future* as something different from *now*. An unknown shadowy region replete with its own dangers and terrors, unknown but no less feared.

As if *now* isn't bad enough!

18. JUSTICE FOR ALL

Along the stern rail of the *Ocean Princess,* the following tense discussion is witnessed by wind, surf and seagulls.

Captain:—I've got a bad feeling about this. I don't like the way he's looking at the water.

Billy:—Think he's planning to go for a dip?

Captain:—Might be.

Johnny:—There's no reason to expect that. We never saw any sign that he can swim.

Billy:—He ain't the Creature from the Black Lagoon. Flippers and gills are about the only things he *doesn't* have.

Captain:—Let's hope you're right. If he gets free in the city, all hell will break loose.

Billy:—Look at him just sitting there, cool as Elvis. I still can't believe he broke those chains.

Captain:—Believe it.

Johnny:—He snapped them like paper streamers, Billy.

Captain:—Ash, did the Coast Guard say when they'd commence the operation?

Ash:—Once we're in harbor, sir.

Captain:—That's cutting it close.

Billy:—Hey, don't complain. It took me three months to talk them into doing it in the first place.

Ash:—They said they didn't want to move prematurely, sir. If the monster falls off the platform, they don't want it to be too far offshore.

Betty:—What are you talking about? What are you planning here?

Captain:—Let's hope they get the voltage right.

Betty:—You mustn't hurt him!

Johnny:—Easy darling. No one's going to hurt Romeo here. Billy's got a nice place for him in the warehouse district.

Billy:—A regular Waldorf-Astoria, doll. And it cost about as much!

Johnny, placing a hand on Betty's shoulder:—But we've got to knock him out to get him under control. Surely you can see that.

Billy:—It's not like we can carry him up another cliff and throw him over again, can we?

Impatient, Betty shakes off Johnny's reassurance. Sometimes—only sometimes, but more and more often lately—her husband feels like a complete stranger to her.

The exchange doesn't go unnoticed. Billy studies his friends from the corner of his eye. He notices the tension locking Betty's shoulders, the stubborn set of Johnny's jaw, the professional calm of the captain. Billy figures he knows a thing or two about human nature, about how people react under stress. Johnny's bullheadedness, an asset in some circumstances (on the island, pursuing Betty and the monster) can be a drawback at other times (sinking every penny he owned into a single safari, a one-shot that gambled everything. And lost). Johnny just doesn't know when to quit, how to say enough is enough. But then anybody who has ever watched him drink, or play poker, or mix with the girls, knows that already.

Billy also knows a thing or two about Betty's overgenerous heart. How she'll give the benefit of the doubt to anyone. Or in this case any*thing,* especially anything male. Billy isn't sure whether this is the result of the unfortunate circumstances of Betty's life: the older brother crippled and bedridden with polio, the dashing young father spilling his life onto Omaha Beach, vivisected by a German howitzer. No, Billy can't say for certain, but it could be, sure. And look at her getting in with the orphanage. A blind man could see the connection. Billy figures he knows a thing or two about the limitations of his friends, maybe more than they realize about themselves. Clearly he is the impresario of this show here, the top gun, the big cheese, the P. T. Barnum of the operation. It bears remembering, Billy thinks. So he'll remember it.

Billy squints toward shore, coming up fast now. A half mile off, maybe less. The big warehouses flanking the port hove into view, the tankers and container ships berthed like happy cattle. Above it all, striding the shore like some wide-hipped Colossus, looms the brand-spanking-new Golden Gate Bridge: the same bridge destroyed by the giant octopus in *It Came from Beneath the Sea*. Billy can't resist a chuckle: that flick was the last he'd seen before shipping out with Johnny on this crazy trip. Seems a lifetime ago now.

For a lot of his companions, it *was*.

Billy's chuckle curdles in his throat and he frowns up at the bridge. Whether this cockamamie plan is going to work, he can't say, but he figures the Coast Guard has plenty of bright fellas working at it, guys who know a thing or two about how to do their jobs.

He sure *hopes* so, for Chrissake.

Johnny peers at the choppers thickening overhead like a cloud of flies. Police, army, FBI, Coast Guard, ABC, NBC, CBS. A wonder they don't all crash into each other, but then, you never saw a cloud of flies doing that, either.

To Billy he says, This won't help our road show. All these people getting a free look at what we want to charge them money for.

—That's where you're wrong, Billy says, clapping him on the

shoulder.—This kind of publicity just makes Joe Public desperate to see the thing for himself.

Betty tosses her head.—I hope you're right.

—Trust me.

Johnny squints at the copters again. A lot of people would be thinking *Enough already*, but Johnny is the type of guy who thinks: *How come no National Guard?*

—Getting close now, murmurs Ash.

Johnny drops his gaze to the harbor entrance that reaches toward them with two long jetties like a pair of lover's arms. He leans into the rail, feels the hard bite of it against his sternum. Beyond the harbor, San Francisco can be seen rearing up against the midmorning, mid-November sky. Hills and houses, plenty of mountains and a couple skyscrapers. Off to their left, Alcatraz lurches out of the water, forbidding and grim like some haunted castle in a fairy tale for adults.

The city waits for its unwilling guest and Johnny wonders, for one of the few times in his life, whether he has perhaps pushed things too far.

The boat enters the harbor, trailing K. on his raft. The impromptu flotilla hangs back, flanking the *Ocean Princess* like bridesmaids. Betty watches as a Coast Guard chopper hovers overhead. Its belly distends heavily as if cancerous or pregnant. Or both.—Don't be melodramatic, she chides herself.

All the men glance at her quizzically, briefly, then look back at the chopper.

It floats above K.'s head like a dubious piece of thistledown, like the ugliest hummingbird ever imagined, its hateful dull gray flanks marked only by a diagonal orange slash. It rests perhaps a hundred feet above K.'s raft. A line appears in its swollen belly, thickens, widens, and slowly the undercarriage splits open and two swinging doors unfold. Betty, watching from a hundred yards away, cannot imagine what might be carried in that bay. Not a bomb, surely? They can't mean to just kill the thing? Billy has promised not, and Johnny. Surely she can trust them.

K. can't imagine what might happen, either. But then, who can say what K. can or cannot imagine? *He* certainly can't.

In any case, something startles him. Perhaps the chopper reminds him, suddenly, of his flying reptilian rival back on the island. Or maybe it's something else entirely—the smell of diesel on his tongue, the buffeting downdraft playing havoc with his antennae. What matters here is the result, which is that K. lurches to his feet on his bobbing floating raft not two hundred yards from shore in the heart of San Francisco's harbor. The raft convulses under his feet but K. manages to stand upright. Wobbly but upright. And when he jabs up with one overlong arm, his claws brush the air a bare ten, fifteen feet beneath the undercarriage of the chopper.

The pilot panics.

(Hard to blame him. His name is Clarence and he has been in the Guard for something less than a year. A pilot of exceptional natural aptitude, he has been tossed this assignment by a commanding officer who detests him and hopes he will screw up. This is because Clarence is a Negro. The commander hopes Clarence will damage the helicopter, perhaps badly, or even crash it and die. Besides this, Clarence knows that the apparatus nestled in the belly of his chopper is experimental and untested; his copilot is a slow-witted redneck from Massachusetts who communicates in grunts; and most of all, Clarence's wife Stella is currently in the hospital, sweating through the birth of their third child after a particularly demanding pregnancy. So Clarence might be forgiven for responding to K.'s abrupt swipe at the chopper's exposed belly by shrieking—Whoa there! and hitting the red toggle next to the altimeter.)

K. lands hard on the raft, loses his balance as it bucks beneath him, goes up on one leg like a tightrope walker. Before he can recover his balance, K. finds himself assailed by a kind of ghostly attacker unlike any he has ever faced—not that he has faced many—an assailant with a thousand grasping hands, a foe who falls back at his every swipe but who ensnares him at elbow and knee and around his throat, who weighs nothing at all and yet hopelessly entangles him. K. reels, unbalanced, the raft pitching wildly underfoot. In fact only part of K. is caught, but he is far too enraged to notice this, or to think (think?) clearly enough to extricate himself from this situation. He has come under attack rarely enough in his life, and this is the first time he has encountered anything so taxing as a net.

Up in the helicopter, Clarence shrieks:—Hit it!

His copilot, a taciturn specimen named Larkin, grunts without moving.

—Hit it I said!

Larkin grunts again.

Clarence reaches across his copilot's impassive face and yanks a yellow toggle. Beneath the chopper, a thousand volts course down a tether cable and burst through the net's uninsulated mesh. K. gasps and staggers, lurching like a schizophrenic receiving shock treatment.

—Lord, mutters the captain, watching through his binoculars from the safety of the *Ocean Princess.*

K. blacks out briefly but comes to a moment later, still on his feet.

The captain watches K. shiver as if cold, then turn his lipless face toward the chopper and let rip a howl of unalloyed rage.—What's this thing made of, anyway? Concrete?

Ash's face has gone gray.—Sir, that was enough juice to knock over a herd of elephants.

The captain's face is hard.—Let's hope they've got enough for

two herds. And if they don't, then let's hope they drop that umbilical before the monster pulls them into the water.

In the chopper the copilot Larkin has turned his cold eyes on
Clarence.—Nigger, you reach in front of me like that one more
time and I'll kill you.

Clarence decides that this is not the time to engage in a discussion of racial equity.—Then turn that dial to two thousand and
hit the switch, he barks.—That way I won't *have* to do it and you
won't *have* to kill me.

Or try to, he thinks.

(In a B movie, naturally, the racial tension would remain unac-
knowledged: either both pilots would be white, or a mixed part-
nership like this would betray no unease. Even in a major motion
picture, the racial element would be glossed, or perhaps resolved
by an incident in which Larkin suffers a life-threatening injury
and Clarence skillfully, one-handedly—perhaps injured himself—pilots the chopper safely home and thus saves his copilot's
life; the shamefaced Larkin admitting in the end that *I was wrong
about you.* A manly handshake follows, wry grins, silent nods of a
brotherhood, forged in danger, that transcends skin pigment. But
as this record is in fact the true chronicle of actual events, it needs
to be recorded that Larkin never ceases hating Clarence for even
a moment and will go to his grave convinced that Negroes, later
blacks, later still African-Americans, are a race of dissolute subhu-
mans genetically predisposed to drug dealing, gang warfare and
the violent assault on white women. In later life he will read many
scholarly books written by bitter, aging white men which use art-
fully culled and selectively arranged statistical evidence to rein-
force this belief.)

Larkin turns the voltage dial to two thousand and punches the
yellow toggle.

K., blinded by a white-rimmed agony he cannot strike, collapses
to his knees, then slumps to one side. Miraculously he stays aboard

the raft, though one arm and both feet trail into the water and the whole float lists alarmingly. The pain fades after a time but his vision swims before him like a sheet of monsoon rain. K. is unable to focus on anything and his cranium throbs like a bell. He has of course never heard a bell. But the sensation is unpleasant and he responds to it by hoisting his feet out of the water, planting them on his raft and trying, shakily, to get to his feet.

—Wouldja looka that, sir! gasps Ash.

—You sure you want to go on the road with this character, Billy?

—More than ever, Johnny. More than ever.

Betty and the captain say nothing. The captain's face is set into scowling lines of expectation: of disaster, of folly, of miscalculation. Betty's face is harder to read, but there is almost a sense, mixed in with the anxiety and revulsion, of *admiration*.

Ash says, Let's hope that pilot has the brains to either get the hell out of there, or hit the switch again.

Evidently he does the latter: K. snaps upright, thrashes briefly, stiffens. This time when he falls, he topples heavily and lies motionless, as if struck by lightning. Which in a sense he is.

REEL FOUR

MONSTER, 1958

I do not agree that the dog in the manger has the final right to the manger, even though he may have lain there for a very long time. I do not admit that right. I do not admit, for instance, that a great wrong has been done to the Red Indians of America, or the black people of Australia. I do not admit that a wrong has been done to these people by the fact that a stronger race, a higher grade race, a more worldly-wise race, to put it that way, has come in and taken their place.

—WINSTON CHURCHILL, ADDRESSING THE PEEL
COMMISSION OF INQUIRY REGARDING THE
CREATION OF THE STATE OF ISRAEL
IN BRITISH-OCCUPIED PALESTINE, 1937

Perhaps the world that these creatures inhabit is coming to an end. Perhaps they need to find somewhere else to live.

—WARREN MITCHELL IN *The Crawling Eye* (1958)

19. BOX OFFICE

1958 is a strange year.

Even K. recognizes this, K. who has lived what many would consider a strange life; K. who has little basis for comparison regarding what might be considered baseline experience, the existence of the not-bizarre.

It's a great year for monsters. 1958 sees the release of *The Wild Women of Wongo*, possibly the worst film ever made; it's the year of deadly blobs, half-human flies, brains from planet Arous, fiends without faces, fifty-foot spiders, fifty-foot women, teenage monsters, brain eaters, crawling eyes and terrors from beyond space. It's also the year that Jerry Lee Lewis marries his thirteen-year-old cousin: parents shudder, while hip teens make jokes about hot rods and great balls of fire. Monstrosities flourish in literature too: Elie Weisel recounts his hellish concentration camp experiences in *Night,* while Nabokov publishes his controversial vampire novel, *Lolita.*

Castro—monster to some, hero to others—continues his revolution in Cuba, while Ghana and Malaya both gain their independence. General Charles de Gaulle comes to power in a "bloodless revolution" in France, caused at least in part by those restive Muslims in Algeria. General Ayub Khan declares martial law after seizing power in a "bloodless revolution" in Pakistan, caused at least in part by those restive Muslims in, well, Pakistan.

NASA is created, and the United States responds to Sputnik with a satellite of its own, *Explorer 1,* but minus the little dog Laika sent up by the Soviets. Later in the year they send Pioneer satellites out past the moon, toward Mars and beyond; metal boxes weighing a few kilos are now flitting around the planet like mosquitoes. Back on Earth, Washington continues sending military experts to Vietnam, even as the French give it up as a bad job. In front yards across the American heartland, families light barbecues and teach themselves to hula-hoop, only to collapse into giggling fits when beer-bellied Dad just can't get the hang of it.

A coup places Karim Kassin in power in Iraq. Mao, in his final year as China's head of state, initiates the Great Leap Forward. Khrushchev formally takes over premiership of the Soviet Union. Pius XII dies and John XXIII is elected Pope. Egypt and Syria unite under Nasser to form the United Arab Republic. Pelé leads Brazil to victory in the World Cup. Johnny Unitas marshals the Baltimore Colts to the NFL championship in what will come to be regarded as the greatest contest in pro football history: 23–17, the Giants lose the first-ever "sudden death" overtime playoff game. And speaking of sudden death, a pair of American physicists apply for, and receive, a patent on the world's first laser, an instrument that uses light to burn holes through steel. Suddenly those sci-fi ray guns aren't a fantasy anymore. Meanwhile Mark Rothko paints *Four Darks in Red* and leaves people saying things like:—You call that art? My kid could do that.

Yes, 1958 is a singular year. But then they all are, one way or another.

For K. this year is a strange one because he never sees the sky, barely breathes a wisp of fresh air. Stars and rain have become as rare as free speech in Hungary, free movement in Algeria, freethinking in

Utah. His world has shrunk, its molecules crowded together or ripped away until his whole life is constricted to the inside of box-cars and tents and iron-barred cages, while around him swirl murmuring crowds of popping flashbulbs and sweaty human flesh.

K.'s understanding of how it all works is limited to what he can see and hear and smell, which is at the same time nothing much and a great deal. Nothing much, because of the limitations placed upon his senses; and a great deal, because most of what he does sense lies outside his comprehension, and so is material for endless rumination.

He wakes each day to darkness and confinement. Hemmed by shackles and confused by the overweening gloom of what his internal clock tells him should be daylight. Sometimes the very ground beneath him vibrates as he hurtles through space in a shell of reinforced titanium alloy, but of course he doesn't know this. In fact he is the guest of honor aboard his own private boxcar, modified to Billy's specs, barreling down the rails at sixty miles per. The car he rides in is a bit more—but not much—than a reinforced cage with bars as thick as his biceps and army-surplus tank plating two inches thick. The whole affair is barely large enough for him to recline in comfortably. Forget about sitting up, much less standing. At irregular intervals the vibrations stop as the boxcar rolls onto some remote siding, and bushels of his preferred foods are slipped through a hatch—bananas and melons, corn on the cob and romaine lettuce, mushrooms and mashed potatoes and walnuts. Never has K. eaten so regally, and his weight has long since returned to normal.

But mealtimes are erratic, and K. begins each day with a session of timeless darkness. Who can say what goes through his mind (mind?) in these black hours. Pictures, perhaps, fragments of memory, whiffs of nostalgic longing like remembered wood smoke. Dreams? Or else things half remembered, half imagined, the borderline lunacy of the prisoner in solitary confinement. (Mossadegh

in Iran a few years ago, Mandela in South Africa a few years
hence.) Emotions too of a sort, unhappiness or despair or flat-eyed
rage. Hope? Probably not. But without words to quantify his feelings, can he be said to truly feel them? Does someone actually have
something if he doesn't know what to call it?

At midday the train arrives at the outskirts of some city or mid-
sized town or even, in farm country, a disused field leased for the
purpose, with a little-used railroad siding nearby. Swarms of
hired hands race to erect the tent, a waxed canvas big top the size
of an aircraft hangar. Setup takes four hours. The bleachers are
arranged in a horseshoe shape facing a curtained proscenium and
an open, sandy ring in the center. Most of the action will take
place in the ring, circus-style, just a few paces from the twitching
hearts of the audience.

During all this, Johnny and Billy blitz the local radio stations
and give statements to the press, who have been notified beforehand. Complimentary tickets shower reporters like confetti on
V-E Day. Showtime is six o'clock sharp and the crowd is there
well beforehand. At three bucks apiece, tickets sell fast; the tent
seats two thousand and there's rarely an empty space on the
bleachers. Programs and souvenirs cost extra: T-shirts from Taiwan, plastic monster dolls from Japan, Halloween masks from
Mexico. They net fifteen thousand per show, sometimes more;
twice that on weekends when they run a matinee. After two
weeks, sometimes three, rarely only one, they pack up and roll on
to the next city or town or fallow field. They have been doing this
for nearly eighteen months now, through the second half of last
year and all of this one. Lou Dalton, the burly lion tamer, has
been heard to mutter:—Been away from home so long my kids
won't even recognize me.

But everyone's afraid to stop, the way the money's pouring in.
It's a cornucopia of Mammon, it's a teat that squirts cash. Sure,

Billy works them hard, but he pays well too and works himself no less than anyone else.

—Hell of a way to make a living, he is heard to say on more than one occasion. If K. could understand the words, he would probably agree.

20. NO BUSINESS LIKE IT

The show starts with clowns who belly-flop and tumble their way through a skit entitled "Monster Romeo and His Sweet Juliet." This features a seven-foot-two klutz-acrobat named Doug in the lead role of the (safely comic) monster, while a woman named Midge, barely five feet tall but with jugs the size of her head, plays Juliet. Think Howdy Doody with dirty jokes; think Mouseketeers, with that never-to-be-seen skit in which Annette's blouse is shucked off. For such is the climax of this farce: bewildered Doug clutching a handful of tearaway clothing while Midge flounces offstage in her underwear. The kids squeal and love it; the fathers pretend not to notice Midge's pumpkin boobs and pumpkin-round butt; the mothers are bored to distraction, shifting their own housewifely backsides on the unforgiving bleachers and wondering why on earth they've spent fifteen bucks on this plus parking, plus sodas plus doodads. Maybe the neighbors were pulling their legs when they said—It's something to see, all right.

For another hour the circus carries on: clowns, horses and trick riders, more clowns, a trapeze act featuring sprightly Olga and wiry Petrov from Romania, black-haired and glamorous in matching lavender leotards, sequins flashing as they elastically flip overhead. Then a lion act, Lou Dalton and his three sluggish, kittenish brutes; and yet more clowns. Admittedly, the circus has a theme, as when the lights go dark and Billy breathlessly declaims through the PA system:—Ladies and gentlemen, witness the nameless terror of the forbidden jungle! And amid the sudden hush, a single spotlight flares down to reveal . . . a poodle. More squeals from the kids, more silent curses from the parents. It is of course another clown act, this one featuring the seven-foot Doug in blond curls, yellow evening gown and stuffed bra, prancing in terror from the poodle, who chases him in frantic yapping circles round the sandy floor of the ring. Everybody relaxes again, half disappointed but half relieved too that the famous monster hasn't made its appearance just yet.

The poodle catches Doug's cuff in its hyperactive jaws and grips tenaciously. Doug skitters away in mock terror, the pup trailing diminutive tracks in the sand as he's hauled from the spotlights. Everyone laughs at the oversized sissy.

Billy's original plan: at just this moment, when all eyes are on the little dog and everyone's dropped their guard to chuckle at its cute antics—just *now* hit the bank of floodlights and hurl K. into an unforgiving wash of light right in the middle of the ring, nightmare face level with the topmost bleachers and glaring down on everyone else like God. In so doing, to use Billy's own words— Scare the *bejeezus* out of everybody in the place.

It was a good plan, in terms of theater, but a hotly debated one. Betty hated it, hated the cheap shock, and Johnny had his doubts. Maneuvering K. into position unnoticed would probably prove impossible. He was forty feet tall and tended to grunt. Even sedated, as he was nowadays, his chains rattled as he moved. Distracting people away from all that seemed a lot to ask of a poodle. Then there was liability: old people having heart attacks, kids bursting into tears, screaming nightmares for weeks afterward. As it turned out, things would be bad enough. But Billy could only be talked out of his idea reluctantly.

After Doug and the poodle exit, nothing happens for several

minutes. The lights flicker, flicker again; come on overbrightly, then die entirely. This is another idea of Billy's: get them thinking about technical difficulties. About what could go wrong. The tent is blacker than any public place anyone's ever been. The crowd grows curious, then restless, then—get ready for it—anxious. You can always sense when the sudden idea spills across the audience, like mercury through the ocean: *Has something happened? Is there a problem they're not telling us?* Heads crane, exits are eyeballed, hushed voices tell the kids that everything is fine in tones suggesting that in fact something might not be.

It is at this moment that Betty makes her appearance.

From offstage, Billy's voice spills through the loudspeakers:—Ladies and gentlemen, let's give a big welcome to the Juliet of the Jungle!

Now *this* is more like it.

Forget Shakespeare. Betty's Juliet has nothing to do with Capulets and Montagues, and everything to do with maximizing her substantial cleavage and brightening her blond highlights to something resembling a fission reaction. This is achieved, and with the help of a low-cut, lime green leotard and white heels, she monopolizes the audience's attention more effectively than the cleverest poodle could ever hope. The men look, to be sure, but the women look too. One of life's mysteries. Or as Billy puts it:—Men look at women, and women look at each other to see what it is the men are looking at. The day ever comes when women start looking at men, I mean really *looking,* the human race is screwed. Starting with me.

So then. This is what the crowd expects. Hearing the name Juliet, they expect to ogle a blond doll in a swimsuit, and when she is duly produced, they duly ogle. And clap: here is the show at last. Whistles and hoots pepper the air. Betty smiles at the crowd, turning to wave at each section while torquing her hips just enough to look like she doesn't know she's doing it.

Brilliantly lit against a black curtain hanging heavy behind her, she stands framed by the proscenium, silent as a mannequin. It's not her job to say anything yet. Billy, the impresario, narrates her story from offstage.—Ladies and gentlemen, he begins in a grandiose nasal roar as the crowd noise dies back.—Behold our Juliet.

There are a few residual hoots and cheers. Billy goes on, You can all see just how pretty she is.

Whistles split the air like tracer bullets.

—And right you are! But sometimes—Billy's voice drops— beauty *isn't* a charm.

The crowd hushes.—Sometimes it's a burden, Billy declares.— Even for a sweet girl like Juliet here. Some things can make even a beautiful woman curse the day she was brought into the world with a face like this.

Betty's not smiling now. She's looking down, angst stamped across her brows like a headline. Fingers twist together before her stomach, but not so high as to obscure her bust. The crowd ponders. The idea that there is something undesirable about blond hair and 38Ds is new and strange, but they're willing to play along for a while, to see where the announcer is going with this.

—But not even in her wildest dreams or most deranged visions, Billy continues, could our lovely Juliet have known what awaited her on that island of nightmares!

Stone silence now under the big top.

—After all, human eyes had never seen its like before. And now—yours *will*!

On cue, a rasping, hideous snarl cracks across the tent like artillery. The noise is shocking: the crowd start in their seats, stomachs tight, biting their own tongues. Little kids wet themselves. It's only a prerecorded howl of K. at his angriest, minus the drugs he's been given to keep him docile, but the saps don't know that. It sounds wretched enough, as it should, played back at twenty times normal volume, shredding the speakers in an insane symphony of crackling distortion. As the echoes fade, the audience hears the rattle and clank of chains. These are not recordings; they're real. The sound of his own voice always agitates K., and he shuffles his feet and flurries his arms in response.

The spotlight is very tight on Betty now, as she turns to face the curtain behind her. Her leotard is cut high on her thighs so her butt spills out each side, the V of the fabric bisecting the double ovals of her bottom. But this happy vision is not allowed to linger long for the crowd: Betty's arms are raised, imploring the heavens, perhaps God, if God exists, or something else, if anything else does. Betty is a conductor, the audience her orchestra. As her arms go up, so do the orchestra's eyes. Timed to perfection, the spotlight on Betty fades to black just as the audience's gaze reaches the shadowy void where K.'s face is. Silently, the curtains part.

The stage manager hits the lights.

K. leaps into existence amid them all, shark-eyed, snake-tongued reality: misery given form, solid and undeniable and taller than Hell itself. Feathers like a bloodsmear across his thorax, claws lashing furrows in the ground. Gangs of teeth glaring at the crowd over his lipless slash. Everybody screams.

Everybody. It's not a voluntary thing. You look at death and perdition and Loki enchained; you scream. It's not a question of cool. James Dean would scream, ditto Jimmy Cagney or the Duke. You see that thing towering over you, the mouth big enough to swallow your kids whole, the claws that could disembowel your wife or the seven-toed feet that could smear your husband into red paste or the acrid dribbling spit that could drown both your parents in one go—and you scream. No shame.

There is always an initial withering sweep of panic, teenagers rushing for the exits, old people smothered, children trampled. Early on in the tour there were injuries: broken bones, a collapsed lung, some psychological problems afterward. Lawsuits threatened until Billy settled with some quick cash and Johnny reworked the intro. Thus, before the show's entertainment even begins, before the house lights drop and with the black curtain still safely closed, Billy strides out in person to assure the crowd that the monster is safely restrained for the duration. Shackled round his waist, chained at wrist and ankle; the only furrows being dug are the ones in the ground at his feet. The alloy belt clamped around his waist is chained to the boxcar squatting on its tracks behind the tent. Mighty the beast might be, Billy tells the crowd, but not even he is capable of overcoming such a ball and chain.

It was decided early on not to admit to drugging the creature. After all, people go to the zoo to see lions, not sedated lions. If the tigers at the circus are stoned, what's the thrill of the tiger act?

Despite all these assurances, there is panic anyway—it's not something that can be doused with a few placating words. But it doesn't last as long, and no one's been put in the hospital since Oklahoma. Except for that old guy in Memphis, and he was due for a stroke anyhow. The family was bought off easily enough in the end.

After everyone's back in their seats, the crowd reasserts its dominance energetically, even aggressively. Flashbulbs erupt in a frenzied riot; every flicker of K.'s tongue, every shift of his feet or bob of the head is greeted by squeals and howls and jeers. Soon enough the taunts flow as the toothpick-chewing hoodlums in the back rows—the first to bolt for the exits, minutes ago—hurl salvos of abuse at K.'s flat-pewter eyes, picket-fence teeth, drooping shoulders.

—Hey you lug! Your mother give you a face like that? You should slap her!

—If I was as ugly as you, I'd be steamed about it too!

—Aw geez, Robbie, you *are* that ugly . . .

Early on in the tour, Billy would cut this short and get on with the show, but now he lets it ride. He figures it's low-effort profit for himself, do-it-yourself entertainment for everybody else: the crowd paying him money to entertain itself while he does nothing but shine the lights on K.

—Give 'em what they want, he says by way of explanation.

Johnny doesn't like it.—They get on my nerves, making all that racket.

—Then go buy yourself an island, Billy grins.—You're rich enough. Buy some peace and quiet for you and Betty. Just wait'll after the tour.

—You know, I might do that. . . .

The show goes on after the crowd settles.

—Ladies and gents, says Billy, if I could just have your attention please.

A few final taunts, greeted by a self-righteous chorus of—Shhhh!

Billy plows on, When this monster first laid eyes on Juliet here [subtle emphasis on *laid*], our jungle Romeo found himself the victim of unexpected feelings for the first time in his monstrous life.

The spotlight flares again on Betty, sequins sparkling, breasts outthrust, fanny wagging. A soft spot remains lit on K.'s face, which has turned cooperatively to focus on the girl, the only illumined object in his field of vision. Thus every mug in the audience can see: the thing's still sweet on her!

The script for the remainder of the skit is loose and heavily improvised, incorporating local jokes, current events, news of the day. The quality is roughly equal to a high school drama, but given the material, nobody much cares. Billy's sketchy outline runs something like this:

BETTY: Here I am, all alone on this mysterious foreign island that no one has ever discovered before. I've gotten separated from the group and now I've lost my way, far, far from home. Help! Is anyone there?

(Enter DOUG *as monster.)*

DOUG: Aaaargh! I'll help you all right, missy!

Doug's costume is recognizably modeled after K., but its effect is, predictably, comic rather than frightening. Compared to the real K., it could hardly be otherwise.

BETTY: Oh! It's Mr. Khrushchev!

This always gets a laugh. Sometimes she says, It's Mr. Castro! or, It's Mr. Nasser! or once, in a moment of daring, It's Mr. Mc-Carthy! but the crowd tittered uneasily at that, as if embarrassed. In Alabama, where the audiences are entirely white, more than one local wit earns big guffaws by hollering out:—It's King!

DOUG: Aaaargh! You're the most beautiful woman I've ever seen.

BETTY: Why, thank you. And how many have you seen?

DOUG: You're the first!

BETTY *(to audience):* Well *that's* not too flattering.

DOUG: Aaaargh! I'm tired of all this conversation. All you Americans do is talk, talk, talk.

BETTY: But we just got started. If you want something else, I guess you should go find yourself—*(Pause. She lets it stretch.)*—a French girl!

Another big laugh at this.

DOUG: Stop trying to confuse me! I'm done looking, so I'm taking you home.

BETTY: To Mama?

DOUG: To me!

He chases her around the ring. Betty runs awkwardly in high heels but Doug slippy-slides and lurches through the sand, giving her ample time to jiggle her way past the front rows. The crowd relaxes into the burlesque, using it to distract them from the alienness of K.'s affectless visage staring down at them like some malignant moon. Doug is familiar from earlier skits; Doug is a clown; Doug exists for them to laugh at, so they do. At this point they would laugh at Doug no matter what he did—such is his blessing, and curse. There's something inherently comic about very tall men, as well as very short ones. So when he two-handedly gropes Betty's ass before tumbling into the sand, they guffaw, and when she stamps his hand with a stiletto heel, they roar.

When Doug finally catches her, K. has grown so agitated that he is growling and snarling and the crowd has—once again—remembered his looming threat. So their laughter is tempered with caution, not to say anxiety or outright fear, and the men's attitude toward Betty, who has lived through the actual events being played out before them, is an unfamiliar mixture of lust and respect.

Billy lets this play out for a while, until the audience starts getting restless. Then he intones:—But she couldn't run forever. It was only a matter of time.

Doug swoops onto Betty, heaves her over his shoulder and tramps across the ring triumphantly. Often this so agitates K. that for several minutes, no dialogue can be heard over his snarling growls, and for a time the act is played out in mime.

No one complains, though. It's a reminder that this story is true.

Eventually, the dialogue resumes.

BETTY: Where are you taking me?

DOUG: Home.

BETTY: Where's that?

DOUG: Moscow!

This is also ad-libbed. Some nights it's—Shanghai!, others it's—Havana! or—Budapest! In California, Doug shouts—Alabama! while in Texas, the biggest laughs come when Doug hollers:—New Yawk City!

BETTY: What do you want with me?

DOUG: You're going to be my queen.

BETTY: You have a kingdom?

DOUG *(shaking his hips Elvis-style):* Got your kingdom right here, doll! *(Sings.)*

> Well since my baby left me
> I found a new island to dwell
> It's right in the middle of Lonely Sea
> In the seventh circle of Hell!

Disgusted titters ripple through the audience. Sometimes the cool cats in the back start singing along, while more than one of the stolid-faced dads sitting on the bleachers are thinking *She's a queen all right* . . .

BETTY: Put me down!

DOUG *(doing so):* Okay, but promise not to run away. I need you to sire my children . . . *(with a Groucho-esque leer at her ass, then to the audience)* . . . which you look all ready to do!

BETTY: Get away from me, you disgusting monstrosity!

DOUG: Aw, don't be like that . . . I'm not a monster, I'm just misunderstood.

BETTY: I understand you just fine. You are a monster, whatever you say! Back in America, we have places to put people like you.

DOUG: Listen, I'm not asking for special treatment. I just want equal rights and opportunities like everyone else.

This is good for a few guffaws too.

BETTY *(to audience):* Won't anyone save me? Where's my Prince Charming, my knight in shining armor?

DOUG: That's me, you silly girl.

BILLY *(from offstage microphone):* But little did our jungle Romeo realize that Juliet was already spoken for—by somebody who was ready to become her REAL-LIFE Romeo.

(Enter JOHNNY dressed in safari outfit, carrying rifle.)

JOHNNY: Hold it right there, big boy! We've had enough of your little games to last a lifetime.

DOUG: Who the heck are you?

JOHNNY *(pointing rifle at* DOUG*)*: You want to make this lady's life a nightmare, well, I'm the fellow who's going to give YOU nightmares for a change.

BETTY: But aren't you that world-famous safari hunter? The one who was with us on the boat that brought us to this mysterious, previously undiscovered island?

JOHNNY: That's right.

BETTY: You were leading the expedition, but advised the captain not to land here because you thought it was dangerous, and when he didn't listen to you, that's when our problems started.

JOHNNY: Yep, that's what happened.

BETTY: So what are you doing here—in the jungle?

JOHNNY: When I heard that you'd been left behind by the group, I knew I couldn't wait around doing nothing. *(To audience.)* Where I come from, that's not what we expect of a man.

BETTY: But it's not like we're friends. In fact, I've never even spoken to you before now.

JOHNNY: But I've talked to you plenty of times. In my dreams, that is. (JOHNNY *is still speaking as much to the audience as to*

BETTY.) Maybe to you I'm just a big game hunter, the leader of some high-class safari expedition that wound up on this crazy island, while you—you're a senator's daughter who came along with some family friends to try to get over the pain of a broken heart.

BETTY: Why, you know all about me.

JOHNNY: Sure I do! I've been watching your every move for weeks now. Your smile, your walk.

BETTY: I don't know what to say.

DOUG: Then don't say anything. Aaaargh! I'm the one in charge here!

JOHNNY: I guess what I'm trying to say is, I've been watching you for a while now, and I love you.

DOUG: Ain't that sweet? But you're out of luck, pal. You want to start a dynasty, go kidnap yourself a French girl. *(Pulls BETTY to his side.)*

BETTY: Get away from me, you brute.

JOHNNY *(leveling his rifle):* Better listen to the lady.

DOUG: You little worm! I'll crush you and whatever army you brought with you.

JOHNNY: I don't need any army.

BETTY: You came here all by yourself?

JOHNNY: That's right. Everyone else waited behind on the boat.

BETTY: Oh, how brave!

DOUG: But stupid. Your little toy can't hurt me. Say good-bye, my queen! *(Grabs* BETTY *and turns to run.* JOHNNY *fires rifle.* DOUG *collapses to his knees.* BETTY *jumps free and runs to* JOHNNY.*)*

JOHNNY: I guess you're not so tough after all.

DOUG: Aaaargh!

BETTY: Oh darling! How can I ever repay you?

JOHNNY: Don't even talk like that. I couldn't bear to have anything happen to you, sweetheart.

BETTY: What about—that thing?

*(*JOHNNY *places a chain around* DOUG's *neck and jerks him to his feet. Though* DOUG *is much taller, his stooped aspect clearly indicates that* JOHNNY *is in charge of the situation.)*

JOHNNY: I think we can do a favor for mankind, by bringing him back to civilization and letting the scientists have a look at him. In the meantime, you'll be safe with me.

BETTY: Oh, my Romeo! *(She swoons into* JOHNNY. *He catches her with one arm, while the other grips the chain.)*

DOUG: I guess now you've got everything you ever wanted.

JOHNNY: You're right about that, big boy. *(To audience.)* It's taken a long time. But now that I've got the woman I love, I've got it all.

(Tableaux. Lights brighten up on K., illuminating him from crown to toes.)

BILLY *(from offstage):* And that's the WHOLE story, ladies and gents, exactly as it happened.

The lighting boys have instructions to wait for applause. It always comes, slamming against the players with the impact of an atomic blast. As the waves of sound thunder out across the sandy ring, drowning out even K.'s intermittent snarls, the lights slowly fade down to nothing. There are curtain calls—five or six, usually—and then one last view of K. before the lights are cut, the curtain drawn, and everything reverts to darkness and void.

21. NOT ENTIRELY ACCORDING
TO SCRIPT

It is tempting to wonder what K. makes of all this. The conceit of the show is of course nonsense, the idea that he somehow lusts after Betty's hourglass figure. It is unclear whether K. lusts after anything. Admittedly, he has a penis, pink and alert, nosing the air from its sheath like a terrier in a wealthy woman's handbag. But no one has ever observed it actually doing anything besides passing urine. K. is one of a kind, thankfully; even supposing he wanted to mate with something, what would that something look like?

But the show needs a hook, and the hook is Betty; and K., for whatever reason, continues to respond to her, night after night. Just as he responded to her on the island.

Not that he finds it easy. For one thing, he's dopey and slow, and this makes it hard to think. Although "think" might not be the right word . . . His senses are dulled. Information comes through patchily or not at all, and much of it is incomprehensible anyway.

He is led from one darkness to another, from boxcar to tent. A few short paces in the open air. Sometimes there is rain, often sunshine or wind. He registers unfamiliar smells: fields of ripening corn, cooling in the twilight; air pollution; axle grease; dogs. Always dogs. Sometimes he hears birds he doesn't recognize, or traffic, or distant radios, or all three. Feels a distant longing to break his chains and start running, any direction will do. But that

longing is quickly smothered by something murky and soft that
seems to trundle through his veins like silt, leaving him pliable
and dumb. Dumb as in voiceless. Dumb as in stupid.

Then he is in the tent. He doesn't know it's a tent; he knows
only that this darkness allows him to stand, unlike the other darkness that forces him to recline. Later it fills with incomprehensible
sounds, animal smells and the overbearing stench of massed human beings in close quarters. He stands enshrouded in shadow behind the proscenium curtain, shackled and bound, but of course
he doesn't understand the logistics. He knows only darkness and
restraint, sound and scent. When the lights come on he sees tiny
humans buzzing back and forth and something tugs at his memory, something to do with the female he carried and the male who
chased her and those noisy stingers that spit smoke and pain. The
whole affair agitates K., and would ruffle him a great deal more if
his mind weren't so dull and cotton-stuffed. Still, something down
in his fundament is writhing, howling, fighting to be heard. These
actions are not expressed in words, but if they were, they would
come out something like this: *Break the chains. They are threads and
are powerless to bind you.*

Grab the female, take her to safety.

Trample the little insignificant creatures if they try to stop you.

And run. Run. RUN.

22. NOT ENTIRELY ACCORDING TO SCRIPT

Betty is worried about something. Something big, but for once it is nothing to do with K. She is worried that Johnny is going mental.

She doesn't have any experience with this, not at all—no crazy aunts in the attic, or any such—so she is far from certain. But the suspicion can't be shaken away, and the worst part of it is, there is no one she can discuss it with. Not even Billy. *Especially* not Billy.

What is happening is that her sex life is changing; more and more, Johnny seems to become aroused only in the presence of some danger, some illicit element. They have long since moved past the phase of making love in the hotel bathroom while the maid made the bed on the other side of the closed door. That had kept his interest for a few weeks, through California and up into Vegas. The first time he left the door open, with the maid stripping the sheets off the bed and Betty hoisted onto the sink just footsteps away, she had flushed and refused to go on with it. Johnny retaliated by stalking from the room half dressed and ignoring her for a week. Miserable, she relented in El Paso, where the maids were Mexican and, if they gossiped, at least would do so in a language she wouldn't comprehend. Betty told herself that anyway it was asking little enough of someone who threw herself so utterly into her relationships.

But the open-bathroom-door phase was brief: by Oklahoma City, Johnny was insisting that the room's *outer* door be left ajar while he bucked into her from the rear. By the time they reached the Great Plains, he was leading her by the hand to seek out public parks in St. Louis, Wichita, Kansas City, and when that paled they moved to taxicabs, mini golf courses, the backseats of city buses. At each stage their public exposure increased and so did Johnny's ardor. The liaisons were brief: he finished in a few seconds, which, under the circumstances, was just fine with Betty.

They were witnessed, of course. Many times. But no one ever stopped them, maybe because the episodes were over so fast. Betty assumed that Johnny knew, but she never asked him. Maybe, she reasoned, witnesses were part of the thrill.

It was only a matter of time before Johnny required more danger than America's public parks and yellow cabs could provide, and this is the development that now worries Betty. She quails the first time he gropes her during the nightly show, while the jugglers twirl under the lights and the tigers wait sullenly in the wings. Behind the bleachers he takes her roughly but quickly, and her sequined leotard looks none the worse when he is done. But he goes past even this, of course; beyond doing it during the clown act that precedes her own appearance. Soon they're having sex (it has long since ceased to be lovemaking) beneath the bleachers as the oblivious crowd files past after the show, its imagination overstuffed with K.'s Picasso-esque impossibility. At last Betty feels compelled to speak up.

—What's the matter with you? she hisses, adjusting the crotch of her leotard.—Why are you treating me this way?

He looks down.—I don't know.

—Do you hate me? Is that it? Are you trying to humiliate me?

—No.

She'd expected threats, tantrums, fireworks. There are none. Johnny looks lost, like a kid caught shoplifting comic books. He stares off to the side, not seeing the boisterous crowd flowing by, chattering about the monster they have just seen, filing through the tent entrance into the chilly Des Moines night.—I guess I'm trying to . . .

—To what?

Still he hesitates.—Remember something.

—Remember something, she repeats.—How can you remember something we've never done before?

He struggles visibly for words. Betty fights impatience, knowing that explanations don't come easily to her husband.—Some feeling, he says finally.

The urge to snort or laugh aloud is overwhelming, but Betty senses this would abort the conversation.—What feeling? Danger? Excitement?

—Maybe, he mutters.

She waits. And wonders if he is going to tell her: *Life with you is an anticlimax.* Or: *I liked it better on the island, when you were helpless and I was the hero.* Or even: *I'm not the kind of guy who can live with routine. Not with sex or anything else.* Any of these statements, though hurtful, would be an explanation of some kind. Would, in theory at least, be better than no explanation.

She tells herself, I am not going to speak for him.

But he says nothing and the crowd trundles past and he says nothing and the mob of customers thins to a trickle and he says nothing and the tent is empty now except for the crew leading K. back to his cell. Still Johnny says nothing, and Betty can't help herself. Her voice comes out small and beseeching and she hates herself for it.—Isn't there anything else I can do, darling?

He exhales noisily.—No, he shrugs, and turns to go.

Betty stares after him. The callousness of it hits her like a slap, leaves her short of breath. There is a dull pain behind her clavicle but she figures, Well, at least there's an end to it.

For a time, she's right.

23. DECLARATION OF INDEPENDENCE

Johnny does have an inkling of what's going on but it's tough to put into words. He's not even going to try; speech has never come as easily to him as action—hunting, tracking, climbing, chasing, shooting—and he's not about to start learning how to talk just so he can explain himself. Not to his wife or anybody else.

But the fact is that sometimes in the early morning, with the sun angling low through the curtains of the hotel room outside Boise or Milwaukee or Denver, Johnny has a pretty good idea, a sort of sense-picture, of why he likes to have sex in places where he might be caught. And not just with Betty either but she needn't know that. Women are different anyway.

If he is very honest with himself, as on those drowsy cold-sunshiny mornings, he sometimes is, he might admit—in a non-verbal, impressionistic sort of way—that he wants to be seen. Why is this? Because he is top dog, alpha male, commander of Betty and master of the territory around him. Or maybe master of Betty and commander of the territory—it's hard to think straight early in the morning, but then that's the point isn't it? So if people want to look, let 'em. Let 'em catch a glimpse. Hell, let them stand and take pictures, home *movies*. It's all they'll ever get, and it only points up the difference between himself and the others. The best they can hope for is the chance to watch him.

He didn't use to be this way. It started back on the island, he suspects. A lot of things started on the island, he suspects. Out there, tracking Betty and the monster, rescuing her but leading a dozen of his fellows to their deaths—it was a terrible time of course. Horrific beyond words. Unspeakable. Something he wouldn't wish upon his worst enemy. And yet. And yet.

And yet he, Johnny, survived to step off that island as its undisputed champion. Betty's ripe hips in one hand, twelve-gauge in the other, and a blackjack between his thighs. The monster limp and helpless beneath its shroud of chains. Johnny ascendant. The only fly in the ointment being the lingering memories of his men's horrible deaths, their screams and curses and sudden wet oblivions; and of course Johnny's own destitution. Well, destitution is no longer a problem. Billy has spun them money faster than Rumpelstiltskin, faster than Dillinger could steal it or Liz Taylor spend it; they'll be hard-pressed to consume their riches within their lifetimes, and here the tour is only half over. As for the horrible memories, they're fading too. Still there admittedly, and still poignant, especially on rainy afternoons with the endless Midwest plains rolling past gray-streaked train windows. But fading.

Problem is, Johnny's resurgent ego yearns for ever-larger injections of danger, of thrill. Hence his sexual olympiad, his need to be observed or at least risk being observed. Betty has clamped down on that, and with this stiffening of her resolve, his own stiffening has waned, his libido in retreat. For now. It is only a question of time, and not much time at that, before Johnny's creativity reveals itself in a new way. As the train rattles from Iowa to Nebraska to Michigan, from Indiana to Illinois to Ohio, Johnny ponders his new scheme, ruminates and percolates and incubates.

Not until Pittsburgh does he approach a woman. Not Betty; it's been a month since he last touched her in passion, under the bleachers in Des Moines. His communication with her is barely more than grunts. But if she won't have him, others will. In the meantime Betty can stew, uncertain whether she is in the wrong, until she's ready to consent to anything to win him back. Johnny knows he has the upper hand here. And this new plan, he judges, will take care of his needs in the meanwhile.

For a time, he's right.

24. B MOVIES, AND OTHER KINDS

Doug needs to catch a break. It's been a long time, way too long he figures. You want a hard-luck story? Doug's got one. Got several in fact. Sometimes Doug makes up movie titles for events from his own life. *Attack of the Drunk Mean Daddy. The Boy from Outer Space That the Other Kids Picked On. I Married a Monster from Idaho Who Left Me and Ran Off with the Goddamn Mailman, for Pete's Sake.*

People think it's good to be tall and maybe it is. Better tall than short. But surely there's a limit, and that limit has got to be somewhere below seven foot two. Seven foot two places Doug well out of the category of Tall Enough to Command Respect, and solidly in the realm of Freak of Nature. Doug's got a lifetime of anecdotes to back him up on this.

He harbors no illusions: it could be much worse. He could be seven foot *ten,* for one thing, or he could be in the diminutive shoes of his best friend, Tony the midget. Four foot three in cowboy boots. Endlessly babied and cooed over and told:—You're so *cu-uute!* Doug has told himself countless times, *Better up here than down there.* What Tony himself might think, Doug doesn't know: his friend is tight-lipped on the subject. But Doug suspects that Tony agrees.

At seven foot two, Doug is looked upon less as a guy with

more-active-than-usual glands, and more as a useful piece of ambu-
latory furniture. It goes well beyond taking down books from high
shelves and changing lightbulbs—although he is asked to do both
with numbing regularity. What galls him is the way he's thought-
lessly expected to perform tasks either too dangerous or too unpleasant for anyone else. Since Doug's temperament is reserved and
his frame oversized, he is often interpreted as being big and stupid,
and thus ready to do anything without comment or protest that
others assign him. Add to this an element of his personality that
seeks to avoid calling even more attention to himself than he already receives, and Doug can be found agreeing to all manner of
jobs that would be refused by a more outspoken individual.

Slopping out the animal cages, for example, as if his extra fourteen inches are some guarantee that he'll do it quicker and more
efficiently than anyone else. Hauling and stacking baggage, even
though his back has nagged him for years. And most of all, giving
K. his twice-weekly injections.

This chore Doug hates not because of the danger, which is
minimal with the monster enchained and still shaking off the ef-
fects of the previous shot. After all, the drug and the dosage have
been calculated by a team of wildlife experts, although none of
them was willing to approach K.—chains or no—with the two-
foot syringe necessary to test their research. This duty fell initially
to Johnny, who plunged the needle into the soft reptilian flesh of
K.'s forearm that first afternoon, and then held on. When Johnny
tired of the chore some weeks later, it passed to Doug as if by
common but unspoken consent. No one ever actually asked him
to do it; but somehow the syringe finds its way into his hands, and
the expectation with it.

No, it's not the danger. Doug hates this chore so much because, in K., he recognizes something of himself: overlarge, freak-
ish, ineloquent, judged, mocked. For that matter Doug loathes
his job too, clowning around and getting laughed at by brats; but

getting laughed at is the only skill he has ever recognized in himself, and besides, Billy pays generously.

It would be falsely melodramatic to say: *When Doug injects K., he feels as if he is injecting himself.* Doug does not, in fact, feel this. But he does feel more than just a flickering sympathy; something more than a gentle soul's compassion for a bound and chained fellow creature. Doug is not a great deal more verbal than K. himself—his vocabulary is made up largely of grunts, gestures, facial expressions, which is one reason he's such a gifted clown—but it is possible that, if he were able to put it into words, he might acknowledge that in K. he has met something of a kindred spirit.

Or maybe not. Maybe he'd just say:—I feel bad for the sucker. Sure is a big sonofabitch, ain't he? Seems a shame to lock him up like some lobotomy case. He oughta be out raising hell someplace.

The caravan makes its way across America's heartland, nosing into the eastern seaboard. Doug's discontent grows as summer slides into fall, as 1958 squints nervously at 1959 and wonders, *What kind of crazy stuff are you waiting to pull?* Past Cincinnati and Pittsburgh, past Philadelphia and Atlantic City (where they park for a solid six weeks, playing to SRO crowds nightly, five matinees a week, and a rival promoter offers Billy a flat million to buy the show outright) and into New York City itself. Madison Square Garden no less, Christmastime.

—New York New York, Billy loves to say.—The town so nice they named it twice.

Johnny shares his good spirits.—If I can make it there, I'll make it anywhere, he croons, faux-Sinatra.

It's hard to know what Doug makes of all this. He is a guy who needs to catch a break, and from what he can see, K. hasn't caught one in a while either. So a little natural sympathy lies smoldering, needing something to fan it into jumping, jittery life.

This night, after the opening show at the Garden, the rest of the crew goes off to celebrate uptown somewhere. Some trendy club in Harlem where his white colleagues—they're all white—can congratulate themselves for going someplace edgy and black. Doug doesn't know where exactly and doesn't plan to attend. He knows what will come of it: lots of drunken camaraderie, professions of goodwill and fraternity that he will allow himself to believe and even become quite moved by, followed by more drinks. Then the knives will come out. The jokes will start. Innocuous at first, basketball references.—Joining the Globetrotters hey Douggo? He'll smile wanly. Then:—How's the weather up there? Doug will grit his teeth. Booze will loosen tongues.—I bet his legs ain't the only things that's long! Titters and calculating glances all around and Doug, not knowing where to look, will catch his friend Tony's eye. But Tony, small though he is, is some kind of magnet for broads. He'll be perched on some Rockette's lap like a lascivious six-year-old, hoisting a beer with one hand, pawing cleavage with the other. He'll wink at Doug, or give the thumb's-up while the titters die away and the women put their heads together to discuss just how big they think . . . but no, of course they'd never . . . —A gorilla like that? (This in a whisper, but not enough of one.)—Please, don't be *obscene.*

So no. Doug stays back rather than endure the false bonhomie and revolted/intrigued glances of bored New York tarts. Better to have a night in, enjoying *The Outer Limits* and his own fantasies of Betty. Doug readily admits he's got the best job on earth, slinging Betty over his shoulder for ten minutes a day, her lungs hanging down against his chest, her quim so close he can smell it. . . . Apart from Johnny, Doug has laid hands on Betty more than any man alive. Can the audience see his excitement through the monster costume? He is beyond caring. Anyway they probably think it's part of the show.

Maybe it is, he thinks. Maybe everything is. Maybe there's no difference anymore between existence and entertainment.

Doug's not stupid. He knows Betty's spoken for, and the line of guys willing to take Johnny's place is so long that he'd be easily overlooked, seven foot two or not. In real life, Betty pays him about as much mind as Betty Grable. In Doug's fantasies, though, she is always interested in him, always compassionate. It's not purely physical, either. Sometimes they stay up all night, just talking.

Doug hurries to K.'s boxcar, syringe in hand. Best to get this done with, then turn in. But when he gets there, he finds the door to the boxcar ajar. Doug stares at it awhile.

Very odd, he thinks, not to say an outright snafu. There is little enough danger of K.'s strolling out, bound as he is by chains and chemicals. But still. It's very sloppy of whoever led the monster back to his cell to forget about shutting the door. Doug will ask around, find out who was responsible and have a quiet word.

Doug slips through the open door, his sneakers silent against the metal floor. The boxcar feels like a looming rectangular cave. A single unshaded bulb burns at the far end, throwing harsh light over K.'s head and torso, bleeding away into shadows. In the light he looks more enormous than ever, an Easter Island statue come to life atop the body of the Sphinx. At such moments Doug feels wonder and awe and terror wash over him in equal portions.

The thing reclines against the far wall, shoulders and head leaning upright, legs stretched the length of the car. Doug stands by its ankles. Now it turns its great eyes onto him and murmurs. Doug grips the syringe tight in his hands like a rifle.

What's behind those eyes? Doug has often wondered. That there is something is undeniable. Doug has seen dogs get beat, has seen shot ducks flop crippled to the earth, seen children wincing under an enraged father. (No need for *those* details.) All of them spoke more eloquently with their eyes than their tongues, but what were they saying? Could it even be put into words? Not likely. Some things are beyond verbalizing—they are too simple, or too profound. Just look at a mother whose child lies buried under a bombed schoolroom. Ask the kid whose dad went to war and never came home. Look into this creature's flat gray eyes as it sits waiting for the needle's sting that—somehow, it knows this—will continue the nightmare. To see that inarticulate mix of longing and fear and fatalism is to know the limitations of words.

Doug strides silently to K.'s wrist, clamped down with enormous shackles bolted directly into the floor of the boxcar, and hefts the syringe. The thing is longer than his forearm, as thick as a baseball bat, seems to carry a weight of malevolence and threat. The fluid inside is a sick yellow. K.'s reptilian arm stretches alongside him like a stone wall.

Doug doesn't want to look up at K.'s serving-platter eyes, shining dully like old pewter. He knows he will be distressed at what he sees, but nonetheless Doug looks, as if tugged by a string that links those eyes with his own. And as their eyes link up he hears, clear as his own thought, the quiet words:—Oh God.

Doug stares. The monster has spoken. He hears it again.

—Just a little more. Oh God please.

Doug continues motionless for some seconds, even as muffled sounds register behind him, in the shadows by the door. Scuffling sounds, quiet animal grunts.

—Oh God, I'm gonna come.

Deliberately, Doug casts a glance over his shoulder. The light is dim at the far end of the boxcar, where two figures huddle in the deep shadow near the open door. Doug's quiet steps bring him close as if drawn by this vision. The man's trousers are cluttered around his ankles, while his naked buttocks rise and fall with urgency above the woman's proffered hindquarters. As Doug draws near, Johnny turns to face him, his mouth contorted in what could be rage. The look in his eyes is murderous.—I'm gonna *come,* he snarls.

—Okay, gasps the woman.

She is facedown in the boxcar, dark hair spilling round her head like a stain. Her legs are splayed like a doll's and her skirt is hoisted past her waist. Johnny clutches her hips as if afraid she'll break free. Doug licks his lips and suddenly Johnny grins up at him. Then Johnny's eyes clench and another brief, inarticulate grunt escapes him.

Moments later his body relaxes.—God, he mutters to the woman's prostrate form.—That was the best.

The woman begins to straighten up. Bewildered, Doug scurries from the boxcar, out the still-open door.

Later he realizes he still has the syringe, still needs to give the monster its shot. But by then his bewilderment has turned to fury. He has masturbated three times already to the image of the woman gasping under Johnny's thrusts. Not Betty, that was certain. Probably black-haired Olga, the Romanian from the trapeze act . . . Instead of sating his fury, these acts have only whetted it. Why should Johnny catch all the breaks? Here he is with the swell girl Betty and all the dough, the fame and glory—everybody knows he caught the monster on some island—and the future staring him in the face brighter than a Vegas light show. And to top it all he goes screwing sexy foreign girls in the animal pens while his wife's out with the crew.

And what does Doug have? A weekly paycheck, sure, but nothing else. No blond wife, no little something extra on the side. And no prospects in sight either. No prospect for much of anything, except an endless road of crummy chores and mocking brats.

So by midnight Doug is well on the way to hating Johnny's guts. By 2 A.M. he's arrived. In a way it's surprising how quickly it all happens, but in another way it's predictable. Doug is a minor-league shortstop who resents DiMaggio; a soap opera walk-on who thinks Marilyn is overrated. He's an overworked employee who hates the boss. There are plenty like him.

Doug steps out of his own boxcar that early morning—the boxcar he shares with Tony and the stunt riders and Lou, the lion guy, all of whom are still out at this late hour—clutching K.'s syringe like a totem. Their train has been shunted onto a siding behind Grand Central, and all around loom unused boxcars and dead locomotives as cold as the corpses of mammoths. Skyscrapers shoulder up around him and the stars are rinsed out by their glare, leaving the sky pale and sick-looking. Doug grew up in rural Pennsylvania and thinks it must be weird to live a whole life without seeing the constellations. Orion and Draco and Cassiopeia are old friends to him. He shuts his eyes now and listens as traffic noises are carried to him across the cold December sky.

Doug holds the syringe in both hands and presses the plunger against his thigh, squirting the fluid into the cold winter air.

The patter of K.'s injection drizzling onto the ground reminds Doug of his father's pissing into the snow, back in Pennsylvania. He opens his eyes. His family wasn't Amish but the Amish weren't far away. Maybe that would've been better, to grow up like that. . . . Now Doug has to piss too, so he does, his urine mixing with the drugs and soaking into the gravel between the railroad ties. A black moonlit puddle like a bloodstain. When he is done, the syringe dangles empty in his hand. His fury has left him and in its place rumbles a blend of trepidation and excitement. Belatedly, Doug wonders what will happen.

Around him, even at two in the morning, New York City seems to be expecting something. That's the kind of place it is. To pass the time it murmurs and hums and tells jokes to itself that no outsider could ever understand.

25. LOVE ME (LEGAL) TENDER

Billy feels terrific. None of Doug's effete bellyaching for him, nor Betty's lovelorn anxieties, nor yet Johnny's greasy, macho preoccupations. Billy is a happy man: Billy's getting rich.

He is not a guy saddled with smoker's cough, alcoholism, heroin cravings or poor self-esteem. He doesn't lose his head over a broad or a card game or a chance on the stock market. Billy is, to his own way of thinking, remarkably free of vice, of anything that might cause sleepless nights. He figures he knows a thing or two about bad habits and how to stay away from them. Sure he watches TV but not too much, worries about his expanding gut (and after a year-plus of the good life, it *is* expanding) but not too obsessively. Follows current events but not too close. Cares about the noble causes of the day—Dr. King, pollution in Lake Erie—in an offhand, good-natured way. Mostly he thinks about his next dollar, or his next several thousand.

Perhaps most important for his peace of mind, Billy is not tortured by the demons of unrequited lust. Not for women anyway. How many other middle-aged guys grope for their lost youth between the legs of some twenty-year-old? Not Billy.

Take Betty. Unlike every other man who deals with her on a regular basis, Billy experiences only perfunctory desire for her, the kind he might feel for a particularly nice car, something stylish, without too much chrome. This should not be taken as a slight. Billy is perfectly cognizant of Betty's figure, face and curls. Ten years ago, Billy would have had trouble walking straight, given the johnson he'd have at the sight of Betty's ankles. But now he has entered a stage, in his forty-ninth year of life, in which it takes more than a beautiful broad to hoist Billy's flagpole. Or maybe it takes a lot *less*. In any case it takes something different. What it takes is money.

Every so often it crosses Billy's mind that he might be a goddamn mental case or something, but he's not the type of guy to let it eat him up for long. Billy figures he knows a thing or two about nutcases—he's worked with a few in his time—and figures he isn't one. Or maybe everybody is. Who the hell knows? As long as the dough keeps rolling in, Billy guesses it doesn't matter much. Look at Howard Hughes. Look at the Shah of Iran. The difference between a humorous eccentric and a wacko in a padded room, Billy knows, is only a matter of how many shekels he's got stashed under the bed.

So it's not to say that he is without appetites altogether. He just keeps them parked off to one side, where they can't distract him. So is that vice then? Hell no, Billy reasons. Vice is only vice when it causes problems. Otherwise, it's a hobby.

Everybody needs one. This is his.

Every couple weeks or so, when the urge grows too strong for him to ignore, Billy finds himself a nice little private hotel suite. Not some roadside dive but something with class, wall-to-wall shag, dimmer switches, a hi-fi. Not the mirrors-and-chandelier phony-European-cathouse look that impresses so many American hicks.

He finds a nice place. Makes a few discreet inquiries. Tracks down the local talent and pays top dollar. He can afford it, and Billy is a strong believer both in the virtue of talent and in the gospel that you get what you pay for. He's also a big believer in supporting local enterprise.

What Billy pays for is the attentions of a couple of luscious broads, one blond, one dark. Or maybe both blond or both dark. The coloring isn't critical, isn't the deciding factor, though he does like a mix. (He had a Japanese gal once, too boyish for his tastes, and a couple Venezuelans. Jesus Christ Almighty.) Apart from that he doesn't much care what they look like. Sure, they can't be deformed or something, but tall or short, voluptuous or athletic, they all have their appeal. What matters most of all is the energy, the zip. Sparkle is a must.

—I don't want any sloths, Billy explains when making the arrangements.—No slugs. I'm looking for whippersnappers, you _____ eir work.

_____ g is, I want girls who are ready to

_____ out how to make a girl feel wel- _____ iting in his suite with a chilled _____ ning bubble bath. (Another re- _____ tub.) Chocolates on the dresser _____ menu for later. Billy wants the _____ business, but that doesn't pre-

_____ ub him down and flatter him _____ lly straining with excitement _____ organ they're being paid to _____ have fun. Let them think he _____.

_____ names like Sandy and Pris. When Billy sug- _____ et's go in the other room, there's never an argument. _____ n the bed he's left his valise, closed and latched.—Open it up, he says.

Always, they exchange glances, as if wondering whether tonight's the night they meet the psycho with the suitcase full of intestines. Often there is hesitation and Billy has to coax them:— Come on, it's nothing bad. In fact you'll like it. Take a look.

With a deep breath Pris or Sandy snaps open the latches on the valise and flips back the lid.—Oh!

The girls stare until one of them says, It's money.

Stacks of singles, brand-new, fresh from the bank like bakery doughnuts. George Washington staring dolefully up at them, as if to say, *This wasn't my idea, Martha.* With that new-money odor that people talk about all the time but actually smell only on rare occasions. Billy is somebody who smells that aroma a lot.

—Touch it, he says, reclining on the bed with his manhood jutting toward his navel.—It's brand-new. It's the cleanest money you'll ever see, it's never been touched by human hands.

The brunette hooker giggles.—Virgin.

Billy smiles indulgently. Somebody always makes that joke, sooner or later.

The blond is ruffling the bound stack of bills like a deck of cards.—How much is this, anyway? Hundreds I bet.

—Something like that, says Billy.

—It's just singles though, says the dark one. Then, perhaps realizing that she sounds petty, adds quickly, I mean it's still a lot.

Billy smiles to show no offense taken, and savors the moment: two beautiful women on his bed, clutching wads of money. Money he's earned, that he's brought here. As he brought the girls. He leans forward, takes the dark one by the wrist, pulls the money from her hand. Tears the paper ring that seals it into a bundle, fans the bills before her. Tickles them against her nipple, brown like a stain on her caramel-colored tit. What is she anyway, he wonders briefly. Italian? Greek, Lebanese? What the hell is her real name? Not Pris, that's for sure. Not Sandy.

—Look at you, she giggles.

Still tickling her, Billy looks over at the blond.—Lie back and open your legs.

This is familiar territory. Pris or Sandy does as she's instructed. Billy reaches for her crotch and rubs it. Not with his thumb or middle finger, but with money. The dollar bill, clean and stiff at first, soon grows warm and pliable and, eventually, slick. Sometimes this takes a while. The girl lies back with a surprised look in her eyes and her mouth open a little, but Billy's urgent rhythms are irresistible. Besides, she's not getting paid to resist.

—Feels good doesn't it? he says.

She murmurs something noncommittal.

—They make it with cloth you know. Paper money isn't just paper. There's cotton fibers and God knows what else in it. Rubber probably. Corn silk. You can run it through a washing machine and it won't disintegrate.

The girl's eyes are closed now.

—I want you to fuck this, Billy rasps at her.—Fuck the money. I want you to come with my money.

—All right.

He looks back at the dark-haired, dark-eyed woman.—You too. Touch it till you come, and then you can keep it all. And no faking. I can always tell when it's fake.

She certainly looks willing. As if, all things considered, this isn't the strangest request she's ever had. Billy releases her wrist, then leans against the pillows and watches. The girls writhe across the foot of the bed, the dark one on her belly, the blonde on her back. They grind dollar bills into their vaginas like hemophiliacs trying to staunch the bleeding. Their eyes are vacant; little strings of drool wobble from half-closed lips. Soon their ragged gasps come faster and faster and then one after the other their bodies shudder and go limp.

Billy lied: he can't tell when a woman fakes an orgasm any more than the next guy. But it doesn't matter. Billy is pretty sure that money would make most people come. Even if he's wrong, what's important is that the girls take some pride in their work. That they put on a good show.

They always do, once he's explained what he wants.

* * *

By now, you might be forgiven for wondering: *Are there any normal people in this movie?* It's a fair question. To which the only possible answer would have to be: *Are there any normal people in the world?* And if there were, would you be willing to pay good money to sit in a dark room and watch them?

Billy lets them catch their breath, then says, My turn.

It only takes a few seconds, with the girls on each side of him and his cock swaddled in a parka of crisp dollar bills. When Billy comes his lips form a little O of surprise and he spills onto the paper, onto the fingers of the girls, onto his own belly.

—Onan never had it so good, he grunts. It is doubtful whether either of the hookers understands this.

They stay the night, repeating the ritual two or three times. In the morning, watery sunlight slinks through the suite's drawn curtains and Billy wakes heavy-headed and gummy-mouthed. His flesh is raw from the merciless scraping of the paper.—You can go now, he tells them, not unkindly.—Take the cash and scoot.

Hookers are not, as a rule, early risers. A little while passes as they rouse themselves from bed, wash their faces, pull on their clothes.

And of course divide up the money. As often as not, Billy leaves them behind while he checks out, the two women sitting cross-legged on the bed, counting out dollar bills one at a time. The bills, no longer virginal, are creased and crumpled and now betray, some of them, flaky spots of dried gunk that obscure the letters and numbers underneath. George Washington's lips, spattered with semen. Numerals shiny and sticky. The legend in bold across the back, now crusted and dulled and obscured by Billy's nocturnal efforts.

In God We Trust.

26. WE THE PEOPLE

December 31, 1958. New Year's Eve, New York City. The show is playing ten gigs a week, SRO. Limited-edition *Monster in Madison Square* sweatshirts are flying off the racks at six bucks a pop. There's talk of a feature film, MGM and Universal both interested. Who'd've thought?

But then again, why not?

Billy's minting enough cash to set up his own bank. Everybody's tired, but everybody's elated too. All of them need a vacation and Billy plans to announce a month off for the whole crew after New Year's. Even the monster seems to feel the strain: the thing's been agitated all week, snarling like a harridan and rattling his chains more or less constantly. Nobody can say why.

—I thought we were keeping him drugged up, Billy says to Johnny.

—We are, Johnny answers, a little defensively.—That same concoction the science boys came up with. Every three days.

—Maybe it's reefer madness, Billy chuckles.

—Maybe he's getting used to it, puts in Betty.—Building up an immunity or something.

—Is that possible?

She shrugs.—Sure it's possible. It happens with other drugs, with other animals. Penicillin doesn't always cure syphilis anymore.

This response leaves Johnny nearly as agitated as the monster.

Billy always forgets that Betty went to college, trained as some kind of scientist.—Think we oughta increase the dose?

—Yes I do, Betty says.—It can't hurt and it might help.

—That guy Doug is in charge of it, Johnny says.—I'll tell him to step it up to every two days.

—Do that, Billy says.—Starting tonight.

On New Year's Eve they're the city's hottest ticket. They've been sold out for months. Tonight, the only address worth mentioning is Madison Square Garden, Eighth Avenue between Forty-ninth and Fiftieth. Black limos pull up to disgorge starlets in ballroom gowns. Wall Street bigwigs rub elbows with senators, Broadway stars, trophy wives festooned with glittering rocks. They hobnob awhile in the lobby before taking their seats, making sure they see everyone else, making sure they are seen. They intend to get their money's worth: for tonight's show, Billy's gouging them at a hundred bucks a seat.

—Coulda been a thousand, he says more than once, but he's smiling.

The waxed-canvas big top is gone, its place usurped by the arena. The setup is reminiscent of a heavyweight title bout with a sandy-floored center ring: the proscenium from the earlier shows is gone, as is the black curtain. K. is led into the arena through a long curtained tunnel leading back to a loading bay door that's left open to facilitate his quick removal back to the holding cage. He will emerge in darkness and the lights will come up once his manacles have been locked into place. It's not their orthodox show, it's not what they've practiced; but hey, kids, this is Madison Square on New Year's Eve. Do something special or get out of town.

The show goes fine for a while. The skits, the acrobats, the lion act, the little poodle, it's all clockwork. Billy watches from a darkened corner, narrates over his microphone, can't help feeling a little bored. The lights go out. Billy sputters into the microphone something about technical difficulties, nothing to worry about, folks.

The clank of chains is audible to any but the dullest in the audience.

Their crew is solid: Billy hires smart kids and pays them well. They have the monster out the tunnel and in place in under a minute. The chains are bolted into steel-reinforced concrete blocks pegged directly into the floor of the Garden. Yes he'd had to pay a hell of a lot for that bit of artistic license, but Billy doesn't believe in doing things half-baked. Not tonight.

The collapsible curtained walkway is down and bundled away in another forty seconds. Billy's watch has a glow-in-the-dark dial: he times it. Not bad.

A whisper at his ear.—All set to go, boss.

Billy clears his throat.—Thank you for your patience, folks. I believe we're got the electrical problem sorted out now, if someone could just turn on the lights?

The lights come up, K. gnashes and thrashes, and the audience roars right back in defiance. Nobody runs for the doors. This is New York, after all.

Tonight makes what, their thousandth show? Billy sighs gently. Something like that.

He'd be a cad to complain, he knows. You might as well complain about big cars, nineteen-cent hamburgers, pretty girls in swimming costumes. Might as well complain about monster movies. Or about America.

You find a formula that works, you stick with it: that's Billy's mantra, even if it's unlikely he's ever heard the word "mantra." You make money. You follow the formula some more. You make more money. It says so in the Constitution, Billy's pretty sure. Or the Bill of Rights, one of those things. If it doesn't, it should. You don't like it, hey, there's plenty of room in Russia.

Billy grins to himself. That's a good one: plenty of room in Russia.

Out in the ring Johnny appears, rifle in hand, to confront Doug-as-monster. Johnny's rifle pops, Doug staggers, Betty lands lightly on her feet. The monster watches it all closely. Billy leans against the wall, he won't need to talk for a while.

At this point the script calls for Johnny to slap chains on Doug and lead him away, but of late the performance has been growing broader, more slapstick—another sign they're all getting bored. Sometimes Johnny chases Doug around the ring, sometimes Betty does; sometimes Betty chases them both, to the delight of the audience. Sometimes the little poodle runs on and raises hell, the whole thing degenerating into Marx Brothers weirdness. Sometimes Doug throws Johnny over his shoulder. And tonight, Johnny grabs Betty and throws her over his own shoulder, then hefts his rifle and aims it not at Doug—no, that would be perfectly in line with expectations. Instead, Johnny swings it up toward K., looming over these proceedings like a natural wonder of some sort. Or an unnatural one. K., who has been growing more perturbed with every passing performance.

Maybe familiarity has bred contempt. Or maybe something else is going on, something deeper and less prone to cliché.

Johnny, with Betty thrown over his shoulder, raises his rifle at K. and fires, *pop-pop-popping* it directly at his oversized, agitated, glassy-round serving-crystal eyes. The blanks fire, the muzzle flashes, the sweet tang of gunpowder flares into the arena.

In retrospect, this is a mistake, because something happens then that no one is expecting.

Something always does.

REEL FIVE

MONSTER, 1959

*In this guerilla warfare there were no front lines or
rear areas; terrorists could strike anywhere and
everywhere. Although the French maintained order
in the cities . . . rebels controlled the countryside at
night. Terroristic actions led to reprisals and to the
fighting of a "dirty war." Both sides showed heroism
but little chivalry, and there were frequent outcries
against torture of prisoners and suspects. Because of
the terrorism, civilian losses were higher than those
of the fighting forces.*

—Collier's Year Book, 1959 (entry: *Algeria*)

*Well look, I don't ask questions because it's against
my principles. But would you like to explain that?*

—JAMES BEST IN *The Killer Shrews* (1959)

27. HUMAN INTEREST

The monster was tall as a house, as two houses. Lime green and lumpy, with a mouthful of RAZOR SHARP teeth like a crocodile's. He glowered down at the busy suburban street, fists clenched, tentacles thrashing. Cars knocked into one another like billiard balls.

The monster roared, RAAAAHH!

—Help! screamed a woman.

—Aiiieee!!!! shrieked another.

Sharon frowns. She's read a lot of comics in her life, more than she can remember. Her brother buys them by the fistful. People are forever yelling *Aiiieee!!!* in them. But in real life she's never heard anyone actually say this.

Then again there are lots of things in comics that she's never actually heard, or seen, so this may be something of a minor point.

At the bottom of the page, a policeman confronted the monster, revolver in hand raised before him like a talisman. He hollered at the thing to STAY RIGHT THERE—

—OR I'LL SHOOT!

This should be good, Sharon thinks. A little tremor of anticipation ripples up her vertebrae. She turns the page.

Bingo. The policeman was clenched in the monster's fist, his revolver smacking useless SPITBALLS into the thing's SCALY

GREEN HIDE. The police officer's cap tumbled from his head while the monster's enormous reptilian eyes widened in a FRENZY OF RAGE. In the panel below, the monster's silhouette reared against the sky as panicked humans fled in all directions, scattering like popcorn. The cop tumbled headlong into the thing's wide-open, befanged maw.

Sharon can't help feeling a little let down. Sure it's fun to see the policeman get eaten, but it'd be even better to actually see him gored by the fangs, crushed and spindled like a stick of gum before getting swallowed down in a wet gob. But the comics never show that, Sharon knows. There's some kind of rule that forbids it. They leave you to imagine it on your own. It's better than nothing, she figures, but still. Sharon hates having to use her imagination.

There was that movie a few years ago, *The Beast from 20,000 Fathoms*. Sharon's never seen it—her stupid parents won't let her—but she's heard abut the famous scene with the policeman who gets gobbled up by the dinosaur. Picked right up off the street, chewed up and swallowed down. One of Sharon's friends snuck into the theater and saw it and had nightmares for weeks afterward. Sharon's stupid father wouldn't allow her to go. Said she was too young.

Sharon scowls. She feels a bit like a rampaging dinosaur herself sometimes, especially when thinking about her stupid parents.

The door swings open and Brad is there, freshly bathed, owl-like, wearing those stupid green-and-orange plaid pants that are so awful it's embarrassing for Sharon to be seen with him. Not that there's anything unusual about *that*.—You got my comic books?

She hands him *True War Stories* and *League of Justice*.—I'm still reading *Terror Tales*.

—How is it?

She goggles her eyes.—Terrifying.

Brad's too little to understand her sophistication.—Good.

—Are Mom and Dad ready yet?

He looks over his shoulder, across the suite that's done up with gold-and-black furniture that smells newer than anything they have at home.—Dunno. Their door's still closed.

She knows what that means, even if Brad doesn't. Either they're arguing, or kissing. Or both.—I hope they hurry up or we won't even get to the party by midnight.

Unperturbed, Brad is already losing interest in the conversation. —Give me that one when you're done.

—Of course, Brat. I'm only reading it because there's nothing else to do.

Brad's already in the other room. Sharon is left alone with *Terror Tales* and the HIDEOUS MONSTER that was RAMPAGING through the town, leaving a trail of BLOOD AND CHAOS IN ITS WAKE.

After a time it occurs to Sharon that she's hearing a funny sound, but not the kind of funny sound common in hotels—thrumming elevators, clinking ice machines. This is a kind of creepy growling. It's been going on for a while but only now edges into her consciousness.—Brat, is that you?

The sound continues, louder now. Also there are a lot of car horns, suddenly.

—Brat, knock it off.

The door opens a crack to reveal Brad's wide-eyed face.—It's not me.

Sharon suddenly realizes the sound is coming from outside.

28. LIVE FREE OR DIE

It's like K.'s dream all over again. Not the flying one, no; this is like his new dream, the one where he's running with the human female clutched in his claw and all the hordes of minute, noisome humans at his heels. Popping sounds throwing pain all about him, lightning and thunder in every direction like no storm he's ever seen before. Lungs burn and thighs ache as he hurls himself forward, toward—what? Safety, perhaps. Refuge. Asylum. Even if he doesn't know quite what that will look like.

Maybe he'll know it when he sees it.

When the human male grabbed the female and then turned to attack him—back in Madison Square Garden, though the name means nothing to him—K. felt something shift internally, some restraint collapse that had bound him. Rage blinded him, literally, a red wash sliding across his vision as animal fury and existential angst collided in a chain reaction of unrestrained id: King Lear meets King Kong. When his vision cleared he was standing free, the foolish cables and shackles tattered at his feet. A whistling roar knived his earholes, and he understood that the faceless, unseen but much-smelled mess of tiny humans was swarming away from him, as frenzied as an ant pile kicked in anger.

It was hard to see: what little light there was glared down in spots. Noise made it difficult to get his bearings, but once free, K. needed to get *out*. His tongue lashed like a snake, caught a draft of fresh air floating in from behind him, and dimly he recalled the huge door through which he'd been led.

A flash of yellow nearby. With a start K. realized he was holding the female. The one called—he had learned this only slowly, but once learned it cannot be forgotten—Betty.

Well now. K. has *learned* something!

He hesitated.

—Johnny! Johnny help me! Oh God, not again!

—Hold on, darling, I'm right here! Dammit, somebody find me a real gun!

K. swiftly made up his mind, such as it was. His business there was done and he turned to go. Something crunched underfoot but he barely registered it, and didn't look back to see the little poodle, a crimson stain soaking into the golden sand of the ring.

Betty has gone hysterical in the monstrosity's grasp. She kicks and screams and curses and pounds K.'s alligator-hide claws and damns God and prays to Him and wishes Johnny were there and hopes Billy goes to Hell and cries. The remarkable thing is: she does all this *at the same time.* Meanwhile a small square part of her, the analytical phylum-genus-species-trained scientific bit, observes her irrational reaction and quietly tut-tuts. Unhelpful self-critical, not to say self-loathing, thoughts flutter through her mind: *This isn't helping the situation any, you stupid girl,* and *The best thing you can do right now is stay calm.* Betty ignores this advice, and goes on screaming and kicking and wishing to God Billy had never had this idea or that she'd had the nerve to say *For God's sake, you must think I'm crazy!*

The monstrosity blunders through a cavernous backstage area

where the gloom is cut by intermittent streaks of fluorescent lighting. Betty barely notices. A huge door swings away and winter's night air slaps her. The cold leaves her gasping and teary but it also sobers her enough to look around.

—Oh no, she whispers.

It's twenty minutes to midnight.

29. THE RIGHT TO BEAR ARMS

Johnny tears through the crowd, trying to find somebody, a cop, anybody, with a functioning gun. He finally collars an officer out front who's trying to work crowd control, ignorant of what's happened in the theater, or else not believing what he's been told.

— Give me that! Johnny yells, pointing at the pistol.

The cop is big and heavyset and ruddy-faced: Irish from scalp to toenails.— It's New Year's Eve so I'll forgive you a little drinking, he says heavily.—Now run along, amigo.

—Damn it, that thing has my wife!

—*C'est la vie*, the cop sighs.— With a little luck he'll take mine too.

If there's one thing Johnny hates it's a wiseass mick, and conversation isn't his strong suit anyway. He coldcocks Paddy with a roundhouse to the jaw that would stun a horse and the man tumbles to the street. Johnny tugs the weapon free of its holster and dives back into the now empty theater.

Behind him the cop is already up on his knees. He spits out a tooth and hollers, I'll have your balls for that.

Bastard must be made of stone, thinks Johnny.

The house lights are up, revealing the obvious signs of panic— torn upholstery, orphaned shoes, a pawnshop's worth of rocks glittering on the floor. The giant guy, Doug, lies sprawled in the front row as if stunned. But there's no other sign of anything untoward. That is to say, no monster. Makes sense, Johnny figures. He tries to think like the thing: if he were it, the last thing he'd do would be to bust himself free, grab Betty—and then go chasing after the crowd that had come to see him in chains. Uh-uh, mac. He'd go dead in the other direction, out the back door.

Johnny bolts down the aisle, across the sandy-floored center ring; slips on something wet and keeps going. He runs through the stage wings, past the green room and out the loading bay, which some Einstein decided to leave wide open. Johnny clutches the cop's gun, solid with a decent balance but not very heavy. He wishes he had something bigger. He wishes he had a goddamn flamethrower and a dozen hand grenades. But he doesn't, so he pushes his way forward, through the loading bay, out into the alley beyond.

He can't see a thing: the streetlights are all smashed. But before he can get annoyed with that, he realizes he just needs to follow his ears. He scampers out into the frosty night, down along a side street and into an alleyway, sprinting to Eighth Avenue at the far end. Where, judging from the cacophony of car horns, the world's biggest-ever traffic jam is taking place.

Or maybe something else.

If Johnny paused then and there, halfway down the alley, and asked himself, How do I feel right now? he might notice something unexpected: that despite his accelerated heart rate and breathing, elevated blood pressure, sense of urgency and imminent doom—or more likely, because of all these things—he's feeling fantastic. This would not be a happy realization, but it would be an honest one. If you said to him, *Hey Johnny, even though this is an awful thing and the woman you love is in incomprehensible peril, isn't there some part of you, however small, that is secretly glad this is happening?* he would be forced to answer, if he chose to be honest: *Yeah. Yeah I am.*

And then he'd feel terrible, of course.

So don't ask him.

And for God's sake don't ask Billy: *What was going through your mind when the monster was thrashing out of his cuffs and snatching Betty and slamming away to terrorize nighttime traffic in New York City?* Because you know Billy's honest answer would have to be either, *Liability,* or else, *Whether it would eat into our margins or increase them.*

And Billy would feel pretty bad about that too. Feel like a real heel for a few minutes, what with all the trouble everyone's being put to on account of his show. But he'd perk up quick enough at the thought that, in all likelihood, publicity of this magnitude would do nothing to harm their revenue stream when they took the monster to Europe.

This is, of course, before he sees the scale of the damage that K. is inflicting on the city and its inhabitants. Before it's all over, Billy will be sweating all right.

K. breaks from the alley like Knute Rockne shaking off linemen, like a broaching whale slicing the surface of the ocean. He strides onto Eighth Avenue, pauses, then cuts across Forty-ninth Street to Broadway. There he hesitates again, one seven-toed foot planted on each sidewalk. Looks south, surveys what he sees. Tries to make sense of it. Fails.

In his claws the female Betty screams and kicks, but he ignores her.

Broadway unrolls before him like an endless flat river, bracketed on each side by metal towers and obscenely bright electric lights. K. is ignorant of both metal and electricity, but he is also past the point where he would have tried to fit these things into a context he understands—by mentally interpreting the skyscrapers as *odd gray stone mountains,* for example, or the lightbulbs as *enormous fireflies that stood still and never winked out.* No, K. has left such efforts behind him, in a boxcar in Iowa, perhaps, or under a big top in a field in Missouri. Now he sees only a blinding wash of electric color boxed in by gunmetal gray skyscrapers. He doesn't understand any of it, doesn't try to, and doesn't let this perplex him.

There is much more of course. Rivers of automobiles swirl and splash in eddies around his feet. The glare of headlights pains him, and he raises an arm to shield his eyes. Soon the cars crumple and crash, and before long the river has become a dammed pool. Or maybe a damned pool. Humans run shrieking in all directions like something out of Dante, smashing each other even as their automobiles did, flopping to the earth in unruly piles, only to hop up again and press on. The question flickers across K.'s mind as to why these creatures make such a racket and run so ostentatiously when the more sensible course by far for a frightened animal is to stay quiet and move with stealth. This observation—landmark though it is in K.'s interpretation of the world, a critical analysis of the behavior of others—fades in a few moments.

From a few blocks over comes the din of car horns. The sound disorients him, as he cannot see its source, so he assumes the buildings are making it. This is alarming in the extreme. It occurs to K. that these huge towering structures might in fact be living creatures—monolith monsters of some sort—and the thought jogs him forward, along the length of the avenue.

—Hey you—you thing! Where are you taking me? Where are we going?

He ignores her. He would have no answer even if he understood the words.

Cars collapse like eggs beneath his feet. Suddenly the avenue is deserted, only derelict autos left to clog it. They bleed fluids like vanquished bulls, K. their infernal matador. K. pauses, turns, squints into one of the windows to his right. It is dark and he sees little. He looks into another and sees only an empty room, a vacant bed, a lamp brightly lit.

Something ignites in the street behind him: a flower of gasoline erupts into a blossoming orange flame ball, and nearby windows shatter. K., reminded of his previous anxiety, strides down the avenue. One car after another crunches beneath him, while behind him roar further explosions. And something else, a disturbingly familiar *pop-pop-pop!* He ignores it.

Then again: *pop-pop!*

K. races on, a little faster, some sixth sense pushing him on.

—Betty! Hold on!

Fury washes over K. then. Will he never be rid of this irritant? Just as he is clueless about his own obsession with the woman Betty, so too is the tenacity of the man Johnny equally mystifying. Why won't he simply go away? Why does he insist on trying to hurt her?

For his intentions are never in doubt. K. clearly senses that the male is a threat. It does not occur to him to wonder, a threat to whom?

K. rounds on his pursuer. There he is: alone amid the wrecked cars, lit by electricity and firelight. Orange flames throw crazy black shadows over the scene and everything in it, including the male, but the garish light is plenty for K. to see by. With a fluid, effortless motion he bends, lifts a little scrap of something and hurls it sidearm. The something is a taxi. This wreck slams into the car in front of Johnny: sparks whirl like lightning bugs and the whole mass of twisted steel flips backward. Johnny vanishes beneath the onslaught as stray bits of jetsam carom crazily down the street for fifty yards, the world's longest bocce track.

—Johnny, no!

The female Betty writhes and shrieks louder than ever. K. lifts her to his face as if to tell her: *There is no more danger. I have saved you from that man.*

—You bastard! You motherless, godforsaken son of a bitch!

The words flutter onto Broadway like ticker tape. K. turns his back on the scene and charges on, past Forty-eighth Street, Forty-seventh, Forty-sixth. His pumping strides gobble up whole blocks like licorice. He leaves behind him a trail of wasted cars and flaming puddles, tires smoking amid the mayhem of bent chassis and cracked pavement. And terrified people. And one—so far only one—motionless body.

It's about ten minutes to midnight just now. Down in Times Square, the crowd's been waiting for the ball to drop so they can holler *Hooo-rah!* and they can hear all the car horns and screeching people. Coming closer it sounds like, and then the waves of panicking New Year's partyers wash into the square like a tide.

—What is it? What's going on?

—Just get out of here, pal. Just run!

The Times Square crowd checks their watches and grin sideways at each other and say, These numb-nuts is gettin a early start on the New Year!

There's laughter, then nervous laughter as the explosions draw close, then an unearthly bellow rips the sky. K.'s shadow rears up against the flickering arcs and flashing neon of Times Square. And then there's no more laughter at all.

Colored swatches of light cut across K.'s vision, flickering signs that leave him even more baffled. (And when did he start seeing color, anyway? This movie is black-and-white, or used to be.) The signs beckon him: REGENCY THEATER. SOLD OUT! *FIDDLER ON THE ROOF.* LAST TWO WEEKS. *THE MOUSE TRAP.* "I WAS ENCHANTED AND ENTHRALLED!"—*NY TIMES. RICHARD III.*

The winter of our discontent, indeed: noise everywhere, sirens and amplified voices, engines, aircraft. Whatever else they are, human beings are certainly not quiet.

* * *

It's the Irish cop who finds Johnny, out cold under a pile of rubble that, miraculously, has managed to stun him without crushing the life from his limbs.

—Come on kid, wake up, the cop snaps. He squats beside Johnny, patting his cheeks.—Look sharp! *Tempus fugit* while you're having fun.

Johnny groans.—Wha—?

—You been hit on the head, the cop tells him.—*C'est la guerre.* Don't pass out now or that concussion'll turn into something bad.

Johnny blinks and says nothing. The pistol is still clutched in his hand.—I'll take that back now, the cop says, checking the chamber.—Gee, thanks for saving me a shell.

— Wouldn't matter if I'd saved them all, Johnny says hoarsely. His head is clearing now and he rolls onto an elbow.—Gonna take more than a revolver to stop that.

The cop's name is Flanagan. He's Brooklyn-born and -bred and he's seen plenty in his time. *Plenty.* He could tell you stories, boy. But as his eyes flicker up and down the firelit avenue, the carcasses of Fords and Chryslers littering it like Shermans and Panzers, he knows he's never seen anything like this before. Not even close.—I believe you're right, he mutters.—Looks like Rommel's been through here.

Johnny sits up.—Sorry about smacking you like that. I needed the gun and there wasn't time to explain.

Flanagan nods, fingering his sore jaw.—I guess I understand. Though I can't remember the last time I let a man punch me and walk away.

Johnny believes him.—I didn't get too far though.

Flanagan grins. Johnny winces at the bloody gap in the cop's smile.—Can't win 'em all, pal. That's what the nuns useta teach us.

—Come on, says Johnny.—We've got to catch that thing before it does any more damage.

—Whoa there, Trigger. You won't be stopping anything when you can't even stand up straight.

It's true: Johnny's knees rattle like an addict's. His vision swarms with a delirium tremens of black speckles and colored lights. He slouches into Flanagan and lies, I'm fine. I just need to let my head clear.

—Sure you do. Which is what you'll do the moment we find a nice quiet place to sit. Saint Pat's ain't too far from here—

—No! Johnny wrenches upright. The effort nearly makes him vomit but he keeps to his feet somehow.—That thing's running away with my wife, understand? I'm not going to just let it go.

Flanagan peers hard at Johnny, looks away down the avenue, squints back at Johnny again. He's seen plenty in his time, he reminds himself. *Plenty.*

Johnny says, I rescued her once before, and I'll do it again.

He's leaning like Pisa but doesn't fall.

—All right, says Flanagan quietly. What he thinks of all this is impossible for an outsider to tell. His face is impassive, his voice carefully modulated. In another life, another movie, he'd have made a great psychiatrist—or maybe one of those streetwise priests who can talk to the kids. But for now he'll have to make do as a cop.—All right then. Let's go get your wife back.

30. CONVENTIONAL WISDOM

The sound is closer now. Or louder at any rate. Brad's exhalations leave a circle of mist on the window, which he rubs out impatiently, but there's nothing to see besides the tail end of a fleeing mob. Traffic sits at a complete standstill, fender to tail fin. Most drivers didn't even bother shutting the doors when they bolted from their cars.

Mom and Dad are still in the other room.

Brad says, You think we're safe or should we run away too?

Sharon squints at an angle through the glass, but can see nothing. The sound grows louder by the moment, a wet groaning retch-howl that slithers into her stomach and pokes around in there. Explosions punctuate the night like fireworks. Maybe they *are* fireworks. Maybe it's midnight already, though somehow that seems less critical than it did earlier.

She's scared but she's also the elder.—We're fine, she tells her little brother in the steadiest voice she can muster. She runs her fingers through his downy ruff.—We're on the fourth floor. Nothing can get to us up here.

She hopes this is true, for her own sake and for her brother's.

Brad rubs his breath from the window and says nothing.

Suddenly the bedroom door heaves open and Mom is there, tossing her hair. Red tonight.—What on *earth* is all that racket?

Brad mumbles, Can't see from here. Sharon says, It's some sort of commotion.

—Well it's New Year's, Mom says. A Salem dangles from her lip as she roots about for a lighter.—What do you expect?

—I think this is different, Sharon suggests carefully.

As if to punctuate her remark there is an especially loud double explosion, definitely *not* fireworks, followed by a testicle-clenching screech. Mom exhales twin streams of exhaust and blurts, The hell is that? Willard, get out here!

Mom joins the kids at the window as Dad shuffles into the room, fussing with his tie.—I hear it, I hear it, he says.—Some kind of publicity stunt I imagine.

Mom cuts him a glance, smoke trailing from her lips like a red-headed dragon.—Why don't you join us before you make your opinion known, darling? She gestures to the obvious signs of disorder, the abandoned cars, the firelight reflecting from up the avenue.—A publicity stunt, all this?

—Hmm—perhaps not, Dad admits. He joins them at the window and peers out, rabbit-like. One hand soothes his pencil mustache while the other jingles loose change in his pocket.—Something more, I would imagine.

Mom drags deeply on the Salem, shaking her head.

—But you can't see it from here, whines Brad.

—Small favors, darling, murmurs Mom.

Dad clears his throat and fusses with his cuff links.—No worry on that account. Whatever it is seems to be moving this way.

—You can just make out some kind of shadow on the buildings up the street, says Sharon.—You have to really crane your neck but you can see it if you try.

—So you can, says Dad. A moment later:—Rather a large shadow, I should say.

For a time they stand with their faces pushed against the cold glass. They use their sleeves as windshield wipers to furiously erase the condensation. Mom chuckles, Anyone looking at us will think we're lunatics.

Nobody answers.

At length Sharon says, You're not afraid, are you Brat? We're still on the fourth floor, we'll be all right.

There is no answer.

—Brat?

She pulls back from the frozen glass but her brother is not there. Behind her, the door to the suite is ajar.—Oh shit.

—None of that now, says her father.

—Oh *shit*, Sharon repeats.

Doug needs to catch a break, but for once he's not the only one. The whole city needs a break right now.

—Help me!

Doug looks around. He's still in Madison Square Garden, lounging among the busted seats and abandoned swag. When K. grabbed Betty and lumbered off, Doug was flat on his ass in the sand, gaping upward in disbelief and dead certain that his time had come to get squashed flat. Instead the monster had bypassed him completely, the hall had emptied and Doug was left to gaze around dazedly before lowering himself into an empty front-row seat. He noticed, in an abstract way, that the performance area looked very different from this angle.

Now what? he wondered.

The lights came up even though everyone was gone. He sat motionless, even as Johnny came charging through a minute later, then the cop. Neither had spared him more than a glance.

—Can someone please help me?

Doug frowns, wondering where the voice is coming from. Far away, probably. Someplace outside. He figures the city's full of voices like that right now.

Looks like he has more movie titles for his life story. *The*

Monster That Swallowed My Job. The Screw-up from Another Dimension Who Stopped Giving the Injections and So Caused a Major Catastrophe.

—Isn't there someone there? I can hear you!

Or his favorite: *The Giant Who Never Got Laid.*

—I can hear your chair, I'm right back here! Help, please!

No—that voice wasn't so far away after all. Doug realizes he's been sitting in a daze, but now shakes it off, cranes his neck. Behind him he sees only rows of seats, either empty or toppled.—Somebody there?

—Well, I *guess* so.

It's a woman's voice, or a girl's: high-pitched and thickly swathed in Bronx. Doug stands slowly and says, I don't see you.

—These seats have me pinned. I can't see you either but I heard your chair squeaking. Is everybody else gone?

She pronounces it "gaw-in." Doug says, Yup.

—Stupids. This is probably the safest place in the city right now.

Good point, Doug decides. He moves quickly, his hesitation evaporated. He strides five or six rows up the center aisle, to a point where a section of four seats has been upended. The seats are bolted to metal runners that join them, benchlike, into a single unit. Now he sees that one of these units has been overturned as the mob rushed out, wedged under the row in front. Beneath them lies a girl.

—Don't worry, he tells her.—I'll get you out.

All that's visible are her shoes, white patent-leather heels poking out from beneath the seat. Funny shoes for a little girl but maybe it's the fashion these days. From the other end of the overturned chairs, a few blond strands are splayed out as if on display. Doug bends his knees, shifts the jammed seats, and carefully pivots them away from the girl.—Can you move?

—Sure. Just a sec.

She stands and Doug realizes she's no little girl. She's short, yes, maybe five two and that's with the heels. But late twenties, Doug guesses. His own age more or less.

—Thanks a lot, hon. Appreciate it.

—Glad I could help, he answers, lowering the seats to the floor.

She watches with a look of appraisal on her face. Doug straightens up, feels her gaze on him, looks away, looks down.

—Whassamatter? You shy?

—Well no, he says, then:—Maybe a little.

—Don't be. Shyness never got anyone anywhere. My name's April.

—Doug.

—Got a smoke, Doug?

Cigarette packets litter the floor like lottery tickets.—Camels or Pall Malls?

Camels if you got 'em.

She lights up and inhales gratefully, always watching him. He steals glances. She's pretty, he decides. Not glamorous: too much nose, not enough chin, brown eyebrows clashing with blond bangs. But kind eyes, sad eyes that droop downward, with heavy lids.

—You're the monster. In the show.

—Yeah.

—Hope you saved your money.

He blinks confusedly and she adds, Looks like you're out of work.

Doug grins ruefully.—I guess.

—And I guess you need a drink too.

—I wouldn't mind, he admits.

Her little starfish hand swings out, grabs his and tightens.—Well then. Seeing as how my rescuer is newly unemployed, looks like it's up to me to buy you one.

K. clomps down Broadway like a Visigoth hunting the Forum. Streets pass underfoot as he hurtles unchallenged past Madison

Square Park, then farther, inducing the junkies in Union Square to go on the worst trips of their lives. K. scatters chaos the way Johnny Appleseed sowed fruit. Deranged matrons clutch their offspring and cower in doorways as he passes. Devout atheists fall to their knees, blubbering prayers to the Almighty. Gangsters resolve to confess, give to charity, be nicer to their wives. Priests wrench off their surplices and go running to whorehouses. Estranged couples dive into each other's arms. The lame don't walk and the blind don't see, but it's close, it's close.

Betty observes none of this street-level excitement. Her view from the center of things is, paradoxically, more limited than anyone else's. All is confusion and misdirection, like standing inside the temple as Samson flexes his biceps. The streets around her are wreathed in smoke and the uncertain flicker of flame and flashing lights, the condemned-banshee screech of sirens and bullhorns. For the services have arrived: the fire department busily dousing the flames in their wake, and the police—out in force on New Year's Eve—blocking the streets, cordoning off the area, keeping the populace safe.

Or trying to. Up ahead is a barricade of squad cars, stubby black-and-white vehicles with a phalanx of men crouching behind like revolutionary Parisians. Betty knows these men are armed, and her thoughts echo a silent internal wail: *For God's sake, don't shoot me!*

A tinny amplified voice cuts the air: someone is hollering through a megaphone.—We have you surrounded! Put the girl down.

—You must be joking, Betty moans.—This isn't Pretty Boy Floyd, you idiots.

For his part, K. ignores both the voice and the barricade. What's one more voice anyway? Or one more barricade among many. Not that this is much of an obstacle. A fallen tree back home on the island would pose a bigger problem. He strides on, three steps away now, two, one, and the cops fall back as K. scuffs through the patrol cars parked three deep across Broadway, knocks them aside like Lincoln Logs. The cops huddle in doorways and under awnings, waving their weapons futilely. The din of rending metal is enough to make them contemplate changing careers. Some of them pray, some cry, some do both while Betty kicks her legs and all but foams at the mouth.—Don't shoot me! she screams at the men.— Don't shoot me, and don't shoot him either! He doesn't know what he's doing.

Her voice chokes off and she is left with only the echo of her own words. She wonders if the police officers heard what she said. Then she wonders why she said it.

And then she wonders whether it's true: maybe *the monstrosity* knows exactly what it's doing. What about that? Had she ever thought of that?

Well, no.

But somehow Betty doubts she'll live long enough to find out one way or another. K. is two blocks past the barricade already. Moving south fast, as if he aims to hit the harbor and start swimming.

A snippet of song runs through her head. *One day soon and it won't be long, uh-huh, oh yeah, mm-hm, that's right . . .*

And then, up at the next corner, she sees what looks like a little boy.

31. ONE DAY SOON AND IT WON'T BE LONG

K. is getting tired of this. He staggers on, his movements as jerky as a poorly animated dinosaur model. K. can't remember such a day in his life. Admittedly he doesn't remember much. But still: there must have been a day when he wasn't chased and shot at and blockaded and so on. He feels sure of this, to the extent that he is sure of anything.

Overhead float the noisy human machines that he hates. Around him spotlights probe like fingers, up into the sky, down from the stars into his face.

The female Betty has gone silent in his hand, limp as spinach. It occurs to K. to wonder why he has gone to the trouble of keeping her safe with him. Hey! That's new! A touch of self-awareness, perhaps—the beginnings of something resembling insight, even *ego*? And if so, can it be said that all this mayhem the humans are putting K. through might, in fact, have some beneficial purpose? But then the question slides away from his consciousness, wiped away like rust under a wash of solvent, leaving his awareness as glassily clear as ever.

He continues down Broadway, roaring defiance.

Meanwhile, Flanagan and Johnny dog K.'s footsteps like—well, like dogs. An Irish setter and a Doberman, maybe. A Shetland sheepdog and a rottweiler. A golden retriever and something left in the woods too long, too far from the confines of domesticity and routine, something that has turned viciously feral and now is barely recognizable.

They round a corner and spot K.'s receding figure shuffling down Broadway. Lit from below by orange gasoline fires; lit from above by ghostly spotlight fingers.

—This way! hollers Johnny, charging after.

Flanagan rolls his eyes.—Ooh la la, he mumbles, but doesn't argue.

Betty screams, He likes music! Play him a song and he'll quiet down.

The boy stares, crew-cut frizz atop his head like a parody of surprise. Ditto the owlish stare.

Betty fights down a sob. Maybe the kid's simple. That would explain why he's out here in the first place. It would also explain the plaid pants. Green and *orange*? Or maybe it's the *mother* who's simple.—Can you hear me?

The boy nods.

K. has paused at the intersection of Broadway and Thirty-third. Betty lolls streetward, hollering as loud as her wracked lungs can manage.

—Listen to me. He calms down if you sing to him. But it's too noisy here. Tell everyone to quiet down and play him a song. Then he'll put me down and stop running.

K. makes up his mind and turns toward the harbor.

—Do you understand? Betty wails.

The boy nods.—What kind of songs? he yells suddenly, his voice a silver thread that Betty can barely hear.

—Rock and roll I think! But maybe anything will work. Tell the police, all right? Find my husband and tell him too!

The boy calls back something she doesn't catch.

Then K. rounds a corner and he is gone.

* * *

Moments later Brad's father and sister are beside him.—Jesus wept, says Dad. His eyes had caught a glimpse of K.'s retreating butterfly wings.—Are you all right, son?

—I'm fine. That lady said we have to play songs for it.

His father's hand rests on Brad's shoulder, fussing with his collar.—Hmm?

—She talked to me.

—Sure she did, Brat, snorts Sharon.—Don't listen to him Daddy. He just wants to be at the center of things.

—No sir! Dad, she told me that if we play rock and roll the monster will stop running away.

—I think we'd better get inside. You've had enough excitement.

—But—

His sister's face leans close.—*Brat.*

Brad experiences a strange mix of emotions. Powerlessness, which is nothing new, is coupled with the certainty that he has been called upon to perform a vital service, which is novel in the extreme. The knowledge that the lady in the monster's hand has told him something critical, something he can't just ignore or forget about the way he ignores so much of the adult world, causes his stomach to clench. Impatience stresses his bladder, casts him ashore on the verge of tears.—We have to do this, he whines.— We *have* to.

—Let's go, Dad says. He steers the teary Brad into the marble-and-brass hotel lobby and makes for the bank of elevators. Brad just has time to register the faces of the hotel staff cowering open-mouthed, bloodless, behind the reception desk.—Your mother will be waiting.

Just as he says it the chromed elevator doors open and out steps Mom like a red-turbaned maharani, only her turban is really her hair piled up in coils and her hookah has taken the form of a dainty Turkish meerschaum pipe.—You heard all that I suppose, Willard? We must contact the authorities.

Dad stops.—Hmm?

—Oh for Christ's sake, show a little initiative. We have a *situation* here.

Brad sees his chance.—She talked to me, Mom. The woman with the monster.

—Did she? Mom inhales on her white clay pipe, jetting trails of smoke through her nose.—And what did she tell you?

—She said we need to play rock and roll songs so the monster puts her down—

—Eva, it's just some figment of the boy's imagi—

—Not it's not, Mom interrupts.—Unless I'm suffering the same delusion myself.

The four of them stand a moment, blinking.

—When you were busy rescuing our son here, who apparently had no need of rescue, I was watching through the window and heard everything that poor woman said. I didn't realize she was talking to you, Braddykins. Mom's red-painted lips smile briefly.— I should've guessed you'd be in the middle.

Brad feels a hot flush of pleasure. Sharon's eyes spit nails but so what?

—Now Eva, begins Dad.

Mom cuts him off.—We need to get this information to the authorities, or to her husband. She mentioned her husband, didn't she?

Brad nods up at his mom, rearing before him like something carved from granite and bigger than anything real.

—Well then. Let's hope *her* husband is a man of action and determination.

Dad says nothing.

—There's a policeman, squeals Sharon.

They all look past the hotel's plate-glass fronting. Sure enough, a thick-set cop is shuffling fast down the rubble-strewn street, his uniform caked in dust and ash. Following him is a man who looks as if he's been beaten by thugs. Dad murmurs, I'm not certain they're quite the authorities I would seek out.

—What's wrong with him? Mom demands.—He's a police officer isn't he? We'll tell him what we know and let him pass it along.

The conversation is moot already, as Brad moments ago raced through the lobby and out the door like some urban fairy sprite, hollering urgently at the two surprised men. Sharon hesitates only a moment before setting off after him.

She hates to grant him this victory, but sees little alternative. Sharon is perfectly astute at sensing which way the wind is blowing.

32. DON'T TREAD ON ME

Billy figures he knows a thing or two about crisis management. Hunkered in a phone booth he barks to the stringer from the *Morning News,* Never mind the lawsuits! I'm in the middle of a bidding war between three movie studios!

This isn't true, not even close. Fact is, the damage K. has already done—the ruined streets, demolished cars, ruptured city psyche—could bankrupt Billy Quinn many times over. But by tomorrow the rumor will be out that three studios are plumping big cash for the story rights, and the actual studios, fearful of being cut out of the action, really *will* be knocking down his door. Billy figures the only way he can insulate himself from financial ruin is to show that he's got the money and clout of Hollywood behind him. All those stars, all that glamour, not to mention all the legal muscle. Billy figures there's not a law firm in town, even this town, that wouldn't think twice before taking them on. And if push comes to shove he can always buy them off.

The hack is jabbering in his ear, something about the monster's taste for human flesh.—Don't be an idiot! Billy snaps.—The thing won't even eat hamburgers. He lives on fruit salad, for Christ's sake.

The hack's voice is nasal and tinny over the phone.—Can I quote you on that?

—You damn well better! Billy shouts, then cuts short his

conversation and dashes outside. He's midtown somewhere, Eighth and Fiftysomething, and the scene's a mess. Like something out of a newsreel: the Blitz, maybe. Confusion everywhere, flashing red lights and the acrid tang of smoke in his nose, lodging in his throat like mustard gas. Billy fights back a wave of panic that momentarily blinds him. He's always had a thing about gas, ever since the Great War, reading about it as a kid in *Life* magazine. Pictures surface in his head, corpses stacked like firewood, men drowned in their own mucus, eyes and mouths stretched wide.

—Goddamn it, he whispers to himself.—Get a grip, Quinn.

With an effort he turns his attention to what surrounds him. Wrecked cars are being cleared away like broken toys. Cracks trace through the asphalt, a few windows gape brokenly like missing teeth, columns sway out of kilter, lintels sag. Nothing catastrophic. Nothing to compare with, say, Dresden or Tokyo or Stalingrad. And nobody dead, at least not so far. That's good, thinks Billy. That's a hell of a lot better than good. The monster is no killer, they can prove it in court, if it comes to court; the monster has never—okay, never *to their knowledge*—taken a life. (*Taken a wife is something else again,* chirps an irreverent voice in his head, but he pushes it aside.) Billy fervently hopes it stays that way. Even if it comes to a lawsuit, well, the difference is immeasurable between damages for some wrecked property, and reparations for lost lives. Oh yes. All the movie studios in the world wouldn't be able to help him then.

A police sergeant is coolly dispensing instructions to a group of men. Billy interrupts him.—Get me the chief of police.

—Who the hell are you? demands the sergeant.

He extends a forefinger along the shattered avenue.—I'm the guy who owns that thing.

Six minutes later he's in a squad car screaming down Seventh Avenue; four minutes after that he's somewhere in Tribeca. The chief of police is rough-hewn and looks like an ugly Jack Palance.

His hair is unkempt, as if he's been pulled from bed, but his flinty eyes are clear as lasers.—I've heard about your circus, Mr. Quinn. You shoulda stuck with clowns and lions. You're in some profoundly deep trouble, is how I see it.

—Listen, says Billy, that thing's not a killer. It's scared and trying to get away from us, that's all. It doesn't even eat meat for God's sake, it's a vegetarian.

The chief chuckles, or perhaps snorts, or perhaps chokes back vomit.

—Just tell me this, pleads Billy.—Has anybody been killed yet?

The chief's eyes slide away, linger, slide back.—Not so far as we know.

Billy exhales deeply.—All right. All right. Listen, there's no reason to kill it. It just needs to be contained so it can't do more damage.

—You inna habit of telling people how to do their work, Mr. Quinn?

—No I'm not, Chief, but I think I can say I understand this thing better than any man alive. I've lived with it twenty-four hours a day the past eighteen months. I know its moods and I understand its psychology.

The chief snorts again at the word.

—Our team has developed a drug to tranquilize it, Billy pushes on.—For some reason it's been less effective than usual recently, but a solid double dose should be enough to bring it down.

—And the girl?

—What girl?

The chief cocks an eyebrow.—This monster that you *know more about* than anyone else, Mr. Quinn. It's carrying a girl in its hand, from your own circus.

—Oh God. Betty?

—I don't know the name.

This is the first Billy's heard of it: he'd been offstage during the initial confusion at Madison Square, and knew only that K. had escaped. His mind spins in useless orbits like a dog chasing its tail.—Well . . . well . . .

The chief is smiling mirthlessly. Billy pulls himself together and says, All the more reason to be careful. There's a life at risk.

—More than one is how I see it, the chief says with heavy irony.—Let's say we trank it like you suggest. Then what?

—Then we'll take it back, and put it—away—

—Back in some cage it can break outta? No thanks, Mr. Quinn.

Billy fights back impatience. He figures he knows a thing or two about the law-enforcement mind-set; it's just a matter of finding the right lever and applying adequate force. Simple mechanics, really.—Chief, the man who resolves this situation will be a hero to the entire city. The man who resolves it quickly and without bloodshed will be in line to stand as mayor, even governor. Listen to my advice, and this whole drama will be a memory by sunrise. Your picture will be on every front page in the city. January first, nineteen fifty-nine. Not a bad way to start the New Year, huh?

The chief regards him for a time, his wry smile nestled among a small topo map of wrinkles.—You're one slick talker, I'll give you that. You shoulda gone inna politics. You're not from around here, are you?

—Ah—Los Angeles, actually.

—Showbiz capital of the world, sighs the chief.—That's some kinda politics, I guess.

Billy grinds his teeth.

The chief goes on, It's awful nice of you to take such a regard for my career, but you're too late. Even if I wanted to listen, it's out of my hands now.

—Meaning what exactly?

—Meaning New York's finest are unable to handle the present crisis, or so hizzonor the mayor sees it. As of ten minutes ago, he requested the National Guard.

This information takes a moment to whiz across Billy's synapses.—Oh Christ.

The chief checks his watch.—They should start to get here in less than an hour. The choppers'll arrive first.

His eyes rest on Billy's face, and for a moment they almost look sad.—Those boys are crack shots, Mr. Quinn. And they aren't known for using tranquilizer guns.

33. FIFTH ESTATE

SPECIAL EDITION

ONLY 5¢   JANUARY 1, 1959

Manhattan Morning News

MONSTER WREAKS HAVOC IN CITY

DOZENS SLAIN–MIDTOWN ABLAZE–MAYOR APPEALS FOR CALM

P. 12: CASTRO MARCHES TOWARD HAVANA AS BATISTA FLEES

BY OUR SPECIAL CORRESPONDENT

NEW YORK, Jan. 1—The Gates of Hell opened just before midnight in midtown Manhattan, and at least one of its denizens broke through in the form of the creature known as "the Romeo of the Forbidden Jungle."

This monster, brought to this country from an undisclosed Pacific island location last summer and now part of a traveling tent show organized by impresario Billy Quinn *(see related story p. 5)*, escaped captivity and went on a terror spree through the central part of the borough, heading south toward the harbor. As of the time this report was filed, local authorities had been unsuccessful in capturing the creature or halting its deadly rampage of destruction.

"I've never seen anything like it," said a visibly shaken fireman who asked that his name remain undisclosed. "From Madison Square Garden all the way to Fourteenth Street, there's hardly a building that hasn't been gutted. I was in Italy during the war," added the grizzled veteran, "and this is worse." Other bystanders reported the smell of dead and burning bodies as "eye-watering," and confirmed that along some parts of Broadway, corpses are piled two or three deep.

A preliminary count puts the dead at fifty-five, with hundreds injured, but the final toll is likely to be much higher. Many victims were crushed beneath the heels of the hideous beast, or else caught in automobile accidents as the creature jogged down Eighth Avenue, apparently seeking the most densely populated streets of midtown in which to cast its deadly net of destruction. *(See photos p. 2.)*

Eyewitness accounts confirm at least ten of the deceased to be police officers, mercilessly killed and eaten during their initial attempts to contain the disaster. One witness stated, "The thing bent over and picked up these two cops in its enormous claws, lifted them to its mouth, tore off their heads, then sucked the blood from their bodies like soda through a straw." The two police officers' corpses, which were later dropped by the bloodthirsty animal, were reportedly "the color and texture of beef jerky."

Multiple eyewitnesses also confirm that the monster had abducted a woman, one Betty or Beth della Montaine, a coperformer in the traveling circus/freak show which had previously enjoyed such publicity and profits from the monster *(see related story, p. 3)*. Mrs. della Montaine is believed to have been stripped naked by the beast, which then slobbered every inch of her naked body with its groping, slippery tongue, but these reports are as yet unconfirmed. *(See artist's rendering, pp.6–7.)*

"I'm stricken with grief at what I have wrought in this fair city," sobbed Billy Quinn, the man directly responsible for the catastrophe. This reporter interviewed Mr. Quinn by telephone only moments after the first reports of the escape became known to this newspaper. *(See complete interview, pp. 9 and 10.)* In response to a question about the monster's known predilection for human flesh, Mr. Quinn responded, "I know I should have been more careful, but I was blinded by greed. This show has earned me so much over the past year, and now all my riches won't undo the damage which has been done. It's as if all that money is now stained bright red with innocent blood."

Confronted with the possibility of lawsuits, Mr. Quinn appeared genuinely contrite. "Bring them on," he sighed dolefully. "Don't hold back. I deserve everything I have coming."

Mr. Quinn later admitted that he was considering closing down his traveling show and seeking a new line of work altogether, possibly entering holy orders.

In a separate statement, Mayor Wagner made an appeal to the public for calm. "In this time of crisis, I know the people of New York City will rally together and keep a collective cool head," read a statement issued by his office just after twelve-thirty a.m. The statement went on to urge all citizens "to avoid panic, to offer assistance to our public servants, and to make decisions based upon the most complete and accurate information available. In that vein, I also appeal to our journalists and newspapers to provide the most accurate information possible."

This newspaper will of course continue to serve the public in this capacity by upholding the highest standards of integrity.

34. EXTRAS

Johnny and Flanagan cut through police cordons, find the chief, spill their story. The chief waves them away, then thinks better of it and calls them back, hears them out. (Night like this, you don't discount *any*thing, is how the chief sees it.) Thinks about their story. Thinks about it again. Thinks it's crazy. Rock and roll? He hates that teenager crap, it gives him migraines. But if that's what the broad wants . . . yeah, *if* it is. This guy Johnny looks about as loopy as Billy Quinn. Flanagan is steady enough, the chief knows him. Good solid beat cop. Of course on a night like this, who can say who's solid anymore?

Quinn has disappeared. The chief is furious about that—if anybody shoulda been taken in tonight, it was that clown. Sooner or later he'll turn up, but still. Shoulda never gotten away in the first place. And besides, he coulda asked him what he thought of all this music-soothing-the-savage-beast horseshit.

You can't blame the broad of course, is how the chief sees it. A few minutes carried around in that thing's hand and you'd be screaming for God knows what. Buddy Holly, the Andrews Sisters. The Dalai Lama. The Pope's shopping list, Nasser's dirty panties. Who can say what runs through a person's mind in a situation like that?

—All right, we'll try it, what the hell. Though if I'm wrong I'll look like a goddamned idiot.

—My wife wouldn't ask for it if it's not important, says this Johnny character. As if his wife is some Mother Teresa everybody should drop to his knees for.—She's a trained scientist.

Trained to do what? is what the chief is tempted to ask, but doesn't. This guy Johnny's eyes bore into him like a wolf's. The chief is not a man to be made easily uncomfortable, but there's something about this guy. In prison there's always somebody to watch out for, not a punk but a genuine tough character, someone who'd stick a shiv in your back as readily as brush his teeth. That would be *this* guy.

—What's the ETA on those choppers? he asks a lieutenant, who tells him, Forty minutes.

—All right. Listen up, men. We've got forty minutes to wrap this up before the Guard commander gets here. Technically we've been ordered to stand down until they arrive, and take no action other than the minimum necessary to contain the situation. In other words, don't do anything to make our problem worse. But ah—hell, I've lived in this city my whole life, and I haven't been a peace officer for thirty years just to stand aside and watch some big bastard make a mess of my hometown. Am I right in believing that you all see it my way?

His men murmur and nod and he knows they're with him. They oughta be—to a man, New York is their hometown too.— These gentlemen here have brought us some information, and I've put together a plan. I'm the first to admit it's a crazy plan, but this is a crazy night, is how I see it. So pay attention, and none of you Einsteins interrupt till I'm done.

The chief's lieutenants gather in a tight circle, listening intently as he talks. If any of them thinks their boss has finally cracked, none of them says so.

* * *

K. charges on, ever southward. Into the Village with its beatniks and hipsters, toward the harbor beyond.

He's below Houston Street now. In Little Italy, mobsters choke on their cannolis; Chinatown's streets are filled with red paper lanterns and panicked, fleeing mobs. South of Canal Street K. sniffs water, the tickle against his tongue like a promise, and his steps quicken. He continues due south on Broadway, past City Hall Park. Water towers squat on rooftops like malevolent bugs, like invaders from outer space. Fire escapes streak jagged tears across building facades. Still K. trudges on, tiring now, past the looming bulk of the Woolworth Building, the slender sandstone grace of St. Paul's Chapel, the phony Corinthian pillars of the Customs House. The smell of water draws him on. He doesn't pause to wonder why this should be. Maybe some buried bit of him recognizes that he arrived in this bizarre land via the sea; maybe he associates escape with the same route. Or maybe not. Maybe it's all random. Maybe *everything* is random.

K. plows through Battery Park's cobbled walkways and waist-high trees, and finds himself standing at the water's edge. Behind him the city roars like a nest of angry hornets, an unruly pool of finger-fish. He ignores the mayhem and looks around him.

In his claw the woman Betty stirs.—Planning to swim back home, are we?

K. sniffs the air with a glistening tongue, but does not answer.

The waterfront stretches away in both directions, blunt, unlovely, a working shoreline: the Staten Island ferry leaves from here, the Coast Guard's brick-institutional office sits nearby. Starlight glimmers on the water, a fat moon throws jittery highlights that pulsate and dance across nervous wavetops. Other lights flicker too: a couple blunt-ended boats bob on the water, observing cautiously. K. does not recognize this particular type of vessel, nor can he read the word POLICE branded across their hulls. But he is learning fast what it means to be someone else's quarry, and the first thing he learned is to treat all unknowns as hostile.

There's something else too, out there in the water. He stares, growls, taps his foot. Slinks off—west now—along the waterfront, like a sullen Brando. But it's not long before his steps grow slow, then stop altogether. Before him he beholds an extraordinary sight. Something that took him a while to notice, but having been noticed, it now commands all his attention.

—Oh God, groans the female.—This is like some ridiculous movie.

K. looks at her and she looks back with an expression of exasperation that he of course does not recognize. Betty tells him, All we need now is a Gene Kelly dance number, or Cagney with a tommy gun in each hand. Or maybe flying saucers,

K. keeps frowning down at her.

—Yeah, that's it, giggles Betty. She feels herself skating toward the shaky ice of hysteria, and feels also that the time to worry about such things has long since passed.—Flying saucers. Invaders from Pluto, that's about the only thing we're missing now.

Here are some things that happen later in 1959.

Attack of the Giant Leeches is released, to critical dismissal but considerable drive-in popularity and surprisingly long-term affection from connoisseurs of third-rate horror schlock. Understandable, maybe—leeches are disgusting and giant ones more so, even though the "monsters" in this movie look like grown men in latex garbage bags struggling through the water. It's *Ben-Hur,* though, that wins Oscars for Best Picture, Best Director and Best Actor. On TV, CBS begins a new weekly program called *The Twilight Zone,* featuring outlandish stories, crazy stuff really. The kind of thing that no one but a child could ever believe. It will prove remarkably durable over the ensuing decades, slyly suggesting the possibility that almost anything—aliens from space, free and fair elections,

Martians bearing gifts, "liberation" at gunpoint—could be accepted as reality, if presented convincingly enough on television.

And a lot more people get killed—in Hungary, Algeria, Belgian Congo, Honduras, Lebanon, Paraguay, and of course the USA and USSR—by supporters of freedom, or maybe by its opponents. Sometimes it's hard to tell which is which.

The 600,000-year-old remains of an early biped, termed Zinjanthropus by Dr. Louis Leakey, is unearthed in East Africa. Compelling evidence of evolution for some, dismissed as an ungodly hoax by others. Lots of others. Meanwhile the five biggest U.S. airlines begin flying those newfangled Buck Rogers jet planes instead of the old ones with the propellers. Eighteen small Arab states combine to form the Federation of Arab Emirates. The U.S. Congress votes 49–49 to maintain the "loyalty oath" for college students receiving government loans. A 668-page report from the Justice Department's Commission on Civil Rights reveals that nonwhite Americans are routinely prevented from voting by means of "discriminatory application of literacy tests, economic coercion, dilatory tactics, and intimidation." That sounds bad all right, even if most of us are pretty vague on what exactly "dilatory tactics" are.

Ray Charles releases "What'd I Say," maybe the single greatest song ever recorded. Maybe.

Israeli elections will see strong support for the Mapai party, whose seats in the Knesset will increase as a result. This happens to be the party of Prime Minister David Ben-Gurion, who earlier said: "After the formation of a large army in the wake of the establishment of the state, we will abolish partition and expand to the whole of Palestine." Back in 1938, he'd said, "Politically we are the aggressors and they defend themselves"—the "they" in question being Palestinians. He even acknowledged, "The country is theirs, because they inhabit it, whereas we want to come here and settle down," but by the time of his political campaign he seems to have misplaced this interesting notion.

Vice President Richard Nixon visits the USSR; Soviet President Khrushchev reciprocates in the fall. Castro installs himself as president of Cuba. The Antarctic Treaty bans military activity on that continent by any nation. Cigarette companies introduce menthol-flavored smokes. And the Association of National Advertisers, stung by allegations of fraud and corruption following a string of quiz-show scandals sponsored by its members, recommends that its member agencies ask themselves the following question: "Would we be willing for the public to be fully apprised of all the facts and circumstances concerning the particular program or commercial?"

The answer to that, of course, is: *Hell no!*

35. GIVE ME YOUR TIRED, YOUR HUNGRY

It is a human being unlike any K. has yet encountered. Very large, taller than himself by far, although at this distance it appears small. Somehow K. knows it is not. It's also an unusual color. K. lacks the names to describe this hue or that—he could only discern shades of gray until a while ago—but he certainly recognizes this shiny coppery green as unlike any normal human flesh tone he's yet encountered.

She stands (K. has decided, for reasons unquestioned, that the figure is female) on a very small island of her own in the middle of the harbor. Staring off to the left, one arm upraised, unmoving. Standing, as the old joke goes, with her ass facing New Jersey. K. has never heard this joke. She burns with a brilliance that K. fails to recognize as the reflection of hidden spotlights focused on her. Against the black night ocean she is radiant, serene as a holy icon. Her lifted hand glows like a beacon, beckoning to him or perhaps warning him off.

K. howls and she ignores him.

He roars again, waves his arms, then remembers Betty and waves only his unencumbered hand. Remembers Betty. He lifts the female to eye level and stares at her, then at the huge green human, then Betty again as if trying to calibrate what thread connects them, one to the other. And fails. K. stamps his foot, paws at the poured-concrete waterfront with claws that tear divots out of the cement.

Betty's voice floats through the noise, the sirens and engine clutter and K.'s own howling. She is half singing, half screaming.—You'll ask yourself what'd I do wrong? Uh-huh, oh yeah, mm-hm, that's right . . .

Something tugs at K. but is quickly gone. Noise assails him from all sides, sets his pulse ticking like a stopwatch. He does not know what to do next. Behind him is noise, flame, humans. (Bad, stay away.) In front of him is the endless ocean. (Not bad, but good luck getting across it.) What then to do? K. is as uncertain as a pinball in midarc. The glowing green woman is the flipper, perhaps. If he goes to her, will she knock him along some further trajectory? Or just let him slip to the drain?

Impulsively, he drops into the water.

Betty screams, but the tide is out and the waves only reach K.'s knees. This level quickly rises, however, as he sloshes into deeper water, toward the mysterious woman. In the black night she glows green, like something irradiated or unhealthy, like one of Marie Curie's nightmares. Like a refugee from Bikini Atoll, or White Sands, or Nagasaki.

Billy sits at the edge of the hotel bed. It's a good bed, firm without too much bounce. Some of those beds, Christ, you get seasick the way they wobble.

He unfolds the piece of paper and reads the phone number.

Billy Quinn is at this moment a man in danger of giving in to fear. Fear of ruin, of dissolution. He is fighting the impulse to run, and at the moment he is winning the fight. But it's touch and go. If he had the rest of his money with him—or at least most of it, piles of hundred-dollar bills stacked neatly in a few suitcases—he'd go rent a car, throw the cases in the back and hit the road. And not stop till he reached Cancun, or Belize, maybe Rio. A gringo with plenty of dough can buy anything he wants in such places, Billy knows. Or has heard anyway. Including anonymity.

A new name, a new identity, a new life. They love gringos down there. The idea of being loved holds appeal beyond measure for Billy just now. Besides, the girls have butts that can stop traffic.

Problem is, Billy's millions aren't stacked in suitcases here with him. His cash—a good-sized chunk of it—is in the bank or tied up in the business. The *show*. The monster.

Yes he has some with him now. And more in a couple Swiss accounts, accessible by number only, no names. It's a fair bit of dough he's got stashed but it's not all of it. It's only *some* of it.

Billy figures he knows a thing or two about himself, and he knows he's not a guy who's satisfied with *some* of anything.

His hand barely trembles as he picks up the phone. He admits to feeling pride in this. A lot of guys, they'd be shakier than San Francisco right now. He lodges the receiver against his ear and lets the industrial hum of the dial tone soothe him.

A few hundred dollars nestle in his wallet. He's got a couple duffel bags in the closet and one big suitcase and that's it. Today's a holiday, New Year's, and the banks won't open until 9 A.M. tomorrow. By then, Billy knows, he'll have been served God knows how many depositions, warrants, whatever. If he runs, he can get pretty far. But think what he'll be giving up. Think of how much he'll lose, seized by the authorities, and all through no fault of his own.

That's what really kills him. It's no fault of his own.

Newspapers reporting widespread destruction . . . Dozens believed dead . . .

Billy wants to puke. The mistake had been turning on the radio in the first place. The newscaster's rabbity voice and tales of woe had brought on the fear that now circles him, shadowy and indistinct, like sharks in cloudy water. Billy knows he has to act, has to stay in motion, otherwise the fear will paralyze him.

His finger dips to the ring of numbers on the phone, and begins dialing.

A woman answers and this throws him a moment. Then he thinks, *Well why not?* and checks that he's dialed the right number.

Instead of confirming this, the woman asks suspiciously, What do you want?

—I'm in the Regency Hotel, Billy tells her.—And I'm looking for some talent.

At this moment, in a pub called Union Jack's on Tenth and Forty-fourth, April is doubled over with laughter as Doug relates the story of when he caught Johnny and Olga together in K.'s boxcar. Only in Doug's rendering, Johnny and Olga have been joined by big-boobed Midge, Lou Dalton the lion guy and a camera crew hired by Billy to capture the proceedings on celluloid.

April straightens up on her stool, still spitting giggles.—Stop this! You're killing me!

Doug taps the bar and orders another round. The barman serves him without taking his eyes off the TV news reports of K.'s midtown rampage.

April tells Doug about her ex-husband Mario, a real heel who talked a lotta garbage. She pronounces it "gah-bij." Doug tells April a little—just a little—about his dad. For a while they become serious, staring moodily at the grain of the bar, the beer signs flashing in the window, till Doug decides it's time for another story, this one about Tony the midget and a couple of Rockettes. Inside of five minutes he's got April crying with laughter again.

An hour after that, with the helicopters buzzing on the TV news that they've long since quit watching, Doug and April have shifted from the bar to a booth. He's got his arm around her shoulders. They're done talking for now, just sitting contentedly and sipping drinks. He can't remember another night when he's talked as much as tonight.

Doug's thinking he's gonna need some new movie titles to describe his life.

36. WHAT HAPPENS NOW

—Find me a boat! the chief had barked, and so they had.

By one of those mysterious, miraculous coincidences—the sort of thing that only ever happens, really, in the movies—the *Ocean Princess* is moored that very night on the west side of the Hudson, not five hundred yards from where K. thrashes his way through Battery Park. The ship is shut down, not even a skeleton crew on board, just the captain and his first mate Ash. If need be they could putt-putt from one end of the harbor to the other, but that's about it. The captain had chosen his mooring for its view of the Statue of Liberty and the fireworks that were rumored to be set off at midnight—nobody knew whether to believe the story or not. These days, the captain reflects sourly, there are lots of stories that nobody knows whether to believe.

Nothing new there. The captain feels tired, bone-tired. Feels like his bones are turning to sponge, as if they're shot through with tiny little tunnels. Hair's gone white this past year, from smoky gray to purely snowy where it hasn't fallen out completely. If he didn't know better, he'd think that his recent tours around the South Pacific haven't been so great for his health. But that's madness, he knows. A lifetime on the sea had left him sinewy and tough, at least until recently.

Ash joins him now on deck.—Think we'll see much?

—Hope to, shrugs the captain.

Come to that, Ash doesn't look so hot either. Deep wrinkles gouge either side of his nose like Martian canals. Ash had never possessed much hair but even that's thinning nowadays. And he's blinking a lot lately, as if having trouble focusing.

Ah hell, the captain thinks. *We're all getting old.*

From their vantage point, the captain and his mate can see Lady Liberty out in the harbor, no bigger than thumb-sized from this distance but glowing green against the dark. They find it hard to focus on her, what with all the commotion from the city behind them. Sirens and car horns and heavy *thumps* like gigantic bowling balls hitting the lanes.

—Noisy night, Ash mutters.

The captain leaves the radio on an open channel, out of habit, when he and Ash set up their folding chairs on the foredeck to watch whatever show is on offer. Ash cracks another Schlitz and says, Wonder what all that brouhaha is.

The captain is silent. He prides himself on his ability to sense when something big is afoot, and right now something unquestionably is. The orchestra of horns and sirens is proof enough of that, even without the occasional muffled *whoosh* rolling like an artillery barrage across the water. If the captain's not mistaken—and he prides himself on not being mistaken very often—things are exploding somewhere.

And judging from the position of those police choppers, whatever's going on is heading their way. The captain wouldn't admit to being nervous about this. But he is more than usually alert.

Ash sets down his beer and says, Maybe I should check the scanner. See what the cops are telling each other.

—Stay here, the captain orders.—Whatever it is, I don't want to know until I'm staring at it.

He gets his wish soon enough. The sirens draw closer, the helicopters float like thistledown, their searchlights spearing the air

like ghostly daddy longlegs. Then there is movement near the water's edge, something groping through the trees in the park, the
spotlights coming to rest on—something familiar. Something altogether too familiar.

The captain hears Ash suck in his breath.—Oh gosh. Haven't
we already seen this movie, sir?

The captain doesn't answer until K. weaves his way to the water's edge and stares out at the blackness. Then he says, Better
check the scanner after all.

His mate scampers below, to call a moment later:—Captain,
you'll want to hear this.

—Calling any available vessel, the radio crackles.—Any available vessel in New York Harbor, please respond.

The captain lifts the handset.—This is Captain Ahab of the
Ocean Princess. We have the white whale in view.

For a moment there is silence over the radio. Ash squints at the
captain and says, Sir?

Then the radio barks back to life.—*Ocean Princess,* we have a
problem here.

—I believe I'm looking at it, replies the captain.—Please advise
what you would like me to do about it. I warn you though, my
crew is ashore. It's just me and the mate down here at the seaport.

—Roger, *Ocean Princess.* Please hold your position.

There is a pause. Ash's eyes flash between K. and the captain.
The captain's eyes are locked onto K., whose eyes are fixed on the
Statue of Liberty. Lady Liberty stares off into the middle dis-
tance, in the general direction of Greenland.

—Is he holding something? he asks Ash.

—Sir?

—Look in his hand—it looks like—

The radio interrupts.—*Ocean Princess,* stand by for the chief
of police.

—Standing by, murmurs the captain.

—This is Chief Cochran, another voice declares moments later.—*Ocean Princess*, we request your services in apprehending this creature.

—Sounds familiar, the captain murmurs.

—I understand that only yourself and your first mate are present on your vessel?

—That's correct, Chief. My crew's off celebrating New Year's.

—Understood. All we need your vessel for is a floating platform from which to direct operations. Is that acceptable?

—It is.

—All right then, please listen carefully—

But whatever the chief is about to say is drowned out when K. lurches into the water, sending up gouts of spray, and swells that roll the *Ocean Princess* so precipitously that Ash and the captain are hurled off their feet.

—We've lost contact, the chief says to Johnny and Flanagan. They're still in Tribeca, the chief hunched into a patrol car's window, dead radio in hand.

Flanagan shrugs.—*C'est la vie.*

Johnny is less sanguine.—Now what?

—Now we get to the harbor and see what the hell's going on, is how I see it.

—Then let's quit jawing and get moving, barks Johnny. His eyes scan the confusion.—Which car is yours, Chief?

The chief hesitates a moment, the expression on his face suggesting: *Just who's in charge here anyway?* But Johnny's not watching, and after a moment the chief shrugs.—This one, he points.—Let's go.

As they roll downtown he's on the radio again.—I want loudspeakers, the biggest you can find. And a record player. Make that two record players. And plenty of rock-and-roll records. Buddy Holly, Bill Haley, whoever you got. Pretend you're organizing the biggest sock hop ever. Bring it all to the harbor on the double.

—Sock hop, Johnny snorts.—I like that.

Flanagan gazes out the window with a *que sera sera* expression on his face.

—If that boat's still afloat, we set up the equipment on deck, the chief orders into the radio.—That way we can follow the monster if it tries to swim anywhere.

—It can't swim, Johnny interjects.

—Otherwise, we set up on shore and hope for the best. Say again? No, the police launches are too small. They'll get swamped for sure, we've already lost contact with two of them.

He signs off and stares at his passengers: Johnny intent, haggard, but with an indisputable fire raging somewhere behind his eyes. Energy radiates off him as if he's a caged feline. Flanagan, on the other hand, is slower, calmer, more wary, less certain that he's gotten himself into something that he really wants to do.

The chief addresses them both.—The National Guard will be here in twenty minutes. Our only chance is to settle this before they arrive. So . . .

He holds up his two hands, fingers crossed.—Let's hope for the best.

Flanagan nods, as if hoping for the best is what he's been doing all along. Now it's Johnny's turn to silently stare past the windshield.

The waterfront is mayhem when they get there. Mayhem barely controlled. The chief glides through the bustle like a shark navigating a reef, alert with a shark's deadly earnestness and expectation. Johnny and Flanagan are the chief's remoras, or perhaps something more sinister. In any case a bubble of calm opens up around them as they slice through.—Christ Almighty, murmurs the chief.—Would you look at that.

Out in the harbor, K. is shoulder-deep in water, making his way, unmistakably, to the Statue of Liberty, glowing like a lodestone in the night. K.'s arms are upheld awkwardly above the water, Betty just visible in the spotlight glare. Flanagan says, Funny way to swim.

—He's not swimming, Johnny says with a suddenly dry mouth.—He's walking. How deep is that water anyhow?

No one answers. As they watch, K.'s shoulders are subsumed by black water, glittering like ink.

Suddenly the press of police shakes off the spell. An officer tells them, Chief, the equipment's on its way.

—We're keeping the reporters as far back as we can, says another.

—It's gonna be hard, though, once they get their own choppers here, warns a third.

—What about the Guard? the chief asks calmly.

—ETA is—well they're saying ten minutes, but it could be any time.

They approach a moored boat. Something strikes Johnny about the vessel, the familiarity of its contours . . . he almost laughs aloud. The *Ocean Princess* herself, a year or two older but looking none the worse. Pity you couldn't say the same for the captain. Lines riddle his face like skid marks and his hair's gone completely white. What's left of it anyway: the guy looks like he's been vacationing at Hiroshima.—Captain. Now this *is* a surprise.

The man's face falls on him, works a moment.—Johnny, isn't it? So it is. Up to your old tricks, I see.

Johnny gestures to the harbor.—Guess I'm not the only one.

The others follow his gaze. K. is halfway across the harbor now, in water very nearly as deep as he is tall. Only the top half of his head can be seen, a lumpy pink knob poking above the wavetops, glimmering in the harsh spotlight beams like a chunk of rose quartz. Cantilevered above the water, snaking upright into the air like some wavering palm tree on a tropical beach, is his arm, whose claws grasp Betty's prone form, as incarcerated in her cell of interlocking claws as any death row inmate. For a long moment that image burns itself on the retinas of every observer: the floating pink lump, the wavering arm, the tiny woman. But then other elements demand attention. The green-washed statue, for example, the monster's apparent destination. (Closed to tourists at this late hour—small blessing, that—as the authorities had considered themselves busy enough handling the New Year's mobs in the rest of the city.) Or the helicopters jostling one another in the night sky, no longer truly dark enough to be called night as fingers of light crisscross the scene, probing like inquisitive kittens but fixing mainly on the thirty or so cubic yards of water surrounding K. The spotlights dive into the water, turning it translucent green against which his murky figure can just be seen, like an insect caught in cloudy jade.

A police van rolls onto the dock adjacent to the *Ocean Princess,* and a pair of officers tumble out.—Room service!

—Get that stuff set up, the chief hollers, and make it snappy!

More buzzing movement, more hivelike activity. Tables are unfolded and arranged on the foredeck, mysterious chunks of electronic equipment are plugged and adjusted and unplugged and replugged. Four loudspeakers, each the size of a child, wait nearby, shy guests at a raucous dinner party. Wires crisscross the deck like veins. This whole operation is directed by a newcomer, some freckled kid with a pompadour piled on his head like vanilla soft-serve, wearing the ugliest maroon dinner jacket (black lapels, silver buttons) Johnny has ever seen.

The chief taps his shoulder.—Who the hell are you?

—Hey daddy-o, I'm Jackie Barton, you can call me the Spinner, like in Jack the Spinner. All the hep cats do, it's like a nickname.

The chief looks as though he wants to spit, or worse.—This is a crime scene, young man. I'll have to ask you to leave.

—Aw, don't be such an L7, Dick Tracy.

The chief takes a heavy step toward the pompadour.—You listen to me, punk—

Jack the Spinner hold up his arms in a posture of exaggerated fear.—Say no more, daddy-o. I'm gone like Marcus Garvey at a Klan rally. But if I go, the wax goes with me.

—What?

—The wax, the tracks, the *stacks*.

Jack the Spinner wags a thumb at the collection of electronics being assembled on deck.—It's my party, and I'll cry if I want to. You rent my stuff, you rent me with it. If I go, my platters go too. Speaking of which, I better make sure they don't ruin nothing. Catch you later, G-man.

He scampers amid the men on board the *Ocean Princess*. Soon only his pompadour is visible as he weaves and bobs, checking connections, wrestling speakers into position. He spits orders as he works, a steady stream of semi-comprehensible gibberish.

—Goddamn monkey talk, the chief grates.—You'd think we got enough niggers in this country without white kids pretending to be more. What's gonna happen when they're all going to school together?

—I can throw him in the water if you want, Johnny offers obligingly.—Make it look like an accident.

—Later, the chief says.—Believe me, I don't like waiting. But he might have his uses before the night's over.

Johnny nods, glances out over the water. Catches his breath. Points.

K. is rising up out of the harbor, ascending visibly with each step as he closes in on Bledsoe Island and the statue surmounting it. K. continues to hold his own arm aloft, Betty's blond hair burning in the spotlight like a torch. As Johnny and the others watch, K.'s claws dig into the earth and he hauls himself up, heaving a weighty thigh onto dry land and then half rolling, half jumping out of the water altogether. Through it all he has maintained his grip on Betty and she has—Johnny's been watching so he knows this is true—remained unharmed.

—Now what? asks one of the cops.

It's the question of the night, all right. The question of the year; question of the decade. Johnny, peering through the chief's borrowed binoculars, is wondering too. Probably every cop, every tourist, every resident of the city hunched in front of the radio or TV is thinking the same thing. Even K., staring up at the statue and then back at where he has come from—the buzzing city, the faceless mob—even K., responsible as he is for this whole situation, might be forgiven for letting the question flicker across whatever consciousness he has.

37. YOUR HUDDLED MASSES

Now what? wonders K.

He stands on the island, the bit of dry land poking from this water—this diseased, filthy, so-polluted-he-can-hardly-tolerate-its-touch-against-his-flesh water—stands and stares up the skirts of the enormous green female. The female is holding something aloft in her hand, and K., perhaps in unconscious imitation, raises his own arm to mimic her.

Betty finds herself cantilevered higher than ever above the black harbor water, and screams.

K. had forgotten her. Now he lowers his hand to peer at her: there she is, whole and moving (slightly) and making sounds (faintly). Reassured on some basic level, K. returns his attention to the statue. He's not sure what to do, though glad enough to be out of the water. He has never been immersed before and he didn't like it. Now that he's out of it his thoughts, such as they are, scatter like roaches in the glare of all the new information his senses are pumping into him. The air is cold. The sky is dark, but peppered with many bright lights, some of which move about him. There is the constant hum of machines, not that he knows what machines are, and distant squealing cries of the small creatures that surround him. There is the smell of smoke and water and many things he can't recognize (oil, pollution, exhaust, hot dogs, fireworks over Jersey City). There is the taste, fresh in his mouth, of the harbor water that splashed him when he walked across to this island. It tastes like waste, and for a moment he is seized with the urge to vomit. This passes.

In front of him is a wall of flat stones, much like the earthen one where he used to receive his native sacrifices . . . so long ago. This wall is a bit taller than he, but there is no Y-shaped woman strung up at the top. Instead there is only a towering, four-sided column of stone, and atop this, the green metal female looming above him: one arm reaching for infinity and both eyes staring toward it.

The towering green female—not a real female, K. understands now, lacking as it does the scent of the living—perches atop her four-sided pillar like a harpy. The column is as tall as she is, and the whole construct is balanced on the earthen wall of stone and brick and dirt. K. butts his head against this earthwall. Having gotten this far he's unsure how to proceed, although something— maybe the statue's trunklike thighs, or its color, or simpy its over- whelming size—triggers some deep recollection of the tree in which he used to make his home. *Up,* urges some deep internal voice. The impulse doesn't come in words exactly, but it's no less powerful for all that.

Before heeding this silent demand, K. turns to survey the strange land he has left. It appears surprisingly peaceful now. On- shore, he sees the flickering shadows of humans passing before headlights, and those lights are numberless beyond counting. Of course, for K. everything is numberless and beyond counting, but that's something else again.

On the water too: reflected moonlight, but also the running lights of dozens of small craft jostling through the harbor. Most of the boats are tiny police launches, excitable as gnats and about as significant, but one is larger. It slides through the darkened harbor like a phantom, like the Phantom, like a ghostly memory from long ago. His eye falls on its stubby white superstructure, his earholes register the low discontented rumble of its engines, his tongue lashes at whiffs of diesel. Does he recognize the *Ocean Princess*? Does he remember his months pinned to the deck like the unlikeliest butterfly ever, growing weaker, then strong again? Can he foresee what might happen to him on this night, in this place, with these people, in this first day of the Year of Our Lord (though maybe not K.'s) 1959?

The short answer to these questions is: no. The longer answer is: no, but. *But* it doesn't matter anyway. *But* it wouldn't help if he could. *But* nobody else can either, so don't waste time thinking about it.

Instinct kicks in like a circuit breaker. K. strengthens his grip on the female Betty with one hand, reaches for the lip of the embankment with the other and heaves himself upward.

Johnny, Flanagan and the chief stand alongside Ash and the captain aboard the *Ocean Princess*. Together they watch K. hoist himself from the harbor. Water runnels off his butterfly wings, clots his brown fur, leaves his antennae impotently dangling. He pauses on the manicured lawn as if to catch his breath, then turns his attention to the short mesa of earth upon which the statue's column rests. In moments he has scrambled up the sheer cliff, gouging out thick toeholds of stone as he ascends. Searchlights pin his unlikely butterfly wings as he moves up, faster than one might expect. The men on the boat—and on other boats too—stare, speechless with surprise.

Atop the cliff he straightens up. His hands are empty.

—Where the hell's Betty? Did he drop her in the water? She can swim like a fish!

—Musta put her down is how I see it—

—No, wait—there, by his foot, see? But he's seen her—oh.

—Has he got her again?

The chief, squinting through the only pair of binoculars they have:—Yeah. He's got her again all right. In the other hand this time. Shoulda made a dash for it, mighta gotten away.

—*Plus ça change, plus c'est la même chose,* mutters Flanagan.

Johnny whirls on the cop.—What's that supposed to mean?

—What?

—That foreign faggot shit you keep spouting, *ploo* this and *ploo* that. I'm getting pretty sick of it. You don't like this country, you can fucking well go back to Tipperary.

Flanagan blinks slowly, his fleshy face a mask of bafflement.— What I said was, the more things change, the more they stay the same.

He points at K., who now stares frowning intently at the bulwarks upon which Lady Liberty's base rests.—Meaning, before he was carrying her in one hand. Now it's the other. It's different from before, but it isn't really.

Johnny looks ready to spit.

The chief intervenes.—We're all tense, boys, there's no need to bicker.

—He's right, puts in the captain.—What's this plan you needed my ship for anyway, Chief? This teenage punk is giving me a headache but he knows his hi-fi equipment, I'll give him that.

—Hey, watch yourself, Admiral Nimitz, protests Jack the Spinner.—Your boy Sinatra is the one causing migraines.

The chief coughs.—The plan is to play this noisemaker as loud as we can, in the hope that our savage beast will be soothed into giving up his hostage.

—Rockin plan, chuckles Jack the Spinner.

—And then ahh—

—Then what exactly? asks the captain with an impish look.— Hope he turns himself in to the authorities? Or takes up a trade? Refrigerator repair maybe?

Then men stifle snickers. Except for the chief, who looks

distinctly unamused, and Johnny, who appears ready to swim across to Bledsoe Island and take on K. single-handed. The chief says, Laugh all you want. We're hoping he'll settle down, maybe even sit or lie down and go to sleep. The thing's gotta sleep sometime. The alternative is to wait for the Guard to show up and start blasting. When they're done—and here he points to the Statue of Liberty—how much of *her* do you think will be left?

This sobers the men. They glance at K. and the floodlit statue, then Betty, and then adjust their testicles.

—Well, put it that way, murmurs the captain.

—Sure, agrees Flanagan.—*Veni vidi vici* and all that.

—The way I see it, the chief goes on, is we grab any straw no matter how unlikely. The guy who wraps up this situation with a minimum of mayhem will be a local hero; the guy who lets it get out of hand will be forever remembered as the idiot who lost the statue. Me, I don't want to be that guy.

There is a pause. The men turn their attention to K.

Ash says, None of us want that either, sir, believe me.

Everybody ignores Ash—even Ash, who like the others is staring openmouthed at K. And everyone continues ignoring Ash even when he points to the monster's ungainly form and asks, What the heck is he doing, anyway?

It is not the easiest of slogs. The base column is ungiving stone, though it narrows as it rises, and there are enough windows to give K.'s claws and toes some purchase. The Lady herself, though, is tough. The statue's metal dermis is slick and unforgiving. It doesn't give like tree bark, nor are there branches and forks—not many anyway—to grab hold of. Besides which, he's doing it all one-handed. K. scrambles as best he can, his claws leaving scratches in the statue's verdigris veneer, thighs flexing to maintain his grip. Even so, he slides back two yards for every three he ascends. Laboriously, he hauls himself ever higher till he is able to reach the statue's arm and the tablet she holds (*July 4, 1776*) and can grip the woman's elbow with his claw. From there the ascent is much easier. K. is able to stand in the crook of the statue's elbow and, reaching up, grasp her neck. Hauling himself precariously to her shoulder, he can reach the spikes ringing her head. He levers his body upward, though one spike bends alarmingly under his weight and another shears away altogether when he tries to throw a leg over it. Heaving against his own mass like a fat person trying to escape the deep end of the pool, K. at length manages to squat atop her brows like the unlikeliest headgear ever imagined. On impulse he reaches below the statue's hairline, above her eyes, where a row of rectangular windows looks out over the harbor. K.'s hand reaches to one of the windows and tucks the female Betty inside, where she collapses in a pile on the floor.

—What a ride . . .

K. straightens up, shifts his backside to rest atop the statue's head, careful to avoid the remaining spikes. (Speaking of unlikely headgear, who thought this up?) One foot rests on each of the Lady's green-robed shoulders; his overlong arms dangle before her face like a snakeskin boa. K.'s claws tickle the air uncertainly, as if they don't know what will happen next.

And so they don't; and nor does K. He doesn't know what to make of the *Ocean Princess*, drawing near to the base of Bledsoe Island, three hundred feet below him. Or the helicopters, driftng about like lethal fireflies, their spotlights flickering eerily across his shoulders. K. doesn't know how long he'll remain perched up here, and he has no idea that Betty has already found the staircase inside and is charging down its spiraling metal steps as fast as she can manage in her ridiculous lime green Juliet-of-the-Jungle costume. Most of all, K. is entirely unaware that he'll be sitting up here, atop the shiny emerald Statue of Liberty, for the rest of his natural—or otherwise—life.

* * *

—Tell those choppers to stay in position, the chief of police orders.—And keep the spotlights tight on him.

—Yessir.

The *Ocean Princess* shuts off her engines and drifts thirty yards off Bledsoe Island. The statue, severely foreshortened, looms above them like a Calder mobile. Like a graven idol: something to worship, to pray to, to die or kill for. In which case K.'s unexpected figure, squatting atop it, is—a blasphemy? An intrusion? A joke? A logical endpoint?

On deck, a row of eyes takes in the scene: the chief of police, the captain of the *Ocean Princess*, Ash, Flanagan, Johnny, Jack the Spinner, numerous milling cops. Together they watch like a single organism, like a beast with two dozen eyes. Billy is conspicuous in his absence, as in

—Where the hell's Betty? demands Johnny suddenly.—I don't see her.

—Me neither, confirms the captain.

—What's he done with her? What's that bastard *done*?

—Take it easy, Mr. Steele, suggests Flanagan, resting a hand on his shoulder.

—By God, if that bastard's harmed a hair on her head, I'll—

He breaks off. None of the other men challenges him: *You'll what? Clean his clock? Rip him a new asshole? Make him regret the day his mama brought him into the world?*

Jack the Spinner points.—What's that?

—Where?

—At the bottom of the statue.

—I don't see anything. You mean between the feet?

—*Below* that. At the bottom of the column, see the doorway, under that archway? Where the stairs are. Isn't that a kitten?

Ash blinks, bewildered.—Kitten?

—You know, a doll!

—Doll? . . .

—I see her, growls Johnny, and grabs the megaphone from the chief's hands.—Betty! Stay right where you are!

The tiny figure waves frantically, but if she yells anything it's lost in the background din.

—You're safe where you are, Johnny bellows.—The monster's on top of the statue. Just stay put and we'll pick you up.

—Hold on a minute, the chief growls.—The girl's not the priority, the monster is. To the hep cat he demands, You ready?

—Been ready, daddy-o. You give the word, we sing like a bird.

—Do it then. And save the poetry.

Jack the Spinner bends to his machines as if kissing them.

Betty isn't sure she's hearing right. The song has been tumbling through her mind so compulsively of late that she can't be sure this isn't some especially powerful hallucination. But no: it's real. That little twinkling guitar chime, the lilting intro that hooks into the first verse, she always forgets that part. So she must be hearing the song with her ears, not her mind.

> One day soon and it won't be long,
> Uh-huh, oh yeah, mm-hm, that's right,
> You'll come looking for me but I'll be long gone,
> Uh-huh, oh yeah, mm-hm, that's right . . .

—Well, nobody said it was Shakespeare, Betty murmurs. To whom she addresses this comment is not immediately clear. She hunkers into the doorway at the foot of the statue's base. If she thought about it, she'd realize how winded she is from racing down all those hundreds of steps. But she doesn't think about it. *The monstrosity* is far overhead but she can't help wishing it was a whole lot farther. To make that happen she's willing to run down hundreds more steps. Thousands.

A strong breeze has kicked in from the water. It's cold, a North Atlantic storm, and her eyes tear up. Betty tugs the bangs from her eyes and tries to concentrate on the song. Clings to it the way a drowning woman might cling to a life ring.

> *You'll ask yourself what'd whup-whup-whup?*
> *Uh-huh, whup-whup, whup-whup, that's right . . .*
> *And you'll sit and you'll whup-whup and you'll*
> *   whup this whup-whup*
> *Whup-whup, whup-whup, whup-whup, that's right!*

She squints at the sky. Lights are moving close as the throb of helicopter rotors threatens to interfere with the song, then overwhelms it completely.

Billy sends the girls away when he's done with them. It's the first time he's ever shooed them off before morning, but this is a night unlike other nights.

Ain't that the truth, he thinks to himself.

Billy has a large suitcase and two duffel bags stuffed with cash. The duffels hold fives, tens and twenties; the big suitcase is packed with neat stacks of paper-banded hundreds. Ten thousand dollars per bundle, and dozens of bundles. They represent all the dough Billy's got on hand at the moment, the fruit of endless patient hours of skimming and doctoring the books and never quite trusting the IRS or the Feds. He remembers the Depression after all, has plenty of good reasons not to trust the banks. Billy suffers no guilt: it's his show from top to bottom, so if he gave himself a few extra percent, who's to say anything? What really galls him is that the dough, though it would represent a good-sized fortune to most people, is only a fraction of his legitimate take. But the rest of it is out of reach, at least for now. For now . . .

Billy padlocks the big suitcase and throws a duffel over each shoulder. Downstairs he pays the hotel bill and takes a yellow cab across the river to Jersey City, where he changes it for another yellow cab as far as Paramus. It costs, but it doesn't look suspicious—on New Year's, every taxi in the tristate area is working, and happy about it.

Billy's plan is to leapfrog yellow cabs to Philly, get on a Greyhound for some godforsaken hellhole like Texas, spend New Year's Day on the road. The cops might look for him but they can't stop every bus in America, and he's been careful to keep his mug out of the papers. Down in Texarkana or wherever the hell he finds himself on January 2, he'll rent a car for a month and drive across the border into Mexico. A good-sized fortune in the States is a goddamn Pope's ransom in Tijuana. A few months will see all this nastiness blow over. In the meantime he can see about accessing those numbered accounts in Switzerland, find himself a villa on the beach in Acapulco, and maybe set up house with some of the local talent.

Billy sighs and reclines against the smelly vinyl of the cab seat. He's not exactly content, but not quite unhappy either. It's been a hell of a ride, but the ride is over. And maybe not before time, he has to admit. A guy works his tail off his whole life, spreading a little entertainment to his fellow citizens—*hell, it's time to settle down, before life settles with you. And it always will, brother. You can take* that *to the bank.*

—Busy night? he asks the cabbie.

—You wouldn't be*lieve,* the cabbie answers.

—Oh I don't know, Billy says. He allows himself a tired little half smile as he gazes at Newark's sci-fi skyline of chemical factories and natural-gas balloons.—Night like this, I could believe anything.

—What the *fuck?* howls Johnny. The helicopters draw closer, circling in on an intercept course with the statue at its vortex.

Moments earlier, the captain had requested permission to launch a dinghy and pick up the girl from Bledsoe Island. His request was refused by the commander of the National Guard.

—What the *fuck?*

Nobody answers: the chief and the captain know that things have been taken out of their hands, and the other men are plain scared of Johnny's incandescent fury. Wordless, he turns to face the sources of his frustration—the helicopters, the monster, even the girl—and now bellows inarticulate quasi-sentences at them all.

The song finishes and Jack the Spinner lifts the needle.—Again?

—Again, barks the captain.

—That Chubby Checker is hep, offers the DJ.—Maybe something with a little more jazz can get through to this cat.

The captain's jaw aches from being clenched so hard.—This "cat" is looking plenty sleepy to me. Just play the same goddamn record as before!

Jack the Spinner offers no further advice.

The chief of police turns to the captain and says, The way I see it, there's not much point in playing that noise anymore. Unless you want to give him something to listen to while they fry him.

For a time the captain says nothing. He prides himself on his ability to see when a certain course of action has benefits—or drawbacks—that are overlooked by others. Right now he figures this kiddie-music horse manure is about the only thing keeping this Johnny character from going off half-cocked. From jumping clear over the bulkhead rail and making a dash for the girl. The illusion of useful action is all that's preventing him from launching himself into something useless or futile, even dangerous.

The captain is about to explain all this to the captain when Ash's sudden cry snaps his head around:—Hey, you can't do that!

The captain lays eyes on Johnny's broad back and tensed

haunches as he holds himself poised on the starboard rail. Then the idiot tips forward and hurls himself into the water.

The Statue of Liberty is 151 feet tall, including her upraised torch-bearing right arm, which is itself forty feet. So the crown of her forehead, where K. now sits piggyback-style with his thighs bracketing her neck, is 110 feet above the pillar that supports her. That pillar is another 150 feet above the flattened stone-and-brick foundation that rises forty-odd feet above the water of New York Harbor.

So then. K. rests 301 feet over the water, 261 feet above the ground that would catch him if he fell. This is almost seven times his height. The equivalent of a forty-two-foot drop for an average-sized man.

Some creatures can survive a fall of seven times their body length: cats, insects, some lizards. A human being would have a tougher time of it. And K.? Who knows? But it's worth pointing out: K. is closer, in appearance and body mechanics, to a human being than to an insect. Notwithstanding the butterfly wings, antennae and so forth.

K. squirms on his perch. One foot here on her shoulder, the other one shifting, toes now against the Lady's flexed bicep. Then he shifts again, trying different spots. His butt squirms against the spikes ringing the statue's head. He looks like he's trying to get comfortable but he's not. Getting comfortable isn't an option, some part of him knows. What he's doing is getting *ready*.

Up in the air the floodlights swing closer to him as the helicopters bear down.

38. QUICK CUTS

Christalmighty this water's cold —

Johnny gasps, swallows a lungful of the brackish Hudson, hurls himself up and chases the water with a deep shot of winter air. Shakes off the shock and starts slapping the surface with powerful Johnny Weissmuller strokes. He's always been a good swimmer and he pulls easily through the water but even so—*damn*—for a minute he wonders if he's screwed up here. Screwed up bad.

The captain's voice is low but urgent.—Can you see him? Can anybody see him? Somebody get that spotlight on! Not the statue you idiot— shine it on the water!

The men peer into the dark. The spotlight sweeps slowly, left to right, right to left. Nothing breaks the surface of the waves.

—Maybe he's swimming underwater, suggests Ash.

Nobody answers.

Betty squints up at the sky. It's so full of lights and beams that it's practically daytime. For all that, though, she can't see much. Ditto with the harbor, although that boat out there has drawn pretty close, sweeping with a searchlight as if trolling for something valuable.

She wants to laugh out loud, wants to holler: *Hey, you louts! I'm not in the water, I'm up here!* But she doesn't bother. She's too tired, and they wouldn't hear her anyway.

She's *so* tired. She shuts her eyes.

Johnny's fingers bump rough cement and the water is shallow beneath him. He knocks around in the dark—*cold it's so cold*—trying to find some way up. The rough current snatches at his ankles, tripping him; he's on the verge of despair when he stumbles across a set of shallow steps chipped into the concrete apron, slick with moss and algae. He won't complain: he'll take anything. In a minute he's onshore, shivering epileptically, stumbling through the dark like Ray Charles. Even so, he's that much closer to Betty.

K. watches the lights against the night, flinging themselves toward him, heavy with threat. Some part of him senses that this will prove to be the final confrontation of his life. Part of his mind knows: *It ends here.*

Johnny wishes he had a flashlight. He wishes he had a knife. He wishes he had a bullhorn to call out instructions to his wife; wishes he had anything, in fact, besides soggy Hush Puppies and and a drenched wallet stuffed with twenties. But no luck. If he wants to rescue his girl, it looks like he'll have to do it the hard w—

Suddenly he's framed in glare: light slamming him like the flash from a howitzer. But it's only the spotlight from the *Ocean Princess.*

—*There's a fire escape a hundred yards to your right!*

He recognizes the voice of the police chief, sqawking through the bullhorn. Reaching for him from the night, he sounds like God.

Betty opens her eyes and thinks, *Is that voice talking to me?*

* * *

K. hears it too, and wonders. Not exactly in words of course; but in his own inarticulate way, he is curious about the tinny voice floating up from the water. So he looks down. This is a mistake, because the threat isn't coming to him from below, but from above. But he doesn't know that.

Then again, it wouldn't help him one bit to know that his death was approaching from the sky overhead, was even now closing in at better than two hundred miles an hour.

—*Take the stairs to the base of the tower,* the voice continues.—*Betty, sit tight! Johnny's coming for you, you hear? Your man is coming for you!*

Your man—damn right. Johnny pauses just long enough to give a thumbs-up to the boat, invisible now in its sea of glare. But as he turns to run for the staircase, the chief's voice collars him again.

—*Look out for the*—

Whatever more he says is lost in the whine and whistle of incoming shells as the helicopters dive toward the island like malevolent wasps.

Pain rips into K. as a small explosion lances through his midriff. Blind with shock and fury, he is flung backward. Only his legs' reflexive tightening prevents his tumbling from the statue. Both overlong arms are flung behind him, but one snakes back to grab at Liberty's upheld arm. The limb doesn't snap off—not quite—but it does bend back alarmingly amid a flurry of popping rivets and groaning metal, as if the Lady is trying to use her torch as a back-scratcher.

Around him K. sees lights dancing. Some of them are real; some are visible only to him. He shakes his head like Sugar Ray Robinson shrugging off an upper cut, and snarls at the pain whose source he can't focus on.

* * *

Aboard the *Ocean Princess,* the men wince in unison as the missile blossoms against K.'s chest—then gasp, in unison, as the monster grows only more enraged at the attack.

Ash watches K. wrench the statue's torch-bearing arm.—He's going to tear the statue apart, sir!

—Not much point to *that,* the captain replies.

—Way I see it, the police chief intones, those boys in the choppers better not get too close.

As if to prove the chief's point, K. chooses this instant to snap off one of the statue's head spikes and hurl it at one of the helicopters. The missile quickly disappears, swallowed up by the ominous night.

—Wonder how many more of those there are? says Flanagan.

—Twelve, says Jack the Spinner.—One for each of the original colonies.

The other men look at him.

—We had a field trip in ninth grade, the DJ mumbles.

The chopper pilot's name is Hawke. He's always thought that was pretty appropriate, pretty stylish: a pilot named Hawke. The dames think so too. Anyway it was about the best thing his father had ever given him, the worthless bum: his name. No point dwelling on that, he knows, but still it rankles.

His copilot is some joker he'd never met before, some kid named Swanson. *Swan's son?* What kind of name is that for a chopper copilot, a gunner? Hawke smiles without warmth. No kind of name at all. The mug should've got a job painting pictures or some such. Writing poetry.

—Target's well in range, this Swanson says now.

—Hold your fire, Hawke commands quietly.

The first explosion nearly knocks Johnny off the stairs: they're slick with rust and barely eighteen inches wide, so this is no difficult thing. He barks his shin against hard iron and unleashes a string of curses fit to make Al Capone blush. Then he hauls himself onward.

—All right then, says Flanagan.—He's got twelve more chances to make a mess of things. The question is, will he?

—Eleven, declares Jack the Spinner.—One broke off before, when he was climbing up. The real question is, why don't you squares just leave him alone?

The other men look at him, again.

—I mean, it's obvious he just wants to go away. He's not even carrying the girl anymore. So why do you have to kill him? Why not just let him leave?

—National security, states the captain.

—Public nuisance, suggests the chief of police.

—Degenerate morals, opines Flanagan.—Stealing another man's wife like that is strictly verboten, not to mention destroying all that property. What kind of example is it anyway, for today's youth?

—But look at me, protests Jack.— I *am* today's youth.

—Exactly, son. Flanagan claps a hand on the teenager's shoulder.—That's exactly my point.

In Union Jack's Pub and Grill on Forty-fourth and Tenth, April leans close to Doug, puts her hand on his thigh as she levers up to kiss him. Doug, startled beyond words, shuts his eyes and kisses her back.

—You know what I like about you? she asks after some time.—You don't talk a lot of garbage. I'm sick of men like Mario who talk garbage all the time.

"Gah-bij awl the toim."

Doug, not knowing what to say to this, says nothing. They kiss some more.

* * *

The next pair of explosions follow one after the next and succeed in knocking Johnny off his feet. He's reached the top of the stairs by now and is sprinting toward Betty, and he lands hard on a bed of gravel and frozen mud, with just enough time to shelter his head in his arms as a shower of copper chips, burnt fur and twisted shrapnel rains down on him. When it's over he lifts his head to see his wife's prostrate form thirty yards away, motionless but for her hair snapping about in the chilly winter moonlight.

He rushes to her.—*Betty*—!

She raises her face just as he gets there, tries to speak but fails. Settles for burying her nose in his armpit as another explosion rocks down from overhead, delivering its payload of corkscrewed metal and smoking flesh.

Swanson licks his lips.—We're within range, sir. The others are firing, sir.

—I heard you the first time, gunner. Hold your fire.

Swanson's mouth is pinched: his fear is practically tangible. Hawke is more than ready to loose the missiles and pull up, but he's enjoying the game he's playing with his copilot. Later on he'll rib the man, gently but pointedly, about the difference between veterans and civilian aviators. After all, Hawke didn't go through two successful tours of duty in Korea—wounded once, decorated twice—by being excessively cautious. There were men who'd fought at Changjin Reservoir who owed him his life, men he'd pulled out of a hot landing zone while rockets exploded around him and his copilot lay bleeding all over the instruments. If it were left up to guys like Swanson, those grunts would never have seen home again.

And *that,* if he had to sum it up, was the difference between hawks and swans.

He's still smiling at this bitter witticism when spike number six

from Lady Liberty's headgear—the one representing Rhode Island—punches through the chopper's midriff, splitting it in two
like a vivisected Atlas moth. The engines violently ignite moments
later and everybody dies.

—The fuck was *that?* snaps the chief.

—Chopper, says Ash. The word escapes his mouth before he
realizes he's spoken.

—There, points Jack the Spinner: for no reason, since the
men's eyes are glued to the fiery wreckage streaming through the
night. Fading white to yellow to orange to, finally, red as it hits
the water and then is snuffed out. A thought occurs to Ash then
and he asks the captain, Maybe we should move the *Princess* off a
bit, sir? In case there are more casualties? We're sort of in the
thick of it here.

—So we are. But what about that asshole Johnny? And the girl.
We can't leave without them. Can anyone see where they've gone?

The floodlight is switched on again to poke and probe along
the statue's base, slicing through curtains of twining smoke and
cascading soot. The visibility's lousy: it's like trying to peer into a
burning house. Nobody speaks for a time until Ash once again
states the obvious.

—I don't see anything, he says.

—Johnny—for Christ's sake, not here!

—Yes, here! Johnny gasps.—And *now!*

His pants are around his ankles. He's got Betty bent over in the
doorway, her Juliet-of-the-Jungle costume knocked askew. They're
wedged in a pool of shadow, safely out of sight of the boat's floodlights. Or so he hopes: to be honest he's not too worried.

His cock knocks against her like a tire iron.—You care which
hole this goes in?

Betty's voice is hollow.—Just do it so we can leave, all right?

* * *

K. spends the last moments of his life swatting at invisible demons, at broadsides of light and trenchers of sound that prove more substantial than hope, joy, freedom, the pursuit of happiness. He is deaf in one ear, half blind in both eyes. His antennae have been shorn away by shrapnel, with the result that he swings precariously from side to side like a Bowery bum. The statue he perches on has taken some hits too: Lady Liberty's upraised arm is gone, her torso is cracked and canted. Great runnels of fuel oil and monster blood track down her face like tears.

Betty gasps as Johnny jabs himself in. Betty doesn't want this, but she reminds herself that she is a woman who throws herself utterly into things—into Johnny, into relationships, even into this silly monster show. And she shouldn't get impatient with Johnny if he decides to throw himself utterly into her in the same way.

It just wouldn't be right, she feels.

Besides—she's too damn tired to argue.

It's tough to know what thoughts course through K.'s mind during his final moments. Some wordless sense of injustice maybe, the tightly clung to notion that he *hasn't done anything to deserve this.* Or maybe something altogether simpler, a plain, one-word response to the noise and light, smoke and pain: fear.

A helicopter missile strikes the side of his head and blossoms against his earhole, leaving him stunned and senseless. K.'s arms are flung backward even as as his thighs slacken their grip. A pair of missiles explode against his chest and the cloying smell of scorched feathers mixes in with the smoke and cordite. K. lurches back as if kicked. Maybe the pain jolts him awake, for he lets out a roar, swipes at Lady Liberty's headgear with a clawed hand, but only succeeds in shearing her head clean off. It tumbles toward the island below in a slow-motion cascade even as K. does too,

K. who is undeniably awake now but could be forgiven for thinking that, once again, he dreams.

It's much more bearable that way.

The men on board the *Ocean Princess* stand mute. There are no words for what they're witnessing—the noise, the fury, the fear, the destruction. The men are preliterate, prelingual. Occasionally they manage a little gasp or grunt or whimper of recognition. Pointless useless meaningless syllables dribble from their mouths like spit:— God*day*-im! or—Fuckin-A! or—Jee-zus H. *Christ!* But they're not really saying anything. There's nothing, really, to say.

In his dream, in slow-motion wide-screen Technicolor, K. flies.

39. DENOUEMENT

Flanagan finds them, but it's the chief who decides what must be done.

No sooner does the monster hit the ground headfirst, bounce, settle, twitch for a time, then stop twitching altogether, than the captain of the *Ocean Princess* barks to Ash, Get us over there!

They lunge forward, roaring into the smoke and mayhem. The water isn't deep enough to berth right beside the island so the men fall into the shallows and clamber ashore. The captain, the chief of police, Flanagan the beat cop, all three clattering with the frigid chill but all equally certain that this is something they need to see.

—Jesus this water's cold—!

Soon enough they're though it. Above them the remains of the statue twist out over the harbor, headless, torchless, smoldering.

—Nice job, boys, whispers the chief of police.—Good and thorough.

—They knew what they were doing, says the captain.—The choice was to kill the monster or save the statue, and the statue never had a chance.

The chief doesn't answer. He'll resign tomorrow. Before summer comes he'll sit down calmly in front of his bedroom mirror and shoot himself in the head with his police revolver. There will be no note.

Flanagan has jogged ahead, flashlight in hand, and found the staircase that Johnny ascended earlier. He waves them over and the three men make their way up. Above them helicopter rotors draw near, spotlights finger the scene, the harbor fills with small boats. Sirens everywhere. It's only a matter of time before the troops show up, and—worse than that—the reporters. For some reason, the men feel an urgency to get to wherever they're going before that happens.

Flanagan gets to the top and pulls up short.—Jesus Mary and Joseph.

—Out of the way! snaps the chief.—We can't see a thing down here.

Flanagan hesitates but does as he's told.

There on the ground lies K., dead as a pagan totem. One arm lies pinned under his torso while the other snakes across the ground, broken in a dozen places. Legs too are forced unnaturally backward, while his head rests slightly askew on his shoulders, as if someone had taken a good solid hold of it and wrenched hard to one side. Everywhere his fur is scorched and torn; blood oozes or bubbles through a hundred craters. He is on fire in a dozen places. His head rests on a pillow of green copper: shards of shrapnel and swathes of what used to be the Statue of Liberty.

K.'s corpse is a landscape. The men approach it cautiously, drawn on by an irresistible urge but still, at this late juncture, repulsed by the creature's *other*ness. The men stay together, moving in a huddle up one side of the torso, past the shoulder, around the breathtakingly malformed head. Their path is lit by unsteady flames and intermittent spotlight glare. Rounding the head, they approach the base of the statue's pillar, where a double staircase mounts to an arched doorway. The chief's eyes linger here. Would New Yorkers ever pass through that door again?

—What's that?

The chief's eyes dart to Flanagan, pointing at a sickly pale blotch a little ways ahead.

All three of them know, instinctively. All three have been wondering where the hell Betty and Johnny had gotten to. Well, now they've found out.

Betty is recognizable, though her neck has been snapped by the weight of something heavy striking her a glancing blow across the head. Johnny, by contrast, has been torn entirely in two. His upper half has vanished completely: his lower half, naked to the ankles, is still mounted on Betty's bare backside.

Flanagan vomits.

The captain prides himself on understanding the darker side of human nature but must admit, this stumps him: how a reasonably sane pair of adults could take a break from fleeing for their lives in order to have sex in the middle of a war zone. And not just any old sex, if the captain wasn't mistaken. The captain recognizes perversity when he sees it—even if his actual, firsthand experience is limited.

Flanagan straightens up, wiping his mouth.—Press is gonna have a field day with this one.

The captain is about to respond when the chief of police cuts him off.—No they won't.

Flanagan turns his heavy face to his superior.—Meaning?

—Meaning we have a responsibility to salvage the reputation of—this poor girl.

After a moment he adds, Mind you, I don't give a damn about this other idiot. But if his pants are down, it says something about her.

—You're going to tamper with evidence, sir?

—Damn right I am, and you're gonna help me.

Flanagan is all for it. The nuns had taught him plenty, but they'd never mentioned this.

The captain can hear boats cutting across the harbor. By

chance, none of the helicopter spotlights have fallen on this particular bit of the island.

Not yet.

—Whatever you're going to do, he says to the others, you better make it quick.

If his pants are down, it says something about her.

What the chief means without saying, is: There are some parts of the movie that don't need to be seen. The dirty parts. The mean parts. The parts where the niggers are given syphilis and the Palestinians are run off at gunpoint and the heroine is fucked up the ass.

These parts of the story would make people uncomfortable, so they have to be left out. The movie's job is to make the audience happy. Not to tell them anything true, but to tell them stories they already know. Even about themselves. *Especially* about themselves.

The chief doesn't know if Flanagan understands, but the captain seems to. The way the chief sees it, that'll have to do.

—Captain, we'll move his body over here. Flanagan, you fix the girl's skirt.

—Sir?

—Pull her skirt down. See what you can do with her underwear. Fix her up a little. The captain and I will take care of this Johnny character.

It's some job, pulling up the pants on half a corpse. Blood and pieces of wet things flopping everywhere. The chief does it because it needs to be done—and maybe the captain does it for the same reason. More than once he wishes that Billy Quinn fella was around to lend a hand, to see what had come of his grand schemes. But that degree of justice is too much to ask, apparently. Maybe they shoulda asked somebody first, maybe what they're doing is technically illegal, but too late for that now.

They have a hell of a time with the belt, and zipping up his fly is just asking too much. They'll have to hope nobody notices. The other half of his body—the handsome half, the leading-man half—must be lying crushed under something. Somebody will find it.

Then the men leave. The boats are pulling alongside the island now, full of reporters and troops clattering up the stairs. The troops will guard the body while the reporters take pictures from every angle and ask urgent questions and talk a lot of horseshit. They'll take pictures of K.'s broken body and the shattered statue, and eventually someone will discover the bodies of Betty and Johnny and they'll take pictures of them too. Young lovers, even more famous in death than they were in life. In a way it's a shame really: tomorrow morning, when their photos are splashed across every front page in the free world, they'll be just as dead as they are right now, so they won't even be able to enjoy the novelty of it. Their lives, or what their lives have turned into. Their moment in the spotlight. Their *show*.

But at least—this is how the chief sees it—at least they'll have their fucking clothes on.

REEL SIX

MONSTER, 2059

There is a certain embarrassment about being a storyteller in these times when stories are considered not quite as satisfying as statements and statements not quite as satisfying as statistics; but in the long run, a people is known, not by its statements or its statistics, but by the stories it tells.

—FLANNERY O'CONNOR, 1963

What's real doesn't matter, Qwestar-71. What gets told is what people believe.

—INDIRA CUNNINGHAM IN
Tomorrow Came Yesterday (2059)

40. CLOSING CREDITS

Twice a year, on the longest and shortest of days, the high priest-ess calls the tribe together. As she explains, We choose the longest day to show that we will never forget our past, no matter how long the days stretch. And the shortest day shows that we under-stand how insignificant we are compared to that which has come before us.

The tribe collects at the priestess's seven-toed feet to listen at-tentively. Most of them. There are always a few chortling boys who fail to give her the respect her advanced years deserve, but the high priestess knows how to deal with them.

—There are those who say that Komo ko and Kama ka do not exist, the priestess intones, because no one has seen them for many years. There are those who say they never existed and those who say they used to live but are long since dead. And to them I say, listen to my story and think on it carefully before you decide.

—I'm not a wise woman: this I know. [In fact she knows no such thing, but let it pass.] Not wise the way our ancestors were. But I am old. I have years, one for each of my fingers—that's seven—and one for each of my toes—that's fourteen. Twenty-one altogether plus I have extra years besides that make me nearly twenty-four, which is why my hair is white and my teeth have fallen out. I am the oldest woman for many generations of our people and I would hope my experience counts for something. And don't forget that the ancients lived even longer than I. The knowledge I have comes from them so remember that before you go saying that what I tell you is mere fabrication and tales for children.

The tribe sits and watches, wide-eyed. There is some shifting of backsides to the rear, a quiet flurry.

—You boys who are sitting there so restless and bored and exchanging looks, let me ask you this: If you're in such a hurry to leave, where will you go? For this night is the longest night of the year and there is little to welcome you on the far side of the embankment. Or perhaps I should say there is plenty that will welcome you but little that you would welcome in return.

She pauses.

—Ah. I see *that* has shut you up. As well it might, children. As well it might.

She pauses again. When she speaks, her voice is carried in the deliberate cadences of an incantation.

Now listen. The ill will between Komo ko, the god of things living, and Kama ka, the god of things dead, stretches back to infinity. No one knows how it started and I for one don't care. What matters is that their battles raged on year after year and for most of those years the battles were won by the god of things dead.

This was a hard time for the earth since it remained a dry and barren place with no water or trees or fish. Just clouds of white smoke and black ash and bitter winds and water so salty that nothing could survive in it.

But one day Komo ko—the god of things living—tricked Kama ka by saying, I give up! You win! To which Kama ka said, Why?

Komo ko thought fast.—I'm tired of being bashed around by your lifeless fists. So I concede. Forget it. I'll go back to my mist-shrouded mountaintop (for this is where both the gods made their home) and stay there and meditate and be glad for what I've got. Fair enough?

Kama ka thought about this and wasn't convinced.—I don't know he said.—We've been going at this a long time. Are you sure you want to quit?

—Oh yes.

—Then take my hand and clasp it as a gesture of your good intentions.

Komo ko reached forward to take the other god's hand, but even as he did so, the god of things living smote a mighty blow on the head of Kama ka, using one of his own lifeless stones to stave in his skull. Kama ka, the god of things dead, then fell down dead himself. Or so Komo ko believed.

Then the god of things living arrived on earth and found only a barren place and said, I will fill it with my children. From his feathered chest he pulled the birds and they scattered into the air. From his butterfly wings he spewed forth clouds of insects, and from his antennae came further armies covering the earth like a multilegged carpet. Fish leapt from his glassy eyes to fill the rivers and lakes and, when these overran, they filled the oceans as well. From his scaly arms slithered snakes and lizards. From his furry anus dropped furry creatures whose blood runs warm and whose young are born alive rather than in eggs. And from the tip of his loins spurted men and women, who coupled without cease and bore offspring every chance they got and whose offspring coupled without cease. As all of us sitting here are well aware.

Then for a time all was well.

But then something terrible happened: Kama ka, the god of things dead, came back. How this happened I don't know, being only an old and tired woman. But I suppose that, being a god, he could do more or less whatever he chose.

* * *

The high priestess pauses, blinks. Her eyes come back into focus.—You boys hush up there. I'm not done talking yet.

The boys fall silent.

Kama ka didn't come back in the same form as he always had—terrible though that was. For yes, even though he again rode sheets of flame across the sky and cried out in a mighty voice that made the mountains tremble, when he himself came to earth he didn't do so as a single god like Komo ko did. That would have been honorable so he didn't do it. That would've been reasonable so he shunned the thought. That would have been fair and just to every living thing and so he laughed at it in derision and rejected it in scorn.

What Kama ka did was this. He came back not as a single god but as a multitude of manlike creatures. And even though each of these creatures was by himself as weak and helpless as any man, when they worked together they possessed a ruthlessness and hate that could only come from the god of things dead. We say this because we have seen it and we know that no human heart could carry such monstrous designs.

Think of the fire termites that live on this island past the earthwall. Individually they are nothing and you can kill them with your foot. But come across an army of them and they can surround you murder you and roast your flesh before sunset. Alone a single one of them can do nothing but shovel a little dirt; together the swarm can build a tower seventy feet tall. And so it was with these men-things of Kama ka. They were like a cloud of pollen that makes a whole village fall ill. They were the spores of some plant that can poison a spring.

They were a sickness.

Now Kama ka was clever. And being clever he camouflaged himself as human beings so that we wouldn't see them for what they really were, which was: bits of things dead but walking as if alive. However, Kama ka was also proud with the kind of hubris that gods are prone to, and being such, he made a critical mistake. Which was: the creatures he sent to plague us—to plague the world—were not quite finished. They weren't quite right.

I hear you asking: What was wrong with them?

To which I'll answer: They were the wrong color.

This may surprise you, that a god would make such a basic mistake. But I have thought long on this and I have decided that Kama ka, being the god of dead things and burnt things and ash and lava and blindness and rot, cannot see colors. His is a world of black and white and gray. I may be wrong about this but it's what I have decided and I think I am right. And it explains why, when he came among our people generations ago, he did so in a colorless and repulsive way. It explains why his visage was that of a maggot or slug, of something that feeds on dead flesh.

So then. We know that generations ago, Komo ko—the god of things living—made this island his home. You youngsters may not believe it but you should. I have no more to say about this. But on the matter of Kama ka, the god of things dead, I would suggest something more: We are not rid of him yet.

He came here, once before. He came here and battled against Komo ko and neither have been seen since. But the lightning has flashed many times since and the thunder has been heard that lasts for days. And the warm wind has blown ashy clouds into all the waters of this island. Our parents told us of this: of the years when such things happened more often than any man could re-member. Ten times in a month, six months in the year. Three years in a row. And since that time there has been quiet but we aren't fooled.

No. We aren't fooled.

We know that the god of things living and the god of things dead are still alive and in the world. We know that one day they will return to this island where they first arrived. We know that they will expect obeisance from us. Komo ko, the god of things living, will receive it. Kama ka, the god of things dead, will not.

What will happen to us as a result, we don't know. Whatever it is, we will accept it as our destiny.

The high priestess rests and the tribe listens to the echo of her words in their heads. There is only one more ritual to complete. An old man of some nineteen years raises his rheumy eyes to hers, and asks through toothless gums:—What then shall we do in the meantime?

The high priestess runs an age-spotted hand through her hair.— We will do two things. We shall couple without cease for that is what human beings are best at. Coupling and bearing children who do the same and so on into infinity. Say what you will about us but we never tire of this.

—And the second thing?

—We wait. We shall wait for whatever happens.

The tribe nods at this. It is the answer they expected.

The story is over now. The tribe gathers itself up and shuffles into the darkness. They find their huts and bed down. Grasping their lovers close, or comforting their children, or clinging to their parents, they fall into sleep. Some quickly and heavily, some uneasily, but all wondering what will happen next.

They know there will be something.

AUTHOR'S NOTE

Information about 1950s nuclear tests is available from numerous sources. *The Nonviolent Alternative* (Farrar, Straus and Giroux, 1981) by Thomas Merton, a Trappist monk and essayist, includes interesting reflections on the use of the word "Trinity"—a term which denotes the unity of God, Jesus Christ and the Holy Spirit— as the name of the testing ground for weapons of mass destruction.

The removal of Iranian prime minister Mossadegh by the United States and United Kingdom, and the subsequent reinstatement of the Shah, is discussed in many places, including *The Clash of Fundamentalisms* by Tariq Ali (Verso, 2004). It is touched upon in *Covering Islam* by Edward W. Said (Vintage, 1997) and explored in detail in *Countercoup: The Struggle for the Control of Iran* by Kermit Roosevelt (McGraw-Hill, 1979).

The quote by Dwight D. Eisenhower on p. 27 is taken from a speech delivered on November 1, 1956, at the Convention Hall in Philadelphia, Pennsylvania.

Lyrics from "The Monkey" by Dave Bartholomew are copyright © 1957 by Alfred Publishing Co., Inc., and are reprinted with permission.

The number of Palestinians driven from Palestine following the creation of Israel is a subject of debate. The figure of 700,000 is quoted in Perry Anderson's "Scurrying Toward Bethlehem" in *New*

Left Review, July–August 2001. Other sources put the figure at close to one million (see the Palestininan Refugee Resource Net at www.arts.mcgill.ca/mepp/new_prrn/, which quotes a United Nations figure of 950,000 in 1950). *In Search of Fatima* (Verso, 2004) by Ghada Kharmi is a memoir about her family's flight from the tanks that were shelling her West Jerusalem neighborhood when she was a girl. This book, and others like it, subvert the commonly aired notion that Palestinians left their homes voluntarily.

Quotes by Golda Meir on p. 93 are taken from *The Times* (London), July 15, 1969, and have been widely reprinted elsewhere, for example in *The Christian Science Monitor*'s obituary of Yasser Arafat, November 12, 2004, ("There is no such thing as a Palestinian people") and the *New York Times* interview with John Le Carré, March 13, 1983 ("They did not exist").

Information about the Tuskeegee Syphilis Study is available from many sources, including the PBS's Online News Hour and the *Encyclopaedia Britannica.* In 1997, then-President Bill Clinton issued an apology to the victims on behalf of the U.S. government.

The quote by Winston Churchill on p. 107 is taken from *The Clash of Fundamentalisms* by Tariq Ali (Verso, 2004) and is widely available from other sources.

The quote from David Ben-Gurion on p. 194 is taken from Perry Anderson's "Scurrying Toward Bethlehem" in *New Left Review,* July–August 2001 ("We will abolish partition," etc.). Further quotes are taken from *The Fateful Triangle* (Pluto Press, 2000) by Noam Chomsky ("Politically we are the aggressors and they defend themselves," etc.) and many other sources, including the International Press Center in Palestine web site (www.ipc.gov.ps).

The quote from Flannery O'Connor on p. 235 is taken from *Mystery and Manners: Occasional Prose* (Farrar, Strauss and Giroux, 1962) in an essay entitled "The Catholic Novelist in the Protestant South."